THE BEST OF
JOHN B. KEANE

COLLECTED HUMOROUS WRITINGS

THE BEST OF
JOHN B. KEANE

COLLECTED HUMOROUS WRITINGS

MERCIER PRESS

MERCIER PRESS
Cork
www.mercierpress.ie

ISBN: 978 1 85635 265 9

A CIP record for this title is available from the British Library

Printed and bound in the EU.

Contents

Life – the Incurable Illness

Remembrance

Food – and Drink!

Men and Other Animals

Keys to the Kingdom

. . . Makes the World Go Round

. . . into that Good Night

Words, Words, Words

LIFE – THE INCURABLE ILLNESS

WATERY EYES

People who wear lonely faces are not necessarily lonesome people. Much the same applies to people who have watery eyes. We tend to think that these are teary eyes. The truth is that tears and eye-water come from two different fountains. Do not ask me where these fountains are situated. All I can tell you is that they are in the neighbourhood of the noodle. Go to your doctor if you want exact information but don't tell him I sent you.

Watery eyes are just about the most priceless possession a man or woman can have in this little globular demesne of ours. Since, unfortunately, it is a demesne where hypocrisy is more abundant than charity, watery eyes can be greatly undervalued by those who are lucky enough to possess them. I myself do not possess watery eyes except when there is a strong wind blowing into my face or, on rarer occasions, when I am the victim of a head cold.

My ancestors, however, were not deficient in the matter of eye-water, and there was one particularly vicious relative who had a good word for nobody but who was greatly liked and respected by his neighbours. They said that in spite of his scurrilous tongue he had great nature. Nature, in those days, was a thing no sensible man should be without. A man with nature, whatever else he might not have, was always accorded respect, and if ever his neighbours were heard to criticise him someone was always quick to point out that for all his faults he had great nature. This generally nipped the criticism in the bud.

Anyway, this relative of mine was a great man for attending funerals. The only reason he went to funerals was to pass away the time. He did not like plays or pictures and besides you had to pay good money before you were left inside the door of a playhouse or cinema. Funerals cost nothing and he never failed to express his delight when he heard somebody was dead. He had as little time for the dead as he had for the living. Ordinary people who were fond of criticising a deceased party when he was alive always stopped the practice when he was pronounced dead.

There were two reasons for this. A dead man was harmless and therefore praise couldn't do him any good. Secondly, the louder the praise given at the dead man's wake the greater the quantity of strong drink given to the bestower of the praise.

But to get back to my relative. On the morning of the funeral he would shave and dress in his Sunday best. Always he would make his way to the front of the funeral where he would be seen by all the relatives of the deceased. He always walked with his head well bent and his hands behind his back. This sort of posture impressed everybody.

At the gate of the churchyard he would precede the coffin party to the grave and stand watching all those who came to pay their respects. Those who did not know him often mistook him for a detective.

At the graveside his eyes would begin to water. He could not keep it back and it often ran down the side of his face. He would produce his handkerchief and blow his nose. Then he would wipe the water away. I once heard a woman behind me say to another: 'God bless that man but he has wonderful nature.'

As the water coursed down his face others who were at the graveside, particularly middle-aged women who were in no way related to the dead man, would sniff at the sight of him. These sniffs were the harbingers of genuine salt tears. They would look at my relative again and, believing him to be genuinely crying, would start off themselves. Soon every woman at the graveside was crying. They could not stop even if they had wanted to. Handkerchiefs appeared by the score and eyes were dried, only to fill again from the inexhaustible well of tears owned by every woman. If there was a fresh breeze his eyes would really swim and very often sympathetic souls would come forward and place the hand of consolation on his shoulder.

When he died he had a large funeral. It was dominated by women. All had a plentiful supply of handkerchiefs but they were never called upon to use them. Not a tear was shed because they had nobody to lead them. Their tear-leader was no more and he who was the cause of so many was buried without a single tear in the end.

CORNS

I once knew a woman who wore out three bicycles in search of a cure for corns.

She spent the price of a bubble car on guaranteed remedies when all that she really required was a larger size in shoes.

I heard of a man who won seventy cups for waltzing but he would have forfeited them all unconditionally if his corns gave him a moment's peace.

Whenever I see a really beautiful, well-coiffured, immaculately dressed woman, I always arrive at one of two conclusion. She is extraordinarily wealthy or, on the other hand, she has very little to do at home. Similarly when I see a stout woman sitting on an upturned box at a point-to-point meeting I hazard the guess that her shoes are too tight or that she forgot to look after her corns that morning before leaving home.

Corns thrive nowhere with such exultant disregard for man's comforts as under the patronage of poorly fitting shoes and additionally a man is never conscious of his corns when he patters about on bare feet. Corns have often dictated the humour of a man's day and not infrequently instituted the beginnings of minor lawsuits because many regard the act of standing upon a corn accidentally under the same light as assault and battery and it would not surprise me to learn that the error made by Napoleon in attempting to subdue Russia was brought about as a result of wearing tight-fitting boots.

Until recently I have had little sympathy for those who suffer from corns. Frequently after football matches where men are compelled to stand for hours in congestion I have scoffed at older colleagues who sat themselves relievedly upon convenient windowsills after leaving the football pitch and proceeded, without regard for caution, to unlace their shoes. The sighs and other ejaculations of pleasure heard upon the occasion were proof of the relief enjoyed and we laughed, some of us, in derision at these comical situations, unconscious of unforeseen martyrdom and blissfully unaware of the latter-day development of constricted paunches which come with ripening of age.

The era of the casual corn-cutter belongs to history because these days there are as many cures as there are corns and the neighbour whose forte was corn-cutting is no longer called in.

There are many who may say boastfully that they have never been afflicted by corns but in the toes of each of us is the nucleus of a horrifying harvest and all that is required is a pair of new shoes to bring them forth. Man for the most part is safe enough from the scourge because if he is once bitten by an ill-advisedly purchased shoe he will lower his sights for future occasions but woman will never see the light. She will persist, God love her!, in carrying the day, and admittedly it is hard to burden a shapely foot with a shoes that looks cumbersome. It is unfair to expect a woman, whose figure is preserved in spite of maturity, to wear flat sensible shoes. If she picks up a corn or two in the process it is a churlish husband who would not bend his knee to bring her relief. It was a wise man who said that nothing should ever be thrown away. The derelict razor blade, unwanted and unsung, can play a powerful part in extremity and whatever is said about peculiar and particular cures, corn-paring is as classic an example of practical art as any.

The principle which would have us credit the fallacy that any instrument which pares a pencil will pare a corn has seen to its own share of sore toes. Wood is dispassionate and unmoving but a sensitive toe is liable to unite with its four brethren into a strong assault force which could readily loosen a tooth in the mouth of the administrator.

Never before, in the history of mankind, have such advances been made in all the sciences but man in his blindness has overlooked evils under his nose. The corn will always be with us so let there be a school devoted to corns. Let there be an investigation made as to their culture and origin. Let the habits of the dormant corn be brought to light and let our womenfolk fulfil their feminine and fanciful indulgences without suffering and discomfort. Let stout men stand with impunity and let us, for once and all, clear the air in respect of corns.

INVALIDS

This world is full of people who look worse than they are. A number of my relatives go around like invalids all the time because they haven't the gall to go around looking healthy. Our family, and yours too, I'm sure, has always been afflicted with its fair share of professional convalescents. In fact, if things were to change I don't know what I'd do without the whining and the complaining and the long faces and the shuffling and the shifting.

I don't think I'd be able to carry on I've become so used to it and there's the dreadful thought that if the ailments were to go away altogether they would surely be replaced by something worse because there's a fly in every ointment and when one fly goes there's another ready to take his place.

I have one particular connection who can be very trying but there may be worse waiting to take his place. He is not a relation. He is a distant in-law but distant as he is he has the same destructive potential as distant thunderclouds, distant rainstorms and distant explosions. He would arrive at any minute. He paid me one of his rare visits last week. It beats me how he always manages to look so pale. He is a martyr, according to himself, to many unknown and incurable diseases and there is no moment of the day or night that he does not endure some form of suffering.

A relation told me lately that the reason he is so pale is that he avoids the sun the way a lazy man avoids work. The sun is anathema to him for the good reason that if he were to expose himself to it there would be the danger of his face assuming a healthy hue.

'You will always find him,' said the relation, 'at the shady side of the house when the sun is about its business.'

When he arrived on the premises he stood at the doorway for a while wheezing and whining and nattering and snuffling and casting baleful looks all around.

'God help us,' said a visitor, 'that poor chap isn't long for the world.'

I recalled about forty years before that an uncle of mine passed the very same remark about the very same man. The uncle is dead and the very same man is to the good.

All eyes were upon him as he stood near the door. Then an elderly woman, struck by compassion, raised herself with considerable difficulty and found him a seat. She asked him if he was all right but do you think he favoured her with an answer after her kindness to him? He sat for a moment and indicated by a series of the most terrifying facial grimaces that his buttocks found the seat unbearable. He rose with the customary wheezing and dragged his feet after him as though they were somebody else's.

Slowly he made his way to the bar counter and fixed his eyes on me as though I was personally to blame for all his imagined woes. I was having none of it.

'You're looking well!' I called out to him. This stopped him in his tracks. The enormity of such a statement was tantamount to blasphemy but before he could utter a word I told him that I had never seen him looking better. The cold truth was that he had a hollow look about him like a sausage roll without the sausage.

'Give me a half o' brandy,' he said. I duly dispensed the brandy, and when he had it paid for he demanded a drop of port.

'Sandeman's,' he insisted. This is an old trick. He knew well that if he called for a brandy and port together he would be charged for the port, whereas only a heartless publican would charge a poor invalid with a foot in the grave for a drop of port.

I am happy to be able to report that he didn't die on that occasion and I have the eeriest of feelings that he will be calling after we have all gone.

Under the Bed

'Where were ye when this man was under the bed?' The question was posed one heady night in Listowel while all around lighted sods impregnated with paraffin blazed on pitchforks and men with glazed eyes sought to dismember each other for no other reason than that they had different politics. You've guessed it! Dev was in town, and while he wasn't the man in question, the man about whom the question was posed was, nevertheless, a significant figure in local politics. He hadn't died for his country or anything like that but he had kept his head and remained under the bed when all seemed lost. At first the listeners were baffled by the question but he repeated it defiantly. 'Where were ye,' he demanded at the top of his voice, 'when this man was under the bed?'

'There aren't that many beds in Listowel,' a wag shouted from the edge of the crowd.

What I'm trying to do here is defend those who hid under the bed when there were murderous gunmen abroad. It was at least better than leaving the country and, if one was shot itself they would have to find him first, and will you tell me what sort of blackguard would pull a man from under a bed with a sick child and a nursing mother inside in it?

What went wrong with this country after the War of Independence was that there was no society for men who had been under the bed. Remember that those who had been under significantly outnumbered those who hadn't. I make out that for every hundred men who went under the bed only twelve did not. At least those are the figures we arrived at here in the pub the other night and many of those present were not a bit ashamed to admit that they were sired, even legally sired, by men who had been under the bed.

We all hid under the bed as children and what could be more natural than that we should return to the scenes of our childhood at the first sign of trouble. I mean, where else would a man with no courage and a powerful instinct for preservation go unless it was under a bed. If we have had ancestors who hid under beds we should not be ashamed of it. At least they didn't turn their coats which is regarded as the most heinous sin of all on the Irish political front. Some day I will be passing through a graveyard and I hope I will see what I always wanted to see – that is a Celtic cross dedicated to the memory of the UBS.

UBS simply means Under-the-Bed-Society and I know of no man in this country who was fully compensated for being under his or any other bed. I have always regarded those who were under the bed as a sort of back-up, a last reserve who would emerge when all fruit failed, when their country needed them most. They were never given a chance and have been relegated to a lousy role in history by begrudgers who had no beds to go under.

Imagine what these men went through as they waited to be discovered by their would-be executioners! They must surely have died a thousand times before they were dragged out and even then they were treated disgracefully because no self-respecting soldier would shoot a man found under a bed. It was beneath them. It was work for Black and Tans. I'll put this question to the begrudgers and vilifiers who would belittle those who went under the bed: Did you ever try to eat a four-course dinner while under a bed? Of course you didn't. You left that to men of sterner mettle who were used to four-course dinners, who always had enough to eat before the Johnny-Jump-Ups arrived on the scene.

Those of you whose fathers were under the bed have a perfect right to ask the question of begrudgers and others – 'Where were you when our fathers were under the bed?'

PIPE DOWN PLEASE

I have written on numerous occasions about pipes. These include tobacco pipes, drainpipes and bagpipes, to mention but a few, but I honestly feel that I have never devoted enough time or study to tobacco pipes. Daily I become more convinced of this when I see growing numbers of people who have no qualification at all or no right to go around with pipes in their mouths. Many people carry pipes in their mouths whose heads, jaws and teeth were never designed for such a purpose. They rarely smoke the pipes. They carry them purely for effect or to give the impression that they know a lot more than they are prepared to divulge. Another conclusion I have drawn is this: When a man has nothing to say, as for instance when he is badly beaten in debate, his clenched teeth are fit for nothing else but the holding of a pipe. In effect it could be said that he is hiding behind his pipe.

For a while after I gave up cigarettes I apprenticed myself to pipe-smoking. I could make no fist of it so one day while watching a local football final I took my pipe from my mouth and flung it in disgust in the general direction of the referee.

Since then I have left pipes to those who know how to smoke them. However, let us now list, for the benefit of the student, some of the many ways in which pipes are misused by those who smoke them and those who pretend to smoke them. If I overlook some of the more glaring misuses it is because I am by nature a soft-hearted and well-meaning chronicler who wishes ill will to no one and who would not like to make a show, as it were, of certain guilty parties in front of their wives and families.

There is in every community a man, sometimes more than one who lives in perpetual fear of being assaulted. There may be good reason for his fear but, whatever the cause, he believes that footpads, thugs and others of evil intent are waiting for him behind every telephone pole, in every open doorway, around every corner and even under the bed in his own home. This is the sort of innate fear that breeds its own particular defence mechanism. So what does our friend do? He buys a pipe and every time he ventures out of doors he places it firmly between his teeth. The idea is to suggest, through his bared fangs, that he is not be molested. It does not matter if the smoke gets in his eyes or if his tongue is a mass of blisters from the excessive drawing.

His likely enemies are wary of him while he has the pipe in his gob. His lips are drawn back from the two rows of clenched molars and there is a snarly look about him that is almost wolfish in its ferocity.

At heart he is as windy as an overblown balloon but lesser men get out his way as he strides through the streets with tobacco smoke billowing behind him. The problem here is that, sooner or later, he will foolishly believe that he is as tough as he looks and risk a collision with a man who is either too short-sighted or too stubborn to get out of his way. A man with a pipe in his mouth is easy meat in a clash of bodies. The pipe automatically leaves the mouth at the moment of impact, and as a result our friend is without his armour for the rest of his journey.

Let us now look at the man who taps his pipe against the heel of his shoe. A man who does this is one of two things. He is an incompetent and daring bluffer or a very proficient fellow indeed. Since there is and always has been a woeful deficiency of very proficient men in this world we may safely presume that the vast majority of those who tap the bowls of their pipes against the heel of their shoes are inefficient, incompetent and always late for appointments.

The tapping against the heel is to imply efficiency, to suggest to onlookers that the heel-tapper is a practised pipe-user who has forgotten more about the art of pipe-smoking and pipe-handling than most ever learn and that because he is practised at one thing it should follow as the night the day that he is practised at everything.

Your heel-tapping pipe-smoker fools nobody and in the long run all he has to show for his gameze is a broken pipe.

Let us now press on to a very rare type indeed. This is he who continually carries a pipe in his hand but never puts it in his mouth. Just when it seems certain that he is about to place it between his teeth he withholds it and waves it in one direction or another to indicate a point in time or a place in distance. He may even use it to stress an aspect of his argument or often he may use it as a pointer for maps, charts and the points of the compass.

The case I would like to make is that he will use it for anything but smoking and this in the last analysis is the greatest misuse of all.

Before I close let me parade another type before the reader. This man walks abroad with a pipe in his mouth and with his head in the air. Yet he is neither fearful nor alert for attack. He is just another proud man with new false teeth and he is using his pipe to exhibit them in public for the first time.

LOSING ONE'S WAY

I have lost count of the number of times I have been stopped in the streets of Dublin by people who have lost their way. When I answer that I am a stranger to the place myself they look at me as if I were to blame for their misfortune. I would dearly love to help these people and send them on their proper roads but I am not omniscient and I am prepared to lay odds that I have been lost more often than they. I can sympathise with them when their questions bear no fruit because I have asked these questions countless times myself and I know the resultant feelings of frustration.

In the early days when ordinary passers-by would explain that they were unfamiliar with the places I desired to visit I would always wait until I saw a member of the Garda Síochána. I discovered that most of the Garda Síochána one met on the streets of Dublin were as familiar with the city as I was myself. That is to say they merely knew the basics, such as the way to Kingsbridge or Amiens Street and even a short cut to the Pillar, but if you asked them where was Mooneys of White's Lane where they sold the clay pipes there would be the familiar lifting of the cap and the inevitable scratching of the head. The best bet was to bide one's time and inspect convenient shop windows until an old woman with a handbag happened to come the way.

I discovered after years of trial and error that elderly women with handbags knew their immediate vicinities like the backs of their hands.

There are many reasons for this. Old women in cities seldom wander far from their own doorsteps, preferring the small neighbourhood shops to the bewildering mazes known as supermarkets in the busy areas of the city. There is another reason. They no longer possess the confidence to mount buses or cross busy intersections. Frail and uncertain, they cling to quieter streets within a short radius of their abodes. They listen patiently when asked a question and sometimes, due to faulty hearing, will ask for a repeat. They take their time and ponder well the name of a shop or the street in question. With a sad shake of the head they will sometimes tell you that it is not there anymore. I well remember asking an old lady who carried a handbag if she knew the whereabouts of a typewriter-repair shop which I had visited many years before but of which I had forgotten the precise situation in the meanwhile. She shook her head to indicate that I had posed her a tough one but at the same time I could see that she relished a challenge, that it was test for her failing memory.

'Ah yes,' she said, ' that would be little Mister Lollery.'

'That was the name of the man,' I said.

'The Lord be good to him,' she said and she made a sign of the cross. Then, changing her bag from one hand to the other, she launched into an account of his death and decline. When he found he wasn't feeling well he sold the goodwill of the shop to a tailor who now had a flourishing business but who hadn't half the heart of Mister Lollery who'd give you the shirt off his back. Before we parted company she told me that he had gone to live with his daughter for a while but after a few months he got 'what I hope you'll never get, sir,' which meant some malignancy, like cancer, against which there was no defence. She was right about Mister Lollery. On the one occasion I did business with him I found him to be a decent oul' skin who looked downright apologetic when he had to take a few bob.

Another good source of directions is your postman – that's

if you're lucky enough to catch one. Then there are publicans. Publicans and their assistants, while they may not know the place themselves, will always find somebody who does. Most people, however, you meet on city streets just haven't a clue so that it's no use fuming or losing one's temper when, after a long period of probing and counter-probing, one is as near to one's destination as one was in the beginning.

In the country, where everybody knows everybody else, it's much easier, and there is little likelihood of losing one's way for long. When you meet a fool treat him like a fool, that is with respect and courtesy, two commodities incidentally for which fools always long. When you meet a smart alec treat him like a smart alec, with a nod of the head and a click of the heels. Never bandy words with his ilk for he battens upon these and distorts them with relish to suit the digestion of his loquacity.

Then there are certain uncommunicative gentlemen who cannot be bothered using their brains and time to ponder questions. These are best left alone because under pressure they could wither you with words.

I recall the plight of a certain gentleman who once lost his way in a maze of country roads. He came upon a small man who was seated upon a milestone at the side of the road.

'Do you know such a place?' asked the man who had lost his way, naming a townland in the area.

'No,' said the man on the milestone. The lost man tendered other places and names but every time he received a blunt negative. Finally the lost man lost his temper.

'What a fool,' he exploded, 'what an ass, what a lout.'

'Fool, yes,' said the man on the milestone, 'ass, yes, and lout, yes, but lost, no.'

MIDDLE-AGED MEN

Middle-aged men, from the first of mankind, have taken unto themselves full rights of pious pontification in every generation right up to this present one. With the immunity that is guaranteed by age and standing they hold forth at length to those under their control. To give them their due it must be said that their pontifications have always been confined to two favourite themes to the almost total exclusion of all others.

These would be, in order of merit, the perfidy, villainy and total wantonness of the youth of today and, secondly, the terrible times we live in.

I remember hearing my own father holding forth when I was a schoolboy. He had just eaten a hearty breakfast and was in the middle of the morning paper. Suddenly he folded the pages, the better to concentrate on a particular item of news. He read it out for us. It had to do with the overthrow of a South American government by means of a revolution which claimed the lives of thousands and the lifelong incarceration of thousands more.

'We live,' said he, 'in terrible times.'

What he should have said was this: 'We have always lived in terrible times, we live now in terrible times and, if experience is any guide, we will continue to live in terrible times.'

When dealing with the youth he was never given to oral expression. So awful were the current crop of miscreants and so heinous their crimes that all he could do was shake his head in horror and disbelief as new stories of drunkenness, debauchery and assorted devilment came to hand. If what he heard from another shocked parent was bad in the extreme he would take his pipe from his mouth and make the sign of the cross with the stem. Then and only then would he permit himself one profound yet simple comment.

'Ah,' he would say with a simultaneous shake of the head, 'the youth of today beats all.'

Nothing has changed since the first father expressed disillusionment at the waywardness of his and everybody else's offspring. We may take it then that the two predominant areas for future parental dissemination will be those we have mentioned, i.e. the youth of today and the terrible times we live in.

In my own youth there were famines, plagues, wars, bombings and all the usual suffering that thoughtless men inflict upon each other. There were revolutions and overthrowings of governments. There were religious and sectarian killings and there were assassinations. There were ceasefires and truces and breaches of both but man learned nothing at all in spite of everything.

That is why I have always maintained that life should not be taken too seriously and that even the most cherished ideologies should nearly always be taken with a grain of salt so that men and women might live natural lives and wonder at the beauty of creation rather than conflicting opinions and the carnage created by man.

There are times when I am reminded of my father. I sit reading the paper and I am aghast at the same terrible news. I am on the point of saying to myself that the times we live in are the most terrible of all and I chide myself for repeating age-old inanities.

With regard to the youth of today I must say that, allowing for circumstances, they are no different to the youth of all the other generations since man first woke up from his sleep wondering about the whereabouts of his son or daughter.

The moral here is that you cannot put an old head on young shoulders no more than you can account for the doings of selfish and heedless men. In short, nothing ever really changes and the youth of the day will always be the bane of those who are safely ensconced in middle-age security, who fear for their possessions and their survival and who forget that they were young themselves.

It will always be thus, and the statements being made today about the youth and the terrible times will be repeated in every generation till Gabriel wipes his lips and trumpets the close of the long game.

As for the past, be certain that it has all been said. If you don't believe me listen to what Shakespeare has to say in *A Winter's Tale*:

> I would that there were no age between sixteen and twenty-three or that youth would sleep out the rest for there is nothing in between but getting wenches with child, wronging the ancientry, stealing, fighting.

Shakespeare surely was attentive to the pontifications of his father. How else could he so accurately convey a middle-aged man's intolerance?

Bucket Handles

I was entering a hostelry in Killarney when I was approached by a man who accused me of never having written about bucket handles.

'Buckets you have,' he said, 'and chamber-pots you have, garters you have and half-doors you have but bucket handles never.' I admitted to the charge and pointed out that my accuser had never written about bucket handles either.

'It's not my job,' he said, 'it's yours.' With that he left me. I do not know the man nor do I know where he hailed from but let us, in the interests of open-mindedness, take up the challenge as it were and have a gander at this business of bucket handles. In the first place there are as many types of handles as there are types of buckets so that we must not presume that the most celebrated of all buckets, i.e. the old wooden bucket, had an old wooden handle for the good reason that enamel buckets do not have enamel handles, so that we are without guidelines of any kind at the outset.

Let us, therefore, take a particular bucket. We have enamel, steel, wooden, tin and galvanised. Let us take your common-or-garden galvanised bucket for no other reason than it is the most common of all buckets and also because it has a galvanised handle. This, at least, is consistency of a kind, and we are now better girded for our investigation having, so to speak, a recognisable subject, to wit, the galvanised handle of a galvanised bucket.

It is an object which is not without artistry. Delicately shaped like a sickle and with curls at both ends it is highly musical in the best metallic sense. It has a pleasant, silvery appearance and, while its intrinsic worth is negligible, it can be used in a hundred different ways, as any handyman will tell you. It is a thing of great endurance, and I know of no instance where the galvanised bucket has outlived the galvanised handle.

It is without peer in the matter of tethering goats, asses, mules and small ponies, and I have seen a pair of galvanised handles from modestly proportioned parent buckets used as hinges on a gate which was created from an iron bedstead. This composition of discards cost not a single penny and yet it served the purpose of an article which could cost a small farmer a considerable sum of money.

I also recall an elderly whitewasher who, in my childhood, used to whitewash our backyard. He had his own ladder and tools of the trade. These latter consisted of a large galvanised bucket, two brushes, one as wide as a handlebar moustache for the rough work and the other purposely narrow as a Chinese pigtail for the whitening of niches, cracks, holes and assorted cicatrices. In addition to these expected paraphernalia there was also a galvanised bucket handle. This was used only when the whitewasher was operating from the higher rungs of the ladder. It served to attach the whitewash bucket to the most convenient rung. Few whitewashers can whitewash and hold on to a full bucket at the same time while also endeavouring to manoeuvre at the top of an unsteady ladder.

What the whitewasher did was elevate the bucket handle which was attached to the bucket and place the extra or spare bucket handle underneath it. He then squeezed both ends of the spare in an arc over the chosen rung so that the bucket hung safely. Whenever he climbed higher all the whitewasher had to do was pull the ends of the spare handle apart and reattach the bucket in the elementary manner aforementioned.

Let it be carefully recorded, however, that the spare bucket handle did not complete its services with this action alone. No indeed, for when the whitewasher returned to *terra firma* for the purpose of mixing more whitewash he used the spare bucket handle for stirring the lime which made the whitewash. Not only this, but when the job of whitewashing was complete the spare handle was rapped smartly against the sides of the bucket to disengage loose flakes and foreign bodies which attached themselves to the bucket during the day's whitewashing.

Your galvanised handle had no peer when it came to lifting the covers of roasting-hot skillets and bastable ovens. All one had to do was insert the handle under the little handle which was attached to the lid and place the cover to one side of the hearth while the contents of the utensil in use were examined to see if they were properly cooked or a few more minutes were required to finish off the job.

Now, because of space restrictions, I will have to draw to a close but not before I make a few final, meaningful observations. As a back-scratcher your galvanised bucket handle is to be seen at its best. Its natural curvature assists the scratcher in a way that few other implements can, and if it served no other purpose than this it would occupy a valuable place in the history of therapeutics.

Lastly, if one should happen to be locked out at night after a dance or carousel there is nothing more effective than the handle in question. It will not break a window if thrown gently in that direction but when it strikes the pane the resultant noise is far more irritating and lasting than if the window were smashed in the first place. I hope that in making these few observations regarding bucket handles we will have answered our friend in Killarney and also shown that there is no subject under the sun about which a decent treatise cannot be written.

INSOMNIA

A word or two about insomnia – that scourge that has divided homes and shattered more nerves than all the income tax assessment forms ever wrongfully designed.

There is not a single, solitary soul reading this treatise who has not suffered at some time or other from the scourge of insomnia. Imagine then what it is like to be a chronic insomniac, to know not what the sleep of the just is, to know not what it is to savour sweet slumber when the day's toil is over.

The trouble is that people have forgotten a very important thing about sleep. First of all it's very difficult to locate when you really want it. The thing with sleep is that you must pretend you could not care less about it. That way sleep will come to you but if you persist in hot pursuit you will never catch up with it.

Some wag once said that you would never find a woman or a policeman whenever you really want one. The same thing applies to sleep.

Another thing to remember about sleep is this: It's not to be savoured like a woman. When sleep comes, take it at once or you may well have to do without it. You should remember that it's not the sleep itself you enjoy. How could you when you're not conscious? What you enjoy is that brief period before you go to sleep and, of course, that longer period in the morning when you don't want to get up.

When sleep makes its opening bid be sure to take it at once. It will not bid a second time in a hurry and you may be left waiting a long time. That's how insomniacs are made. Don't muck around with your sleep. Sleep is a very tricky business, best defined as a cross between lightning and quicksilver. When confronted with insomnia the thing to do is to really concentrate on staying awake. That way sleep will come in good time.

Insomnia is no fun. I am not trying to make light of it. Why should I? I know not the hour nor the minute that it will lay hold of me.

When I was a *garsún* in Renagown in the Stacks Mountains there was no such thing as insomnia. I'll grant you that a man or a woman might stay awake occasionally thinking of a distant sweetheart but that wasn't insomnia. That was a form of sleeplessness which could easily be cured by joining forces with the missing party. The farmers of the Stacks Mountains when I was a boy blamed insomnia in their labourers exclusively on books.

'Books,' they would say, 'are the sworn enemies of sleep.' But this could have been because farmers' 'boys' who had a habit of reading books late into the night were unable to get up in the morning and a farmer's 'boy' who could not get up in the morning was worse than a hen that could not lay an egg.

The reason why there was no insomnia in the Stacks Mountains when I was a *garsún* was that feather ticks were the order of the day. Let me tell you now, those of you who have never slept on a tick of green goose feathers do not know what sweet sleep is like or what it is to dream the sweeter dreams. A tick of green goose feathers transported a man straightaway to the sublime climes of slumberland.

Pills and potions won't cure insomnia. They'll satisfy it for a while and make it hungry for more but they won't dismiss it for good.

Diphtheria came and went in the Stacks as did scarlatina which sounds like a ballet dancer but danced on human life instead. We were exposed to everything except insomnia but now that the feather beds have vanished there is talk of this newfangled sleeplessness in places where it was never heard of before.

FOUL TALK

Quite recently I beheld a youngster fling a stone at an old woman as she made her way past the back door of my premises on her way to the post office. Greatly shocked, she turned around and, upon beholding her tormentor, was about to reprimand him. He beat her to the punch, however, and assailed her elderly ears with a torrent of four-letter words, to the amusement of his adoring mother who stood talking to another woman nearby.

Indeed, in my time, I have stood with ever-increasing disbelief while parents almost suffocated themselves with laughter at the awful sayings and dreadful doings of their own children. I am also aware of large numbers of parents who consider it great fun, entirely, when their offspring use a four-letter word. They even go so far as to insist that these toddling prodigies hold forth through the medium of effing and blinding for the benefit of friends, relations and other admirers who might happen to be in the vicinity. Over-indulged by doting parents, the children exult in expressing themselves illicitly. Indeed, there is many a parent who believes that every foul utterance should be preserved for posterity.

Nobody can now deny that the use of the four letter word is at its most prevalent ever. When it was used in my boyhood days there was awe and shock. The user was branded as an authentic transgressor of the first water, bound to end his days with a rope around his neck and certain to sizzle, endlessly, on the scorching spits of hell!

This loathsome form of expressing oneself is also more prevalent among parents but I believe that this can be partially explained by the fact that it has now become too costly to smash plates and saucers as a means of letting off steam. Banging doors is even more expensive because sooner or later a carpenter will have to be called in while the cost of replacing broken windows has risen to astronomical proportions. The cheaper alternative is to avail of the four-letter word. This might be, in view of what I have said, justifiable in itself, provided no children are listening.

Expensive as are the banging of doors, the breaking of windows and the smashing of delph, I would opt for these safety valves instead of the four-letter ones. There is no satisfaction like the satisfaction that comes from a well-banged door and no outlet for frustration so beneficial as the smashing of a dish, plate or saucer. Likewise the flinging of saucepans and pots here, there and everywhere is a highly rewarding exercise. Effing and blinding, on the other hand, is not lasting and the treatment has to be repeated *ad nauseam*.

I was once witness to a row where the female of a partnership flung an alarm clock through her sitting-room window when her spouse arrived home with four of his cronies at one o'clock in the morning. Since I was one of the cronies aforementioned I had a front-line view of the proceedings. We arrived with two dozen bottles of stout and a span new deck of playing cards with a view to indulging in a spot of poker. All would have been well had not our host insisted that some rashers and sausages which happened to be in the fridge at the time should be fried on our behalf. As the contents of the pan sizzled there arose the unmistakable aroma of frying rashers. Whilst our entry and subsequent comings and goings in no way disturbed the woman of the house, the smell of frying rashers quickly penetrated her slumber.

'Who's there?' she called harshly.

'Only us,' her husband responded foolishly.

'Who's us?' she demanded.

As he started to reel off the names of his companions ominous noises began from upstairs. Two of our number silently vanished. The rest of us stood idly by. Down the stairs she came with only her nightdress on and nothing in her hands save a well-developed alarm clock.

'Out!' she screamed, and with that she let fly with the alarm clock. It whirred harmlessly if speedily over our heads and crashed through the sitting-room window before landing on the street, where it alarmed at great length.

Some weeks later I met her on the street and apologised profusely for invading the privacy of her home at such an ungodly hour. She gladly accepted my apology and informed me in a dulcet voice that not an angry word had crossed her lips since the flinging of the alarm clock.

'I won't have to smash a thing now for months,' she explained, which all goes to show that there are better ways of unleashing our frustrations than effing and blinding and that a good alarm clock can be used year after year without any real damage to its structure.

FEAR

I am convinced that fear is the only malady that man will never conquer. By degrees, slowly and painfully, disease after incurable disease is being taken on and overcome by man's persistent efforts. It is man who mostly manufactures fear. We can elude the wild beast, destroy him if necessary. We can survive the elements at their worst by taking precautions. There are disasters from time to time but only because man has persistently underestimated the elements.

But where does fear begin? For me, it began in the school, the very place where it was not supposed to begin, and it didn't begin with teachers. It began with *garsúns* a little older than myself. A year is an awful difference in a *garsún*. Often, when there is such a difference between two small boys, it is much the same as a confrontation between a lightweight and a heavyweight. All other things being equal, the boy with the year advantage is a cast-iron certainty to win out. I was afraid of bullies at school and they were afraid too of bigger boys or of brutality in their homes, and so forth and so on *ad infinitum*.

Two distinct advantages in any confrontation between schoolboys were squints and scars. Let the boy with the squint be a disaster as a pugilist, he had, nevertheless, the edge on his opponent if he played his cards right. He could look at him in the eye with the most advantageous consequences because, when confronted with a squint, the chap at the receiving end hasn't an earthly from what quarter the attack is about to be mounted or whether the left or right hand is going to be deployed as a decoy.

Often, too, a chap with a squint would seem to be looking over the shoulder of his opponent, giving the impression that aid might be forthcoming from that quarter in the event of emergency. In my time I was frequently confronted by a squint. I would sooner face a chap twice my size than one with a squint.

A scar, however, was another kettle of fish. A chap with a scar on his face was rarely called upon to defend himself. The scar was better than a weapon to him. Better still, it had the value of a battle citation, and the bigger the better. In my time I have seen *garsúns* with scars swagger through crowds of bully boys who would normally interrogate every innocent who passed their way. The bully-boys would always make way for the scarred. There would be nudgings and eggings-on by ringleaders but nobody wanted to find out if the scar had been earned in combat or by accident. The result was that the scarred veteran of six or seven had a right of way wherever he went.

The same applied to a chap with a lame leg or a crutch. However, one needed to be a very good actor to get away with a lame leg and if one presented a lame leg without a scratch or a swelling or some other outward sign of injury, the jig was up. Bandages didn't always work either. Bandages could be peeled off by the bully boy and God help the invalid if there were no marks or bloodstains underneath.

Of course, all these subterfuges were created by fear. The innocent quail will pretend to be possessed of a broken wing when danger threatens her young. She will divert the passer-by or the overly curious by giving the impression that her wing is really broken. Man is no different. He uses subterfuge to save his own skin most of the time.

Spectacles were also a great subterfuge. A young chap, when offered to fight against his will, would take off his glasses and pretend he couldn't see. He would, instead, volunteer to wrestle, wrestling not being a very dangerous exercise so long as the victim allowed himself to be pinned to the ground.

Fear was at the back of it all, mostly fear of what might happen. How's that Shakespeare puts it in *Julius Caesar*:

Cowards die many times before their deaths;
The valiant never taste of death but once.

Yes, indeed, as I said at the beginning, there is no known antidote for fear unless one faces up to it. This is not always wise because it is how orphans and widows come into being.

Fear is a malady but it need not be that bad a malady, like miserliness or grandeur. Take it away and we are without the body's last line of defence. A modicum of fear is necessary as well as good. It brings us prudence which is another name for our guardian angel.

Without a leavening of fear, most people would be unbearable. On top of that, the human race would annihilate itself in no time at all because without fear we would be at each other's throats morning, noon and night. We would be without respect for each other, and courage, one of man's finest possessions, would be absolutely worthless.

So maybe it's a good thing that we have cowards and that they die many times before their deaths. Fear, I believe, is one of the most essential ingredients in man's make-up.

When I was young I often heard it said of a man that he was without fear. This could not have been true. The man in question, I am certain, was merely better at concealing fear than most men. He was possessed of fear without doubt but he always gave the impression that he was not, and this is a great sign of a man. He can carry the day by keeping his cool. We are all, give or take a taste, possessed of the same leavening of fear but it is how we handle that fear that distinguishes us from the coward, and this is the very essence of our treatise here today.

I remember after a football game, many years ago, several of us players who had remained behind in the village were surrounded by a hostile mob as we were about to leave. Our enemies, egged on by a well-known blackguard, were whipping themselves into a frenzy and it looked as if we faced a terrible beating. Then one of our party spoke in low tones which only we could hear. He was a half-back.

'Don't give it to say to the hoors,' said he, 'that we're afraid of them. Stand fast now and we'll get out of this no bother.'

So saying, he leaped forward in front of the egger-on and challenged him to single combat. The egger-on crumpled, and suddenly the danger which threatened had evaporated and we were allowed to leave the village in peace.

Our half-back, as we all knew well, was not exactly the bravest man in the world. In fact he always maintained that he was cowardly.

'I'm windy,' he used to say, 'but don't tell me because I already know it.'

Yet he concealed his fear and succeeded in averting a potentially nasty situation. How did he bring himself to do it?

Very simple. He knew exactly how little courage he had but, little as that was, it was more than the amount possessed by the egger-on. In fact, I doubt if the egger-on had any courage at all. Men with courage don't behave the way he behaved. Only men with too little courage and too much fear behave in such a fashion.

Now I have to leave you, for I am also possessed of a fear, and it is a fear common to all writers. It is the fear of boring his readers, a crime of which every writer stands terrified of being convicted.

FEMALE WRONGS

In recent times there has been no scarcity of radio and television programmes concerning the victimisation of the female of the species, concerning the reluctance of the male of the species to involve himself in household work, concerning his unwillingness to participate in all meals and his unwillingness to participate in the washing-up. There's no doubt but that he has gotten away with murder for generations.

Let me be among the first to say *mea culpa*. With ninety-nine percent of the male population of the Republic of Ireland I plead guilty to the crime of non-participation in household chores except on very rare occasions when the woman of the house was indisposed. The only defence I can offer is that after initial efforts to render assistance I was thereafter never encouraged to take part. I was accused of doing more damage than good and wrongfully accused of doing so deliberately in order to avoid involvement in such goings-on in the future.

I will concede, however, that there are many glaring injustices being perpetrated against the Irish female and if I have been guilty in the past I hereby resolve never to be guilty in the future.

Bad as we are in respect of victimisation of the female we are only trotting after our ancestors. When I was a *garsún* it was unthinkable for a woman to present herself in a licensed premises unless she was on the warpath after a drunken husband who had neglected to carry home his wages and was content to see his wife and children starve so long as he could fill his gut with porter. Even then women were frowned upon and the one thing, acceptable to male customers and male barmen, was to send in a child to tell the offending wretch that he was wanted at home.

I remember too being astonished to hear cluck-clucks of disapproval when a woman wearing a black shawl went up the centre aisle of the church. Fine if she went up the side aisles or remained at the rear of the church. Bad, however, as these sins against women were, at the time there were far worse. Women were supposed to eat less and were expected to decline offers of strong drink when offered same. It was fine for men to drink but not fine for women.

One outstanding case of bias against women I will never forget. It was during the twelve o'clock mass many, many years ago. There was always a long sermon in those days, a long rambling sermon that most Mass-goers could make neither head nor tail of. It went on and on and on until half the congregation was either asleep or dozing. Then came the announcement out of the blue that the man in the pulpit had been shocked out of his ecclesiastical wits only a few short days before.

There he was, passing through the town square, when he beheld a woman staggering in front of him. When she fell to the ground he went to her assistance and was astonished to find that she was drunk. He raised a finger of admonition to the congregation and there was a silence in the church the like of which I personally had never experienced before.

'A drunken man, after all,' he said, 'is only a drunken man but a drunken woman is a drunken woman.'

He stressed the words 'drunken woman' and one got the distinct impression that a drunken dog was a noble creature by comparison. He forgot to mention that there had been drunken men falling about the streets of the town since the opening of its first tavern. In fact I once wrote about the longest drunken stagger I had ever seen. I have long been a student of drunken staggers and it totally eclipsed all others for length and mis-direction. It was of course executed by a man, a drunken man. Up until that time I had never seen a woman stagger but they were the more culpable, drinkwise, in the eyes of the clergy.

'Frailty,' wrote Shakespeare, 'thy name is woman.' Alas poor Shakespeare. He should know better than any that the only thing frailer than a woman is a man. Even I know that and I'm no Shakespeare.

Even Milton erred in his attitude towards the English female: 'Wisest men have erred and by bad women been deceived.' Surely he knew that men are the acknowledged deceivers and for every woman who deceived a man there are a hundred men who deceived women.

When I was growing up, and even still, a woman of the house never sat to table until every other member had been seated first. When did we ever see a man on his knees scrubbing a floor? When I see it I'll eat the scrubbing brush.

The Music of Humanity

Many years ago while in the village of Carraigkerry during a carnival I found myself in a public house in the middle of a huge crowd of people. I believe I have referred briefly to this incident before but a letter from a reader in Leeds requests me to recall that marvellous occasion for her. She comes from the district in question and was a young girl when the incident occurred.

It was Sunday night in the height of summer as I set out from Listowel with three companions. Happily all are in the land of the living save one. The deceased is Dan Kennelly, the well-known Listowel publican. The living are Jerome Murphy, the popular Listowel auctioneer originally from Glashnagook, Knocknagoshel, and the other is Jimmy Boylan, a retired upholsterer from the city of Cork.

It was Jimmy Boylan who came to my aid when I strove to resurrect the occasion. He has a prodigious memory and, as luck would have it, he happens to be holidaying in these premises right now.

'I often think of that night,' he said, 'and the magic that was in it.'

Anyway, to proceed with the tale, we departed Listowel at approximately seven-thirty. We stopped in the beautiful village of Athea to slake our respective thirsts, and after spending an hour in extremely congenial company in two of the village's more engaging public houses we proceeded on our journey.

Carraigkerry was packed to capacity or, as the man said, you couldn't draw your leg. However, crowded as the streets were, the public houses were crammed entirely, and it was either a brave man or a genuinely thirsty one who would venture through the portals of any one. We decided, therefore, to postpone a public-house visit for a while so that we might take in the musical delights on offer.

There was no scarcity of musicians. I remember we encountered the late and great Jack Faulkner, who welcomed us officially. Jack always said that his full name was Jack Wilberforce Faulkner, but the trouble with Jack was that you never knew whether he was codding you or not. Otherwise he was a great soul with a profound sense of humour, and his welcome put the seal on what was to be a memorable occasion.

Eventually, because of the attention we paid to the many musicians who played out of doors, we found ourselves mentally exhausted. Mental exhaustion is the very thing to put an edge on the thirst so once more we found ourselves drawn to the public house. We chose the nearest one to where we found ourselves. We were warmly greeted by patrons and publican alike. Standing room was made for us and we were welcomed into that most intoxicating of brotherhoods often referred to by the abstemious as the drinking classes.

Here were no gentlemen as such nor were any landed gentry apparent. Here was the heart's blood of the Irish countryside with its own music, its own money and its own capacity to absorb strong drink in all its forms and all this, remember, without the least vestige of hostility, rancour or coarse language.

Our wants were simple. Four Irish whiskies. Clutching our glasses to our breasts we stood in the middle of the crowd exchanging pleasantries and warmly responding to the many fine welcomes extended unstintingly by the good folk of West Limerick.

Then we heard it, faint at first but gradually growing in

volume until our voices were stilled, so rapt was our admiration for the heavenly music which assailed our ears.

It was fiddle music, of course. We looked around for the musician. He stood nearby with his eyes closed, his bow moving gently across the strings and an unsurpassed melody pouring out from the soul of the venerable instrument which he clasped.

'What's that you're playing?' one of our party asked.

'I'm not playing,' he responded with a smile.

'But it's your fiddle,' we told him, 'and it's your hand that is directing the bow.'

'It is not my hand,' he explained, 'it is the hands of all men.'

He went further for our enlightenment and informed us that it was the stirrings of the throng of people which governed the movements of the bow.

'Look,' he said, as the crowd swayed, 'the people are pushing against my arm. It's their music, not mine.'

What he said was true. The bow moved over the strings, impelled by the human beings all around.

'It's the music of humanity,' said the fiddler, 'praise be to God for all things.'

SALUTE YE ONE ANOTHER

At a wedding recently I was taken to task by a pleasant young female because of a piece I wrote many moons ago which dealt with saluting people. Now I have written about saluting on several occasions but it is the opinion of the young lady in question that I should discourage people from saluting other people. Her reasons are valid enough. She says that people who drive cars are endangering other people's lives when they salute other drivers. She also maintained that pedestrians should concentrate upon their own comings and goings rather than salute acquaintances and friends, not to mention run-of-the-mill passers-by. I did not argue the toss with the girl at the time but I promised her that I would deal with the subject, for the final time, when the mood caught me.

Not saluting people will, I believe, ultimately do far more harm than good. For instance, let us suppose you are driving along any given roadway and an acquaintance salutes you with a wave of the hand from the driving seat of another car which happens to be travelling in the opposite direction. If you deliberately refuse to return the salute you could be the cause of affecting the unsaluted party's concentration and thus contribute to a crash or even loss of life.

What this young lady does not seem to know is that the people of this world, regardless of their stations or ages, are in constant need of reassurance. With no one to reassure them there are many people who would just disintegrate or become antisocial. In the absence of a system, state-sponsored or otherwise, whereby people would be reassured regularly we are left with the simple salute. It is, in my humble opinion, the only inexpensive means of reassuring neglected pedestrians and motorists that there is somebody out there who cares. I'm out there for instance. I feel that everybody must be saluted without reason. Obviously if you are in a dangerous quarter of a large city where crime is rampant you would be well advised, especially if you are a female, to suspend your saluting activities until you return to safer climes or, better still, climes where you are known.

Saluting strange men in dangerous surroundings is akin to a deer saluting a cheetah or a lamb saluting a lion. Imagine a rabbit out for an innocent stroll suddenly pausing and address-ing a nod or a wave of a forepaw to a hungry fox. Beware then where you salute!

Reassurance, like common sense, is one of the world's rarer commodities. If there was enough reassurance to go around, there would be no despondency or depression but then, says the gentle reader, what would happen to depression-treaters and despondency-treaters and what would happen to the employees of chemical concerns who manufacture pills and potions for the lifting of depression? This is the problem about providing solu-tions for the pressing problems. The birth of a solution means the birth of another problem.

However, let us press on. Some people go to extraordinary lengths not to salute other people. I have seen them in action. It has even happened to myself. A man who owes me a few quid which I don't require always covers his face with his umbrella when we pass by. If he hasn't an umbrella he disappears into shops or up alleyways.

Then there are what I call natural slighters who set up in-nocent acquaintances and even neighbours for a cheery salute and then, at the last minute when the other party has committed itself to a salute, the setter-upper doesn't salute at all. This has the same effect on the unsaluted party as a thwarted sneeze.

Then there are those who will not return salutes for the simple reason that they have been unsaluted by the saluter in the past. Then there is jealousy. I knew a woman in our street who cocked her snoot in the air at all those who she believed were better off than she was. Take it from me my friends you are better off saluting regardless of the provocation to which you feel you have been subjected over the years. Not saluting precipitates chain reaction. If you fail to return the salute of an acquaintance then the sons and daughters of that acquaintance may end up not saluting you or yours. The end result of all this could lead to nobody saluting, nobody doffing or waving or winking or yoo-hooing. You want this to happen? If you do, then don't salute people!

Believe me when I say that a large percentage of the world's population is starved for the want of a salute. When I was a small boy there was a man in town who used to give us youngsters a halfpenny to salute him when there were people around on occasions such as race days or after football games or coming from Mass. He would give us the halfpenny with the instruction that we were to say 'Hello Mister Moogle. How are you Mister Moogle'.

Of course his name wasn't Moogle. I can't disclose his real name because his descendants are still in the neighbourhood and if they become aware that I mentioned their ancestor's hunger for salutations they might never salute me again. This happens all the time. The tragedy is that while I would know why I am not being saluted the vast majority who go unsaluted do not know the reason why. This can be very frustrating, and they resolve there and then not to salute 'that so and so', as they call the non-saluter, ever again. I am certain that there are many people who simply pine away for want of a salute. Remember this when you feel like cocking your snoot in the air. You may unwittingly be bringing about the downfall of another, or is this what you have in mind in the first place? If so, you are being grossly unchristian and will one day be called aside and asked to explain yourself by you-know-who.

Of course it must also be said that there are large numbers of people suffering from delusions of grandeur, which I have always regarded as one of the worst maladies known to medical science.

We had a lady in our street once and she would salute nobody. My father, God be good to him, would say that she was right, 'for,' he would ask in his homely way, especially if he had a few jars taken, 'who the heck is anybody anyway?'

Then there are unfortunate folk who suffer from surfeits of rebuffs over the years and will not risk saluting horses and even donkeys. I have seen sane men salute cows and bullocks in secluded places. I dare say some of them do it to keep their hands in.

In conclusion I would advise the gentle reader to salute wherever possible, even if no encouragement is provided by the party about to be saluted. Better still, we might cleave to the dictum of the ancient maxim: Salute ye one another in the highways and the byways, at the going up of the moon and the going down of the sun. Amen.

REMEMBRANCE

A Night to Remember

Did I ever tell you about the time my father risked his life for his family and his neighbours? It was pay day 1933, the first or second day in November to be exact. He was paid monthly, like all teachers at the time. As usual in the pub that night he had one too many. He always did on the nights of pay days.

Accompanying him was a stalwart neighbour who shared in his good fortune. We shall call him Jack. As was their wont they entered our house by the back way but the moment they stepped inside the back gate they were assaulted by several men wearing white garments. A fierce fight ensued in which no quarter was asked or given.

It lasted a full hour, during which not a single utterance escaped the mouths of the men in the white sheets. At first my father thought it might be the Ku Klux Klan but during the engagement he asked himself why the dreaded southerners would make such a long journey just to attack a middle-aged schoolteacher and his elderly friend.

Eventually the fight ended and the assailants fled, leaving behind them their white garments.

In the kitchen of our house my father and his friend saw to their wounds. They congratulated themselves on their courage. Of the two, Jack had suffered the more. He had a loose tooth and a black eye, whereas my father was lucky enough to escape with scratches and minor abrasions. The commotion had awakened every member of the family. Some brandy which was reserved for medicinal purposes was produced. My father and Jack finished it off in no time at all and sat themselves wearily down while they tried to identify their assailants. My mother asked if they might have been from the other world, members of the banshee family or even the Puca, but my father was convinced the creatures were human, 'For,' said he, 'I struck one of the scoundrels twice and I heard him grunt the same way as a human might under the circumstances.'

'They were humans all right,' his friend Jack concurred. 'The chap who struck me smelled of strong drink and he also called me a wretch.'

At this stage the girl who worked in the house entered the kitchen. She was, we all knew, governed by full moons and would watch a full moon all night long until the stars faded from the heavens. She had seen the invaders from an upstairs window and yet she wasn't distraught or incoherent or anything like that. In fact she seemed to find it difficult to hold back the laughter. We thought she was on the verge of a bout of hysteria. The moon had affected her thus at least once in the past. All she could do was point at my father and his friend and hold her laughter at bay.

This annoyed my father no end. Was it for this he and his friend had risked their lives!

'Speak up woman,' he commanded curtly, 'tell us what you saw. Were they human or were they supernatural?'

'They were sheets,' she responded with a smile, 'the sheets on the washing line.'

'But who struck me?' Jack asked.

'Himself,' said the girl. She always referred to my father as himself. 'Himself struck you when the sheet was wrapped around your head. He said you were a wretch.'

'But,' my father expostulated, 'where did I get all these scratches and abrasions?'

'Clothes pegs,' the girl explained. 'When the wind whipped

off the sheets the clothes pegs hit you.'

There followed a long silence. All of us, save my mother, crawled back upstairs to our beds. Later that night after Jack had gone home my mother told my father she was proud of him.

'I know what it's like,' she said, 'to get a slap of a wet sheet, yet you faced a line full of them thinking they were out to get your family and your wife. What you did was heroic and I'm honoured to be married to you.'

It Never Rains But It Pours

Ever since I was a boy I have been fascinated by the pronouncements and conclusions of local weather forecasters. These men knew their suns and moons and their winds and skies but were modest in the extreme about their accomplishments.

'Tis many a long day now since myself and Mickeen McCarthy borrowed Jack Horan's ass to draw a four-man slean of turf out of Dirha Bog. On our way we met Sir Stafford Cripps and Mr Chamberlain which were the names given to two elderly brothers who dwelt in the farthest-in house in the bog.

'Will the day hold fine?' Mickeen asked.

Sir Stafford raised wrinkled eyes to the western horizon and sniffed the wind.

'There's no rain in that,' he said and he turned to the brother for corroboration.

'The crows are flying with their backs to the wind,' Mr Chamberlain announced, 'and by all the powers that be you'll get no rain today.'

The next soul we encountered was Sonny Canavan and he making horse stoolins of dry turf on a bank near the roadway.

'Will the day hold fine?' Mickeen asked.

'Would I be here?' Canavan asked, 'but for I knowing we'll have no break.'

This gave us great heart because the Ballybunion Pattern Day, which is the fifteenth of August, was only two days off and Mickeen had a buyer lined up for the turf if we could have it on the side of the road by evening.

'Listen,' said Canavan and he raised a finger for silence.

We listened, and far away from the west came a sullen deep monotone interspersed with the faint cries of far-off seagulls.

'What does it signify?' Mickeen asked.

'It signifies,' said Canavan, 'that the sea is near today and when the sea is near you'll see no break.'

Greatly heartened, Mickeen produced a paper packet of Woodbines and tendered one each to Canavan and myself. We then sat on our behinds, our backs supported by the stoolins and our legs stretched in front of us, content in the knowledge that we had the day long to handle the job before us. We spoke about the war. The following day Churchill and Roosevelt were to meet at sea. Earlier that year Hess had flown to Scotland.

'If Hess had landed in Dirha instead of Scotland,' said Canavan, 'we'd have an extra man for the slean and we needn't be recruiting townies.'

Earlier that year, as well, the *Bismark* had been sunk.

'I'll tell ye once and I'll tell ye no more,' said Canavan, 'that Hitler lost his chance. He got his fine days too but he didn't make hay.'

So the conversation went on and on until the shrouded sun began to rise in the noonday sky. We took our leave of Canavan who returned to his stoolins and we made haste for the house of Jack Horan. At either side of the roadway the larks rose singing and the mellow booming of bullfrogs bore witness to the simple joys of bogland life. Now and then a billy goat would raise his head from the herbage to inspect us, and mild, summer breezes rustled the tinder-dry heather.

'These are mighty times,' said Mickeen. At Jack Horan's we were greeted by his wife, who told us that himself was in bed but that we could have the loan of the ass for five Woodbines. The cigarettes were handed over and we set about tackling up.

'Will it hold fine?' Mickeen asked of Mrs Horan.

'Will it hold fine, Jack?' she called through the bedroom window. There was no immediate answer but after a short while Jack Horan emerged in a long nightshirt down to his toes and a cap on his head. There was a cigarette in his mouth. The ass was now tackled and the rail in place.

'Will it hold fine?' asked Mickeen. Jack Horan took the cigarette from his mouth, topped it and carefully placed the butt behind his left ear.

'Look beyond,' he said, and he pointed a black-nailed finger towards where the blue mountains of the Dingle range stood out from the background of a clear sky.

'When the wind is from that quarter,' said Jack Horan, 'the weather will stay settled.'

Along the bumpy roadway we walked at either side of the plodding ass. The larks sang louder now and soared exultantly heavenwards, leaving behind them wonderful trails of song. Suddenly I was struck on the forehead by a solitary, outsized raindrop. A minute passed and I was struck by another. Then came another and another until it seemed that every raindrop in the sky had specially convened for an all-out assault on Dirha Bog. The rain came down in blinding sheets until streams began to flow at either side of the roadway. The ass slithered and fell, and the passage which led to our slean of turf had now become a gurgling stream.

'Never mind,' said Mickeen, 'we still have a smoke left.'

From his pocket he produced a paper packet of Woodbines but, inside, the cigarettes were wet and soggy as bog-mould.

'It was said before,' Mickeen announced, 'but I'll say it again. It never rains but it pours.'

CREAKY STEPS

There used to be a creaky step on the stairs of the house where I was born and reared. As an alarm system it was without equal and no matter how carefully one trod on it, it always reacted noisily.

It was a step for which I had no love but nothing would induce my father or mother to have it repaired.

'That step,' said my father, 'always informs me of the home-coming hours of my sons.'

It was indeed a third party. It was also a traitorous double-crossing slat of timber which creaked ominously and often cockily when one of us was out longer than he should.

We used to try avoiding it but somehow it succeeded in passing on the information to the next step which creaked informatively no matter how light one's footfall. This led me to believe, and I have had no reason since to doubt it, that all stairs, great and small, are possessed of this single traitorous step.

My father was proud of our step. In his eyes the other steps in the flight were common fellows not worthy of notice. Years afterwards when we had grown up and gone our separate ways in the world he still cherished the step and refused to replace it, and events proved he was right for the step was to fulfil a role similar to that played by the Capitol geese when they saved Rome or Killorglin's puck goat when he forewarned his friends and neighbours of approaching invaders.

It was the second night of Listowel Races and my mother and he were fast asleep. Night is not quite correct since it was two o'clock in the morning but you know how people say night when they really mean morning. For instance, the song that runs: 'Who were you with last night?' should, I have no doubt, read: 'Who were you with this morning?' If the girl in question was home before twelve the song would not have been written. Nobody minds a girl having a night out but a morning out is a different matter.

But where was I?

Yes, it was two o'clock in the morning and my father was snoring away to his heart's content. He was, as snorers go, in a class of his own. In this respect the Tonic Solfa held no terrors for him and he cavorted between high do and low do like an apprentice operatic singer.

Sound asleep as he was, when the step creaked he awoke immediately and seized a poker which he always kept handy. He did not go out on the stairs but called out from the safety of the room.

'Who's there?' he shouted.

No answer at first but when the step creaked again he knew that the invader was at least intimidated and contemplating retreat. My father waited a few moments and then went out on the landing, clutching the poker. He was, it is only fair to say, followed by my mother.

'There's nobody there!' she said.

'Correction!' said my father; 'you mean there's nobody there now!'

'Maybe 'twas the cat?' my mother suggested.

'Nonsense!' said my father. 'No cat could cause a creak like that.'

Months later, when we were all at home for Christmas, he told us about the incident. He gave a description of the intruder. 'The scoundrel must have weighed fifteen or sixteen stone,' he said. 'He was also remarkably fit, either a wrestler or a fighter.' My father deduced all this from the two creaks. 'But for that step,' he concluded, 'we would all have been murdered in our beds.'

'There was only the two of us in the house!' said my mother.

'When I said "all of us" I meant the two of us,' my father announced.

The following night, St Stephen's Night, the step betrayed us individually and collectively as we entered at all hours from dances and parties. My father didn't really mind the time but he liked to know what was going on.

I have on my own stairs a similar step and sometimes, when I go to football matches, the missus says: 'If I'm asleep when you come back, don't wake me up!' I promise I will do this and always I keep my promise. But one night the step creaked and she woke up. I spent the next two hours describing the match. In the end she asked, 'What woke me?' I told her it was a creaky step. 'Nonsense,' she said. 'We have no creaky step.' I left the room and told her to listen. When I came up to the step in question it creaked in a most objectionable manner. When I returned to the room, she was satisfied.

'You know . . . ,' she said, before she went to sleep.

'What's that?' I asked.

'Nothing,' she said, 'but it's just that I've always wanted a creaking step in the house.'

I like the step myself because it is more than likely that it will be an asset to me, the same as my father's was to him. A creaking step is as good as a dog and it eats very little – just a fragment of wax polish now and then.

CORNER-BOYS

To be a corner-boy one must be fit for nothing else. It is a career into which men are born, not thrust. A corner-boy can, in his own time, become an institution.

Nobody loves a corner-boy, not even other corner-boys, so how, the gentle reader might well ask, can it be called a career?

It was a wise man who said that as long as we have corners we will have corner-boys. We are therefore, as it were, stuck with them. They have become part of the fabric of our society, although some unkind observers are likely to maintain that they belong to the outer edges of the fabric or to that part which is more frayed than the rest.

This is not so. We have had corners since the very dawn of civilisation. Therefore, we have had corner-boys since the very dawn of civilisation. They have established themselves through long tradition which is more than can be said for those drop-outs who simply stayed at home. Corner-boying is a career, without material reward maybe, but a career nevertheless.

Indeed, it might be said that as surely as faith without good works is dead, so also a corner without a boy is dead. There is nothing sadder than a corner-boy without a corner. There are others who have searched in vain for the right corner and never found it. A corner-boy takes one look at a corner and he knows instinctively that this is the corner where he wants to spend the rest of his days.

It may be occupied by other corner-boys at the time but then it is a poor corner that can only accommodate one boy. Most corners maintain two, three, four and even more. As a rule, however, there is only one constant corner-boy. Others come and go and are no more than part-time corner-boys but your resident corner-boy never deserts his post unless he is forced to do so by circumstances outside his control.

He has, as indeed we all have, his natural enemy. The writer's is indifference, the thatcher's is stormy weather and the sea captain's is fog. The corner-boy's is rain. He can withstand hail, snow and storm but not rain. Snowflakes can be brushed away. Hail rolls off harmlessly, but rain penetrates and so he must abandon his post through no fault of his own. On really wet days you won't see any corner-boys. Make a point the next rainy day you're out of doors to examine the corners you pass. You're more likely to see a polar bear than a corner-boy.

Some years ago I had a conversation with a corner-boy of my acquaintance. As a rule, corner-boys are not conversationalists. They are listeners. By virtue of their exposed positions they are prey to passers-by. If these happen to be loquacious or simple-minded or merely drunken people, the corner-boy is forced to lend his ear to the musings, ramblings and general verbal output of his tormentors. He must do this or vacate his position. Only the years bring him immunity and in time an amused smile is his only reaction to whatever he is told.

The conversation I had was unique in that it afforded me the deepest possible insight into the mind of a corner-boy. It was, as I recall, a dull afternoon in midwinter. I had intended going for a walk but the skies had an intimidating look about them. I could well be letting myself in for a comprehensive drenching, I told myself. I crossed the road and stood irresolutely at the corner, asking myself would I go or would I stay.

'Quiet today,' I threw the question at the corner-boy in residence. He did not reply. He produced a cigarette box, extracted a cigarette, the sole occupant of the box in question. He put the cigarette in his mouth and deliberately threw the box on to the roadway.

This was an old ploy. He had several such boxes in his pockets, each containing no more than one cigarette. If he produced a box containing more than one cigarette he might be expected to part to other corner-boys or to acquaintances in the immediate vicinity. The next thing he produced was a match which he lighted by scraping it against the wall at his rear.

Then he spoke. 'It's always quiet,' he said. 'I'm here thirty years, man and boy. I've never seen it otherwise.'

I was pleasantly surprised that he answered. I knew him to be a man of few words. I had at best expected a grunt of agreement. I decided to press my advantage. Here was a man of the outdoors, a man who might be versed in the vagaries of the weather.

'Do you think it will rain?' I asked. He looked upward and cogitated. His gaze remained riveted to the sky for a long period during which time he consistently wetted his lips with his tongue and thrice drew deeply on his cigarette. Then he answered:

'Hard to say,' he said.

'The forecast says it will,' I told him. He scoffed and spat, topped his cigarette and quenched the glowing ash with the sole of his right shoe.

'Forecasts,' he scoffed again. 'Yesterday they promised bright spells and if you had binoculars you wouldn't find the blue of a child's eye in the sky. As for the day before. You remember the day before?' I nodded eagerly, not wishing to interfere with his recollections.

'They promised us a ridge of high pressure.' He was laughing now. 'A ridge of high pressure they said and what did we get? I'll tell you what we got. We got a downpour.'

'Do you remember Neddy Connor?' I asked, entering into the spirit of the thing.

'I do indeed. Why wouldn't I remember him. Wasn't he related to my mother. There's a man could forecast the weather. He had a nose for rain. He reminded me of nothing but a pointer the way he'd cock that nose, warts and all, into the wind.

'"Thunder," he'd say, and you have thunder fit to burst your eardrums. "Snow," he'd say, and before the day was out the roofs of the houses would be white. "Rain," he'd say, and, by God, you got rain.'

'He was some forecaster,' I said, 'and that's a fact about his being able to smell rain.'

'Rain,' he spat out the word derisively. 'Who the hell wants rain anyway?'

'Farmers,' I suggested. He scoffed at the mention of farmers. Let me say here that he was a natural scoffer. Every single scoff was more pronounced than the one before. They were mocking, ironical and sarcastic.

'Anglers,' I said. 'Anglers want rain.' I said it to provide him with material for another scoff. The scoff came, more pronounced and effective than its predecessor.

'Fruit growers,' I suggested. He had no sympathy for fruit growers either. 'Then you have ducks,' I said. 'Ducks always want rain.'

There followed an unprintable exclamation.

'Nearly everyone wants rain,' I said.

'Well, I don't. I don't want the damned thing,' he shot back. 'In fact, the last thing I want in this world is rain.'

'But there has to be rain,' I reminded him.

'Who says so?' he asked aggressively.

'Everybody.'

'Not me. I don't want it.'

'But if you have no rain,' I told him, 'everything will wither up.'

'I'm the opposite,' he said. 'Rain withers me up.'

'How could rain wither anyone?' I asked.

'When it rains,' he explained passionately, 'I have to go home. There's nobody at home. There's always somebody here. I'm happy here. At home I just sit and wait for the rain to pass. The longer it takes to pass the more I wither. Let it rain by night. I don't mind it raining by night. Let it rain any time except when I'm standing at this corner.'

I was quite unprepared for his tirade against rain. I have presented his sentiments as best I can recall them. He looked quite exhausted after holding forth. He looked upward and muttered an imprecation. He had no buttons on his coat, but he drew it together symbolically, indicating that he was about to depart.

He pulled up his coat collar and suddenly, like a frightened coot, he crossed the road and disappeared around a corner further up the street. A raindrop struck me on the forehead. Another did likewise. In no time at all the skies opened up and the rain came down in earnest.

I hurried indoors and surveyed the dismal scene through my front window. The corner was deserted but I had a better understanding of the denizens who frequent it. The corner-boy had said but little but in that little there was much. In a few words he had explained his case. *Vir sapit qui pauca loquitur.*

PLAY THE FOOL

'If fools were scarce he'd make two.' Don't ask me where I heard that statement. It could have been anywhere – radio, television or the pub. It could have been the street. It matters not, however, where it was heard. What really matters is that I remember it and present it here for your titillation.

It recalls for me too how facilely we dismiss people with the disdainful observation that they are fools. 'Don't mind him,' we say, 'he's nothing but a fool.' But is he a fool? He may talk like a fool and be regarded as a fool by those who would be better advised to retain their sentiments but for all this he knows how to make out in the world. I'll give you an instance.

Years ago we were all seated at the dinner table in my father's house. There was a good dinner in front of us. Midway through the meal a young man entered. He was from another part of town but he used to run with us as children and consequently a place was made for him at the table. He had just returned from England where he had left his job and come home for a holiday. He dined well. In fact, as my father was later to recall, he polished off twice as much as any of us. He regaled us with tales of his life abroad in a slightly affected accent. When he finished eating he accepted a cigarette and when the cigarette was alight he took his leave.

When he was gone he came in for some severe criticism. Listowel, then as now, was no different from any other small town in its capacity for character assassination. We referred to his accent and we referred to his tall tales and we referred to the payslips which he had shown us. It was the fashion of the time for young chaps working in England to bring home their pay-slips, especially overtime ones in order to show how well they were doing across the sea.

We had several good laughs at his expense but then my father made one of his rare observations. He was a man seldom given to commentary and when he spoke it nearly always made sense. 'You think he's a fool!' he opened as he cleaned out the bowl of his pipe with a penknife. We did not answer. We were not meant to. He looked at each face in turn, pursed his lips and returned to the evisceration of the pipe bowl. 'I say he's a very clever fellow indeed,' my father went on, 'a far cleverer fellow than any of you.'

At this stage we felt we were entitled to a laugh, and laugh we did, although it was a rather hollow one for we suspected that he was setting us up as he frequently did. Like a skilled boxer he would allow us to indulge in our little vagaries for a while and then flatten us with a series of clever punches.

'He's no more a fool,' he went on, 'than I am. In fact if I was pressed in a court of law I would say that I was a bigger fool than he is.'

More laughter. Then my younger sister intervened. 'But,' said she, 'you're a schoolmaster.'

We all laughed, my father the loudest of all.

'Let us recap,' he said. We listened attentively although all of the males of the household, myself excluded because of my youth, had indulged in a few pre-prandial drinks earlier in Alla Sheehy's pub next door. 'Firstly,' my father had opened, 'he's no fool because of his timing. He knew when we would be having our dinner so he called at that time, knowing full well that he would be provided with an excellent meal free of charge. Secondly, he got himself a free cigarette in spite of the fact that they are severely rationed, and thirdly, he promised that he would call again, which means that he is a very smart chap indeed because the chances are that he will call again during a meal and so provide himself with free fare for a second and maybe a third and fourth time before he decides to go back to England.'

We sat chastened while my father filled his pipe with the cut plug to which he was addicted. Before applying the lighted match to the innards of the pipe bowl he spoke as follows: 'I say to you,' he said solemnly, 'the man who would burn him for a fool would have wise ashes.'

My mother who had been silent up to this joined in. Now she didn't always agree with my father.

'Often,' said she, 'a fellow only seems a fool,' and she went on to tell us about a neighbour of her acquaintance who played the fool to suit himself when she was a young girl in the foot-balling province of Ballydonoghue which lies between Listowel and Ballybunion. 'Everyone,' my mother continued, 'thought he was a fool. This was because he played the fool so well that nobody ever sent him on errands which called for responsibi-lity and nobody asked him to help with the turf-cutting or the hay-making.'

My mother went on to explain that no local farmer would trust him with a shovel lest he do damage to himself or others. Bad as a shovel might be the prospect of what he might do with a pike did not bear thinking about so they left him alone. They even went so far as to cut his turf for him. He had no land so they did not have to make his hay.

'But he was no fool,' my mother insisted, 'he was an able buck and as soon as he went to America they found out that he was far from being the fool he was painted at home. You see,' my mother went on, God be good to her, 'in America it's a case of have it yourself or be without it. 'Tis us here at home that were real fools. We fed and we looked after him and when we had him reared he left us without as much as a thank you. He was able to use a pike and well able to use a shovel but work didn't agree with him.'

To further buttress the fact he was no fool he married well. She was a lady twenty years older and when she eventually worked herself into the grave on his behalf he came back to Ireland and married again, this time a schoolteacher.

'And to think,' said my mother, 'that we thought him a fool. 'Tis now I know who the fools were.'

So there's a messy moral. Play the fool to be thought a fool and you'll even get away with murder!

GAMBLES

The gamble is a thing of the past.

Too much money for one thing and too many motors for another.

I once participated in a gamble for a fat goose. There were eight of us at the table and knaves were cast to see who would partner whom. The game was '31' or, if you like, '25', with 11 for the best trump. Our group qualified for the final and there was an air of tension in the kitchen as the cards were shuffled. The issue was to be decided on the best of five games. In short, the first man to win three games would be the outright winner of the goose.

Cards were cut for the deal and I drew lowest. The man next to me was warned to watch his cut in case I had 'put them together'. As the games progressed there were sighs and groans. Knaves were ruthlessly struck by fives and aces of hearts fell foul of knaves. Diamonds were kept but to no avail. Luck was the deciding element and finally the game was won by a man with a cap on his head and a week's beard on his face. He won it on the last day's trick and he hit the table a resounding belt of his fist as he did so. It would have been sacrilegious to win the trick silently.

Post-mortems were held but it was agreed that he had played his cards well. 'Kind for him,' said one old woman, 'all belongin' to him was gamblers.' It transpired that he had won a turkey the year before at a '25' drive in Templeglantine and went to the last four in Athea when a tractor of dry turf was at stake.

There are still gambles for turkeys, geese and hams, but the days of the big gambles are gone. I do not mean that the prize was enormous when I say big gambles. I mean that a widow woman's gamble was as important a social event as the Stations. Contestants paid a shilling a head, and when the prize was won there was tea and bread and jam. Afterwards there was a bit of a dance. There were rows, too, occasionally, but these were accepted as the natural hazards of the course. Suspected renegers were challenged with all the passion of the Old West and if there weren't six-shooters there were bony knuckles eager to tip a tune on the defaulter's head.

Some were not above concealing the ace of hearts, most versatile of cards, in a waistcoat pocket or trousers fold and it was all right as long as you got away with it. In fact, those who succeeded in breaking the rules successfully were regarded as daredevils and were looked upon as lovable characters as long as they weren't caught out.

Keeping the game in was an art in itself and woe to him who didn't stick the high man. The fall of the lift was always in but today it is no longer observed. I dare say there are enough restrictions in the world without adding to them.

When the cards were put away the kettle went down and cups appeared. There were no saucers since it was only to be 'a cup out of the hand'. There were several loaves of shop bread specially bought for the occasion and there were two or three large pots of mixed fruit jam. Jam was regarded as a treat in those days because I remember a farmer's boy who once complained about his diet to his mistress. 'Maybe,' she said sarcastically, ''tis bread and jam you expect?'

Gambles generally began a week before Christmas and there was never a night without one. A man would get word that he was expected to play for a goat in Knockanure on Thursday night and he was warned by messengers not to miss the turkey in Carrickkerry on Friday night. I once knew a man who cycled twenty-seven miles to play for a goat. He told me so himself. Goats were valuable acquisitions. The skin was used to make a bodhran for the Wren boys on Saint Stephen's Day and the meat was given to greyhounds. It was supposed to be good for no-course duffers and three-quarters. A three-quarters was a dog who looked like a greyhound and ate like a greyhound but who failed to perform like a greyhound.

There were gambles for greyhound pups and holy pictures, gambles for she-goats and pucks, asses and ponies, cows and calves, turkeys, geese and bonhams. These last were mostly pet bonhams and difficult to rear unless there was an old woman in the house who understood their ways. 'Twas often that the ioctar of the litter turned out, in the end, to be the best of all.

There were times when local blackguards would come along while the gamble was in progress and stuff the chimney of the house with a wet sack. The kitchen was quickly filled with smoke and it was always wise to count he cards after incidents like these.

The gamble is gone, all right, but its heyday will come again when people realise that the best joys are the simple joys.

THE SPIRIT OF CHRISTMAS

Many years ago on our street in Ireland there lived an old woman who had but one son whose name was Jack. Jack's father had died when Jack was no more than a *garsún* but Jack's mother went out and worked to support her son and herself. As Jack grew older she still went out and worked for the good reason that Jack was only good for three things. He was good for eating, he was good for smoking and he was good for drinking.

To give him his due he never beat his mother or kicked her. All he did was to skedaddle to England when she was too old to go out and work. Years passed but she never had a line from her only son. Every Christmas she would stand inside her window waiting for a card or letter. She waited in vain.

When Christmas came to our street it came with a loud laugh and an expansive humour that healed old sores and lifted the hearts of young and old. If the Christmas that came to our street were a person he would be something like this. He would be in his sixties but glowing with rude health. His face would be flushed and chubby, with sideburns to the rims of his jaws. He would be wearing gaiters and a tweed suit and he would be mildly intoxicated. His pockets would be filled with silver for small boys and girls and for the older folk he would have a party at which he would preside with his waistcoated paunch extending benignly and his posterior benefiting from the glow of a roaring log fire. There would be scalding punch for everybody and there would be roast geese and ducks, their beautiful golden symmetries exposed on large dishes and tantalizing jobs of potato stuffing oozing and bursting from their hip pockets.

There would be singing and storytelling and laughter and perhaps a tear here and there when absent friends were toasted. There would be gifts for everybody and there would be great goodwill as neighbours embraced each other, promising to cherish each other till another twelvemonth had passed.

But Christmas is an occasion and not a person. A person can do things, change things, create things but all our occasions are only what we want them to be. For this reason Jack's mother waited, Christmas after Christmas, for word from her wandering boy. To other houses would come stout registered envelopes from loved ones who remembered. There would be bristling, crumply envelopes from America with noble, rectangular cheques to delight the eye and comfort the soul.

There would be parcels and packages of all shapes and sizes so that every house became a warehouse until the great day when all the goods would be distributed.

Now it happened that in our street there was a postman who knew a lot more about his customers than they knew about themselves.

When Christmas came he was weighted with bags of letters and parcels. People awaited his arrival the way children await a bishop on confirmation day. He was not averse to indulging in a drop of the comforts wherever such comforts were tendered. But comforts or no comforts the man was no fool.

When he came to the house where the old woman lived he would crawl on all fours past the window. He just hadn't the heart to go by and be seen. He hated to disappoint people, particularly old people. For the whole week before Christmas she would take up her position behind the faded curtains waiting for the letter which never came.

Finally the postman could bear it no longer. On Christmas Eve he delivered to our house a mixed bunch of cards and letters. Some were from England. He requested one of these envelopes when its contents were removed. He rewrote the name and address and also he wrote a short note which he signed 'your loving son Jack'. Then from his pocket he extracted two pounds which he placed in the envelope. There was no fear the old woman would notice the handwriting because if Jack was good at some things, as I have already mentioned, he was not good at other things and one of these was writing. In fact he could not write his name.

When he came to the old woman's door he knocked loudly. When she appeared he put on his best official voice and said 'Sign for this if you please, missus'. The old woman signed and opened the envelope. The tears appeared in her eyes and she cried out loud, 'I declare to God Jack is a scholar.'

'True for you,' said the postman, 'and I dare say he couldn't get in touch with you till he learned how to write.'

'I always knew there was good in him,' she cried, 'I always knew it.'

'There was good in everyone missus,' said the postman as he moved on to the next house.

The street was not slow in getting the message and in the next and last post there were many parcels for the old woman. It was probably the best Christmas the street ever had.

LOVE LIES BLEEDING

There is a Latin saying, the authorship of which escapes me right now, that I always recall during the aftermath of domestic upheavals, especially those ones which are confined to husband and wife. The phrase, by the way, has just been attributed to Terence by a gin-and-tonic drinker who also happens to be something of a Latin scholar. Terence, as every publican knows, was brought by the Romans as a slave from Tarsus and wound up writing comedies until he was twenty-five years of age, when he embarked on a voyage from which he did not return. *Amantium irae amoris integratio est.* Thus runs the observation, which means simply 'Lovers' quarrels are the renewal of love.' Oh, how true!

My first confirmation of the truth contained in this Roman adage occurred when I was quite a young man. As I was walking through a certain street in my native town a chamber pot whizzed past my head. It is difficult to describe the sound of a whizzing chamber pot but it differs from other whizzing objects in that it also whirrs and whistles as it flies past. I had a quick glimpse of the lady who threw the pot. She stood in the doorway of her house, her once beautiful face wrecked and dehumanised by the fury which she had brought upon herself. The scoundrel at whom the chamber pot had been aimed took refuge behind me as soon as he saw it in her hand. He had fled the confines of the marital battlefield in his pyjamas after being pelted with a half-full cocoa canister, a turnip and an alarm clock. These missiles were already strewn around our feet. I fled the scene but our friend stood his ground, albeit at a safe distance.

This is the first chapter of the story. The second chapter begins an hour late as I am returning from my morning walk. I am astonished to see the lady who flung the aforementioned missile in the passionate embrace of the person who had managed to evade them. They kissed and cooed and cuddled and closed the door in my face with a bang as I passed.

How right was Terence the playwright. Earlier than that particular incident, however, there was another which deserves to be recalled. So far we may have deduced that reconciliation follows rows and we may also, therefore, deduce that there cannot be reconciliation without a row, which brings me to the second incident.

Picture a busy fair day in a small town forty years ago. The streets were chock-a-block with cattle and people. Among these people was an innocent farmer unused to the ways of the world. He had disposed of his cattle and was walking the streets lapping up the passing scene. Also among the throng was a travelling man and his wife. They were arguing when suddenly the male of the partnership seized the other by the hair of the head and brought her to the ground where he proceeded to strike her with open palm. The farmer was astonished to see that nobody intervened. This should have told him something but it didn't. Bravely he seized the traveller to restrain him. While he was thus occupied, the traveller's wife seized an iron kettle which happened to be hanging with other wares outside a hardware shop. One would imagine that she might seize the opportunity to get even with her husband. Alas, it was the unfortunate farmer to whom she enragedly addressed herself.

'Let him go, you streak of misery,' she shouted at the farmer and she hit him with the kettle on top of his head, felling him at once.

Later when he woke up in hospital he had time to ponder

the foolishness of his action. As he was being taken away in an ambulance earlier, he saw that the tinker woman and her man were warmly embracing each other. He should have let well alone and allowed things to develop naturally. The traveller and his wife would have made it up anyway. They would have no other choice, just as the couple in the first incident had no other choice. He learned, poor fellow, that lovers' quarrels are the renewal of love and that he is a very foolish fellow who interferes with the course of custom.

INNOCENT BYSTANDERS

A woman accosted me in the backway recently. Her father, she informed me, was a peace-loving man who was never involved in an argument in his life. He was a daily communicant and as pious a layman as ever entered the sacred precincts of a church.

'He never raised his hand to one of us,' she said, 'and he adored my mother.' A tear appeared and there was a sniffle but she resumed control of herself and also resumed her gentle barrage. She told me that her father had once unwittingly been an innocent bystander for a very brief period of time. It was in the early 1960s. Some preachers or evangelists were holding forth outside the market place on the evening of the horse fair.

They spoke about God and the sinful ways of the world and, among other things, about the life of the world to come. The woman's father had stopped for a moment to listen. Although a devout Catholic, he was a reasonably tolerant fellow and, while he would have no objection if the interlopers were booted out of town, he would not altogether approve, for instance, if they were hanged.

As he stood, his mind wandered, and it was during this period that a tinker man, for no apparent reason, rushed from out of the recesses of the market place and struck him flush on the jaw. He did not fall. Rather did he stagger around the street and the roadway before being directed homewards by a passing Samaritan. A member of the civic guards pursued the tinker man but all to no avail. He might more profitably have pursued a snipe.

The guard concluded later that the tinker man, for all his

ferocity and hostility, may have been basically a devout or even a militant Catholic. Who hasn't heard of the church militant! According to the guard, the tinker man may well have mistaken our friend's unfortunate father for a member of the itinerant evangelists who were endeavouring to preach the Gospel.

'I mean,' said the garda, 'why else would he have struck him?'

It was the talk of the town that evening. I remember it well and as I endeavoured to console the woman who had accosted me I remember how my father reacted when he heard the news from a neighbour.

'All he was doing,' said the neighbour, 'was minding his own business, and if a man can't mind his own business we had no business dying for freedom.'

Slowly, deliberately, my father took his pipe from his mouth. He frowned when the neighbour continued on about the injustice of the whole sorry business.

'Really,' said the neighbour in outrage, 'all the man was doing was standing there, just an innocent bystander.'

At this my father exploded although he was a civil man and quiet to boot, slow to anger and of a placatory nature.

'If,' said my father heatedly, 'he was an innocent bystander he must be prepared to accept the consequences and I say hats off to the tinker for showing such restraint for he might have kicked him as well.'

Such was my father's dislike of innocent bystanders that he would cheerfully have charged them with responsibility for all the woes of the world and for the outbreaks of all its wars.

As the woman chided me in the backway I managed to slip away. She stood there for a while chiding some neighbourhood curs at the injustice of it all.

Poor creature! She innocently believed that because a man is an innocent bystander he is guaranteed immunity from assault whereas the opposite is the case. He is a legitimate target for every passing blackguard and is simply inviting assault by his mere presence.

'Of all God's creatures,' said an angry relation of mine one time after he had been severely frustrated, 'the innocent bystander is surely the most provocative.'

'I would have thought,' my father suggested, 'that the adder or the viper would qualify before the innocent bystander.'

'No, no, no!' said the relative emphatically, 'they, after all, are only snakes and unless provoked themselves are relatively harmless whereas the innocent bystander sets out to provoke from the moment he bystands.'

He went on to cite an instance of this particular form of provocation. Apparently he was one day on his way to catch a bus which would take him to the city and to a very important appointment. As he hurried around a corner, who should happen to be obstructing his way but an innocent bystander who stood with an umbrella in his hand looking at a concrete wall. A collision followed but our intrepid traveller continued on his way.

Shortly afterwards, as he rounded a second corner, who should chance to be standing at the other side deliberately barring the relative's way but another innocent bystander. There followed a second collision which floored both the bystander and the relative. Rather than retaliate, the relative bravely rose to his feet and struggled manfully towards the bus stop.

By now, badly battered, his gait had slowed but he managed to remain upright. Then, just as he entered the station, who happened to bar his way for the third time but another innocent bystander who chanced to be needlessly studying the sky overhead. So slow was my relative's pace at this stage that the ensuing collision should have been inconsequential. Alas my unfortunate cousin was at the end of his tether and very nearly collapsed. He had just enough spark left in him to deliver a well-judged kick to the skywatcher's posterior. He would have kicked him a second time but instead settled for a straight left, at which particular punch he had developed a proficiency over the years. Expecting some form of accolade from my father he sat himself down exhausted at the end of his narrative.

'You should be ashamed of yourself,' said my father. 'You permitted three vile criminals to go free when you might have reported their obnoxious and murderous behaviour to the authorities. You have granted them a licence to further provoke God-fearing people and you have shamed yourself and your family by not acting responsibly towards your fellow man. It is we who shall have to suffer from your lack of patriotism until the three innocent bystanders you encountered are safely incarcerated or under the clay.'

So saying, my father rose, donned his hat and went out into the world. The relative and I were agreed that there was some substance to what he had said and were glad that we were not innocent bystanders intent on their provocative ways within the ambit of my father's peregrinations.

CALLS OF NATURE

When I was a *garsún* there were no toilet rolls in our house.

The same applied to every house in the street. There were, of course, many alternatives. The most common was your accurately divided newspaper or magazine, cut carefully into rectangular pieces consisting of an approximate area of thirty square inches. These would be neatly sheafed together and the top left-hand corner would be perforated with an awl.

Through the perforation a slender cord was thrust until equal parts of this cord extended from each side of the sheaf. Both ends were then knotted together and the whole hung from a nail in that place, referred to as the privy or closet.

In country dwellings where there were no such edifices, the countryside itself, meaning its more privately appointed groves and dells, was used for calls of nature.

Logically, one could not expect to find sheaves of paper hanging from the bushes and trees in these isolated places. Mankind, however, always inventive and ingenious in awkward circumstances, turned to the leaves of the trees for a fully comprehensive toilet service.

Where leaves were not available there was other greenery, satin-textured and otherwise for those of different tastes.

The most commonly used plant was the dock and your ordinary dock leaf was without peer in this most private and embarrassing of functions. Any stout-stemmed plant with broad leaves substituted admirably. Then you had an abundance of lichens, mosses and other tender cryptogamic plants without peer in this field.

Indeed we have mention in history books of queens and empresses being favourably disposed towards the softer members of the moss family.

Purely for the record's sake, let me say that in China long before Chairman Mao's ascendancy the emperors and nobles of that vast country were in the habit of using goslings and ducklings for this chore. After each exercise the creatures were released, unlike hare-coursing, where the victims are used again and again regardless of their feelings in the matter.

Let us return, however, to our friend the countryman and extend the theme of toilet materials a little further if for no other purpose than to enlighten today's pampered public in the event of their being caught short as it were in public places far removed from fully equipped public and private lavatories.

Your countryman, in the absence of mosses, lichens and dock leaves, could always turn to mother earth herself and her fleecy cloak of rich green grasses. Those unfortunate enough to be the possessors of tender or inflamed or indeed hypersensitive posteriors sought other than grass for the removal of impurities, defilements and what-have-you.

These unfortunates would betake themselves to the vicinity of a small stream or river and, upon finishing the business in hand, might sit themselves down in a shallow but fast-flowing stream. There, happily, they might ponder while the cleansing waters did the dirty work, so to speak.

In these blissful surroundings such afflicted souls might listen to the soft music of murmuring waters or hearken to the delightful melodies of the innumerable birds which people the trees and bushes standing along the banks of these beneficial waterways.

There is the danger, however, that these absent-minded re-cumbents might submit more than their posteriors to the laving waters, for it is a known fact that unexpected floods have often carried off the unsuspecting and the drowsy without as much as a tweet of apology and with no regard for the feelings of those left behind.

Such is nature, gentle and advantageous one minute and the next, savage and remorseless.

These unexpected disasters should serve to remind us that, although it is the most commonplace of human functions, it should never be embarked upon without careful investigation of the immediate lie of the land. Otherwise tragedy and misfortune may raise their ugly heads.

In the absence of an indoor toilet, those seeking outdoor relief would be well advised to check the ground beneath their feet and to examine the textures of the foliage and grasses in their immediate vicinities. The approaches should also be taken into account for in the great outdoors you never know from whence danger is likely to threaten.

A small scenic glade is the most admirable of all retreats in this respect. The drowsy buzzing of bees and the whisper of gentle winds in the overhead foliage have much the same effect as a muted background orchestra although there are many who prefer to read a book or magazine while so preoccupied.

It is vital to locate a place well removed from the alarums and bustle of the world.

It is often wise to follow cowpaths for these end under shady bowers in the quiet corners of green fields or they lead to serene, secluded, out-of-the-way places beneath lofty river banks. Your only danger here is from frolicsome bull calves who will simulate the stance and rage of their elders and indeed often chance an assault if they think they can get away with it.

Some readers may find it surprising in this day and age to find people who cannot avail themselves of indoor toilets. These unfortunates suffer mostly from nervous disorders or claustrophobia and there are also a few, an adventurous few, who risk the outdoors purely for the sake of adventure.

In Listowel up until a few short years ago there was a man who used to climb trees in order to relieve himself. God help an unwary passer-by and a thousand woes to him who upon hearing a rustle overhead felt obliged to gaze upwards.

Anthropologists would do well to study men of this ilk. It might prove conclusively that man is indeed descended from the great apes and that now and then much of this apishness surfaces unbidden. It might account also for much of the horseplay, vandalism and violence so prevalent at the present time.

To return to our Listowel friend, it must be said in fairity to the man that he chose only remote arboreal retreats. His preference for the outdoors ended on a January evening, when the bough upon which he was perched was assailed by an unexpected gale of wind. Already the bough was slippery from the rains of the previous night.

Our unfortunate friend was more or less in what we may call a 'lavatory trance' when the calamity occurred. In vain did he try to maintain his balance but the odds, alas, were stacked against him. He was caught, as the saying goes, with his trousers down.

With a fearful shriek he fell to the ground breaking, upon landing, his collarbone, some odd ribs and his left leg. He would not climb a tree now for love or money nor indeed for any other reason no matter how pressing.

There was another individual, an acquaintance of mine now happily married in Canada, who refused all indoor amenities on the grounds that they tended to soften the human race and make them too dependent on gadgets and aids.

The individual favoured the tops of cliffs – seaside, landlocked and riverside – and let it be forever to the credit of his innate acrobatic endowments that he never once came a cropper.

Townspeople who may have originally come from a country-side where such outdoor practices were condoned and tolerated have become softened by indoor life and by the availability of bathrooms or water closets. A sight which once might have pro-voked no more than a sly smile now causes outrage and fears are expressed for the safety of innocent children as well as women.

Country people are more aware of the vagaries of inconsist-ent bladders. They know what it is to be stuck, so to speak, and their sympathies are wholeheartedly on the side of the man who is unable to retain his impurities.

At this juncture the reader will be sure to ask why the victim did not avail himself of a public toilet especially since most towns boast fine examples of these. Easier said than done. There are many country people who will not entrust themselves to the interior of a public toilet for love or money. One might be locked in and allowed to languish for days, even forever. A public toilet is like a prison in some respects. It is also impersonal and who knows what might befall an innocent countryman were he to risk a visit there.

No. Better to risk prosecution by availing oneself of a byway, an archway or the side of a convenient and empty motor car. This way a man is dependent on nobody but himself and may retain the link with the great outdoors where his heart really belongs.

Window-Peeping

If you are a peeper-out-of-windows at night please read on. I would improve your lot, not criticise it. If you are interested in establishing the truth regarding movements of passers-by after the witching hour you should not rely solely upon your own vision.

For instance let us suppose that a man staggers all over the place as he passes by your window; it does not mean that he staggers as he passes every window and he may not indeed be the drunkard you think he is. The stagger may have been precipitated by an effort to avoid a dangerous hazard such as a banana skin and, as so often happens, the manoeuvre may have gotten out of hand because the hazard was not expected. Now if the window-peeper had consulted with other window-peepers up and down the street it might emerge that only one stagger was involved and that, far from being intoxicated, the after-midnight meanderer was as sober as the window-peeper.

The need for collaborators to determine the truth about the movements of witching-hour wanderers is most pressing. A discreet advertisement placed in one's local paper or in the neighbourhood newsagent's window calling for the assistance of interested window-peepers to monitor the movements of late-night revellers and others could well bring the desired results and bring together a team which might monitor the passage of the aforementioned revellers from one end of a given thorough-fare to the other in so comprehensive a fashion that any and all members of the team could testify under oath in a court of law that such a person had gone home rotten drunk on such a night and that another person had gone home sober as the judge who happened to be presiding over the court in question.

Some uncharitable readers are certain to ask what business it is of window-peepers at what hour or in what state a man goes home at night.

The truth is that any person out of doors after midnight is everybody's business. Who is to say but that it is not a burglar on the prowl or it might well be a mugger intent on mischief. None of us should be free from the scrutiny of window-peepers, but we are also entitled to fair play in the sense that we would be expecting a truthful and accurate account of our movements.

I have often found a pair of eyes monitoring my midnight movements from certain windows. I happen to know also that the owners of the orbs in question have long since convinced themselves that a man of my ilk would not be abroad after midnight unless he was coming from or going to a drink-ing session. Reports keep coming in from unsolicited sources suggesting that because of my previous character I could not possibly be engaged in any form of philanthropic mission, that alcohol and alcohol alone had to be the basis for any late-night excursion in which I might be involved.

How inaccurate can people be and how many innocent men have been vilified in the past! If there were individual observ-ers I might be absolved on occasion from suspicion of having been participating in post-midnight, alcoholic orgies. It might ultimately be established that myself and men like me are not nearly as bad as we are painted. It might even emerge that I was preoccupied with the laudable task of conveying a drunkard to his doorstep instead of leaving him to his own foolish devices out of doors after dark.

The pooling of knowledge has always resulted in an im-provement in man's perilous position on this wayward sphere, whereas uncorroborated evidence has often resulted in grievous miscarriages of justice. I would therefore recommend that these after-dark peepers get together not just for my sake alone but for the sake of humanity as a whole. However, on a personal basis I would be deeply indebted to window-peepers everywhere were they to foregather at an early date and provide a comprehensive account of my witching-hour comings and goings so that an accurate record may be left for posterity.

The Prophet

Few characters have appealed so much to readers of these essays as the Prophet Callaghan. He is dead now with over a score of years but his memory is fondly treasured by those fortunate enough to have known him. It's not because he was such a prodigious drinker of whiskey and porter that he is remembered; rather it is because he was such a dab hand at quoting from the scriptures and other apocryphal sources.

In fact this was why they nicknamed him the Prophet. His uncanny ability for coming up with apt quotes at just the right moment first came to light during the war years after he had cleaned out a pitch-and-toss school in Listowel's famous market sheds one rainy Sunday afternoon. With his winnings of several pounds, a small fortune in those days, he repaired with his friend Canavan to Mikey Dowling's public house in Market Street but was refused admittance on the grounds that it was after hours.

It was the same story in every pub from Pound Lane to the Customs' Gap. The forces of law and order, to wit the Garda Síochána, were unusually active. The guards would explain later in their homely way that there had been letters to the barracks and that certain lawbreaking publicans had been mentioned in dispatches.

As Callaghan went homewards that night with his friend Canavan he remarked as he jingled the silver coins in his pockets 'What profiteth a man if he gain the whole world and he can't get a drink after hours?'

Another Sunday night the guards raided a pub in Upper Church Street. This pub was always regarded as being relatively safe because it was so near the garda barracks. Anyway Canavan and Callaghan were 'found on'. When asked by the sergeant to account for his presence on a licensed premises after hours Callaghan responded that he was only following the precepts of Saint Matthew.

'I don't follow,' said the sergeant.

'Ask and it shall be given,' Callaghan quoted, 'seek and ye shall find, knock and it shall be opened, and lo and behold,' Canavan continued, 'I knocked and it was opened and that is the reason I am here.'

'All those,' said the sergeant, 'who live by the sword shall perish by the sword.'

'My God! My God!' said Callaghan, 'Why has thou forsaken me?'

And it came to pass that after seven days Canavan and Callaghan anointed their outsides with soap and water and their insides with poitín and they came down from the mountain to the fleshpots of Listowel. In the town was a great circus and multitudes had gathered outside the doors of the taverns when the circus was over. Canavan and Callaghan were refused admission to all the hostelries so they journeyed to Ballybunion where they had not been before and they were graciously received and given credit and presented with cold plates for it so happened that there was an American wake in progress.

The days passed and Callaghan arrived at the Ballybunion publican's door with a bag of choice cabbage and a bucket of new potatoes.

'There's no need for that,' said the publican.

'Lo!' said Callaghan, 'I was hungry and ye gave me to eat. I was thirsty and ye gave me to drink. I was a stranger and ye took me in.'

Once at an American wake in Listowel Callaghan appeared

to be exceedingly drunk. The man of the house told him he had enough when he proffered his cup for more drink.

'You're full to the brim,' said the woman of the house.

'I say to you,' quoth Callaghan, 'all the rivers run into the sea and the sea is not full.'

He was a sick man the day after and the day after that again, but the skies cleared when his friend Canavan arrived with the news that there was another American wake at McCarthy's of Finuge.

Quoth Callaghan, 'As cold waters to a thirsty soul is good news from a far country.'

THE COUNCIL OF DIRHA

Good luck and success
To the Council of Trent,
What put fast upon mate
But not upon drink.

(Overheard at a wake)

When the above couplet was conceived there was fasting on Fridays. Nowadays, Lent apart, we may eat meat with impunity throughout the entire year. The Church was quite clear in its strictures regarding the consumption of meat and meat products on days of fast and abstinence. Then in 1966 Pope Paul promulgated new laws for Roman Catholics. Fast days, which had included all the weekdays of Lent, the vigils of Pentecost, the Immaculate Conception and Christmas and the Ember Days, were reduced to two, i.e. Ash Wednesday and Good Friday. In the same decree Pope Paul reaffirmed the laws of abstinence from meat. However, he allowed episcopal conferences to substitute for abstinence with other forms of penance, especially works of charity and exercises of piety.

Hobside theologians of the time were known to smirk at the expression 'works of charity'. They deduced in their own indigenous fashion that to be charitable one had to be rich. Since neither they themselves nor their associates were remotely connected with wealth they regarded themselves as being incapable of charity. When it was explained to them that charity had other connotations such as love of one's fellow man they were quick to point out that because of their innate worthlessness no one, save their own family, placed any value on their love.

However, this is another matter. It is with the pre-Pope Paul period of fast and abstinence that I propose to deal now. Before I do let me say that fireside theology was reduced to a very fine art in those days. There was no opposition from television, and the country was also far from being motorised. Consequently there was genuine profundity in most fireside exchanges. The subtler arts of sarcasm, irony and cynicism all flourished and were brought to such a degree of excellence by common country folk that ordinary comment was almost totally outlawed.

The first serious council held by hobside theologians to which I was witness was held in Dirha Bog *circa* 1935. So great was the fear of excommunication in those distant days that even today I am not at liberty to mention the name of the house owner. The council was well attended, and present at the time were such venerable sages as the late Sonny Canavan and Jack Duggan. The main spokesman, however, was a *spailpín* by the name of Billy Drury, a brother of the poet, Paddy. The main item on the agenda on that memorable occasion was whether the consumption of black puddings on a Friday constituted a breach of the laws on fast and abstinence. Pork steak and puddings were a common enough diet at the time. Every countryman kept his own pig and when the creature was fat enough to be butchered substantial quantities of pork steak and home-filled black puddings were distributed among the neighbours.

It was universally accepted even amongst the most extreme heretics and schismatics that under no circumstances was the eating of pork steak to be countenanced on Fridays or on any other days of fast and abstinence. Puddings, however, were a different kettle of fish altogether. If I might be permitted the use of a widely used saying of the time, 'there were puddings and puddings'. It was with this aspect of the matter that the

Dirha theologians concerned themselves. When is a black pudding not a black pudding or, to put it another way, what are the chief characteristics of a sinful pudding?

Billy Drury opened the proceedings with a story explaining at the outset that it was to be taken in lieu of his conclusions on the subject in question. I now propose to exploit the Drury paradigm to its fullest.

Some years earlier he had worked with a farmer to the north of Listowel. In a croteen at the lee of the house there was a prime pig fattening. When the time was ripe one of the children of the house was dispatched to the house of the local pig butcher. Duly the pig was killed and butchered, the meal salted and barrelled, the pork steak cut away and the blood readied for the filling of the puddings. This last chore was always undertaken by the woman of the house. Eventually all the puddings were filled, boiled and placed in tall tiers so that they might cool. When they were sufficiently cooled the man of the house, without a word to anyone, produced a frying pan, greased it with lard and placed it on the red-hot Stanley range which dominated the kitchen. He then went to the tiers of pudding and withdrew a substantial ring for himself.

'Will you sample one of these?' he asked Drury.

'I'm your man,' Drury responded. The man of the house placed both puddings on the pan, where they immediately set up a sibilant sizzling. This was followed by a heavenly smell as the puddings started to cook. Both men sat happily by the range while the fat spat and the puddings crackled. Then came the unexpected. Down from the bedroom in her long flowing nightdress came the woman of the house. First she looked at the pair by the range and then she looked at the pan.

'Do ye know,' she said with a sting to her voice, 'the day we have?'

When neither answered her she pointed out that it was Friday and that if either one partook of the puddings he would be risking eternal damnation. Both men shuffled uneasily in their seats. The man of the house rose but Drury stayed put. The man of the house preceded his woman to the bedroom, casting a cold look at the frying pan and an even colder one at Drury. To make a long story short, Drury consumed both puddings in their entirety.

The hobside theologians digested the Drury story and cogitated upon its many implications while they filled or relighted their pipes. Finally a man from Affroulia spoke up.

'You committed a mortal sin,' he said, 'and that's the long and short of it.'

Others disagreed, and for a while the argument ranged back and forth. It was Drury, however, who had the last word.

'I was a witness,' said he, 'to the filling of the puddings. The blood was salted. Common oatmeal and massecrated onions was all that was added. If a sin was committed then it was a venial one and a very watery venial at that. If,' Drury continued, 'the puddings was filled by the likes of Mary Flaherty and if I was after guzzling two of them then it would a mortal sin for Mary Flaherty's puddings is stuffed with every known groodle from spice to pinhead oatmeal.'

At this stage there were murmurs of approval from the council. Mary Flaherty's puddings were known and prized from the Cashen river to Carrickkerry.

Drury was quick to press home this point. He listed the numerous ingredients of the Flaherty puddings, from the chopped liver of the pig itself to the minutely gartered gristle. He pointed out that the two puddings which he had eaten on the Friday at the farmer's house were not legitimate puddings and by no stretch of the imagination could they expect to qualify as whole or legal puddings under the act. Drury went on to state that one of Mary Flaherty's puddings was a meal in itself and thereby contributed to the breaking of the law laid down by the Council of Trent.

The council relighted its pipes and cleared its throats. In the end it held that Drury had done no wrong. Had the puddings in question been up to the Flaherty standard there would be no doubting his guilt. The puddings were inferior, therefore incapable of contributing to a sinful situation.

The conclusions of the Council of Dirha were accepted locally until 1966, when Pope Paul's promulgations changed everything.

FOOD – AND DRINK!

MIXED GRILLS

I have a dream. It is to write a thesis on the mixed grill before progress reduces it to an absurdity. This would be the definitive work on the subject. It would be found after Mixed Enterprise (Econ.) in *The Encyclopaedia Britannica*. When my name would crop up people would ask what's he done that's so important? There would be a shocked silence from the erudite after which would come the confidential whisper briefly outlining my single achievement. The name Keane would be synonymous with the mixed grill. When I would pass by a crowd people would say reverently and proudly: 'There goes Keane, the mixed-grill man.' I would be introduced as Mister Mixed Grill himself. In my obituary notice there would be mention of my most notable achievement. 'Keane was the man,' it would read, 'who rescued the mixed grill from oblivion.' My descendants would come to be known as The Mixed-Grill Keanes. That is my dream. I often ask myself if it exceeds my rightful expectations but no answer comes. I believe, however, that it is my destiny. Some men were born to free sewerage pipes, others to pick plums. I was born to write about mixed grills. This is not my first time. I have written several short pieces for radio and newspapers but this is not enough. Once more then into the breach.

Your classic mixed grill, the constituents of which I will disclose shortly, rose to ultimate prominence in this country towards the end of the Second World War. On the same day that the Americans landed in Okinawa another American who happened to be a relation of my mother's landed in Ireland. His first act, after landing, was to make a beeline for the nearest hotel where he ordered a meal for himself and the members of the reception committee. He also allowed the latter to pay their individual parts of the bill, having first graciously declined to accept it himself. My mother was obliged to foot his part of it. It was not a notable occasion. There was no sparkle to the conversation. How could there be with a question mark hanging over the matter of the bill. There was no wine. In those days wine was offered only at wakes, weddings and christenings. Ordinary people like ourselves required nothing with our meals except pepper, salt and mustard.

I remember to have ordered a mixed grill on the occasion. It is a repast which I remember with affection and respect. What's that Wordsworth said:

The music in my heart I bore
Long after it was heard no more.

It consisted of one medium-sized wether chop, two sizeable sausages, four slices of pudding – two black and two white – one back rasher and one streaky, a sheep's kidney, a slice of pig's liver and a large portion of potato chips which were something of a novelty at the time and were, indeed, quite foreign to many parts of the countryside. Accompanying this vast versification of varied victuals was a decent mound of steeped green peas, a large pot of tea and all the bread and butter one could wish for. It was a meal fit for a ploughman and I can proudly recount that not a vestige of any individual item remained on my plate at the close barring the chop bones alone. The total cost of this extraordinary accumulation of edibles was three shillings and sixpence which was the precise amount I had in my pocket. In those days, not like now, young gentlemen would know to the nearest halfpenny the exact amount of cash on their persons. Tipping in those days, for a chap of my age, was unthinkable.

Since that unforgettable occasion I have demolished more than my share of mixed grills. They were an ideal choice for those who were not prepared to gamble everything on a meal which consisted solely of cold meat or steak or indeed chops, be they pork or mutton. If the steak or the chops were tough all was lost whereas, in the mixed grill, one could find immediate redress in any of the other constituents individually or collectively.

The mixed grill was, of course, an ideal plate for peckish persons. While none of the ingredients on their own could be described as a substantial course they nevertheless succeeded in substantiating each other. If, for instance, the white pudding was not of the required consistency or if the black was too lardy one could ignore both and still make do with the other members of the confederacy.

The mixed grill's greatest single attribute was its variety. All of the ingredients I have mentioned have individual characteristics which set them apart but none is capable of really standing on its own. It is the unification of all the members which gives the mixed grill its strength and intensity, not to mention vivacity and colour. Some readers may carp at the fact that I have deliberately not included eggs in the association and in all fairity I should say that authorities are divided as to whether fried eggs should be included or not. I would probably agree that they should but only on condition that a major ingredient such as the liver or the kidney was absent. Traditionally, therefore, all things being in order, your fried egg is purely optional and by virtue of long association has a closer affinity to rashers.

Some of my readers will now be surprised to learn that I have not eaten a mixed grill in over a year. Strange behaviour for a man who has been so generous in his praise of mixed grills.

Perhaps, however, not so strange when recent events are taken into account. Early last summer I was on my way home from the capital when I decided to stop at a wayside watering place for a pint of ale. As I sat minding my own business contemplating my diminishing measure my nostrils were assailed by a most appetising smell. I quickly finished my pint and headed for the dining room where I was presented with a menu. There was such a diversity of foods on offer that I could not make up my mind. I, therefore, ordered a mixed grill. Here is what I got: one apology for a rack chop, two shrivelled sausages, a small wrinkled rasher and an egg more raw than fried. Finally, to add to the parody, a writhing mass of badly burned onions. There was also the half of a tomato and two leaves of lettuce which I refuse to take into account. Having no wish to offend the waitress, who seemed a decent sort of girl, I bolted as much as I could of the mess, paid my bill and said goodbye. I should, of course, have referred the whole business over to Bord Fáilte but I am a tolerant man and decided to refrain from complaining. Maybe the chef had an off day or a tiff with his wife before starting for work that morning. Who knows what choice error from the vast gallery of human misery attached itself to the poor fellow on that forgettable day.

I haven't eaten a mixed grill since. I have often felt like one but I'm afraid that I will be deceived or disappointed and so I have decided to wait for better times when people will take pride in their work once again and the mixed grill will once more titillate and tantalise those who appreciate its wonders and its subtleties.

While Stocks Last

There have been some great questions and answers relating to the licensing trade in various towns and villages all over the country but I'm sure I'll be forgiven if I highlight three from my native county and, in so doing, I would like to remind readers how mindful I am of the natural wit and repartee of other places.

The most famous of the three refers, as one would expect, to that great bastion of life, liberty and the pursuit of happiness which is referred to on maps and signposts as Ballybunion, so called because it was a stronghold of the O'Bannions who, in turn, were watchdogs for the O'Connors, lords of the Barony.

It transpired in those halcyon days, when there was a more liberal view taken of licensing transgressions than there is now, that there happened to be a member of the Garda Síochána standing with his hands behind his back outside the Castle Hotel. The time was a summer's night in the middle of July and it wanted but three minutes for the witching hour. Up the street there staggered a gentleman who had been asked to vacate a premises on the main thoroughfare. He was, to put it mildly, somewhat annoyed. Truculently he addressed himself to the minion of the law.

'Tell me guard,' said he, 'what time do the pubs close in Ballybunion?'

'After Listowel Races, sir,' came the mild answer.

Then there was the night in the village of Duagh which is a historic and delightful spot lying halfway between the towns of Listowel and Abbeyfeale. The carnival was in full swing when a brother and I arrived from our native town, having been informed by a relative from the area that there was an extension in the public houses of Duagh on the night in question because of the carnival. Alas there were some conflicting rumours. A local dignitary advised us that as far as he knew there was no extension, that it was business as usual, with closing time at ten o'clock.

'However,' said he, 'you would be well advised to play it by ear and keep an eye open for the Squad.'

By Squad, of course, he meant members of the Garda Síochána who sometimes on Sunday nights would conduct raids on licensed premises and who sometimes would not. Some publicans insisted that the guards were affected by the moon and were, therefore, unpredictable while other publicans would testify that guards were merely acting on instructions from a higher authority such as a sergeant or a superintendent.

Anyway the brother and I happened to find ourselves on the premises of the late and great Dermot O'Brien who was to Duagh what the Caesars were to Rome.

'Tell me Mister O'Brien,' my brother addressed himself to Dermot, who happened to be on duty behind the counter, 'how long more will the pub be open?'

'This pub,' said Dermot O'Brien, 'will be open while stocks last.'

Then there was the night in Killarney after a Munster football final. The pubs were cleared on time. It had been an exhausting day and the publicans were weary from it all. A lone guard stood outside a local hostelry as the crowds departed. Up the street came two Corkmen who had just polished off a steak and chips in one of the town's numerous hostelries and who now needed something intoxicating to assist with the meal's digestion. They had tried several public houses but all in vain.

Wearily they eyed the lone member of the Force, a stoutish

chap in his fifties with long years of unblemished service behind him.

'Tell us,' said the leading Corkman, 'do you know where two fellows would get a drink around here?'

'No,' said the custodian of the peace, 'but I know where three fellows would get one.'

HUMBLE PIE

Wise men will tell you that we benefit from suffering, setbacks and letdowns. It's the same with eating humble pie. A man who hasn't been made to eat humble pie has had a diet without roughage.

I would look upon the eating of humble pie as a major developing factor in the human character. My first dosage was administered when I was a schoolboy. I became involved in a fight with a chap who happened to be in the same grade as myself. There the resemblance ended, for he was smaller than I was, thinner than I was and as unlikely a candidate for a bout of fisticuffs as a man with two broken hands. Confident of success, I indulged in a preliminary bout of shadow-boxing prior to the victim's demolition.

A number of other schoolboys had gathered, rubbing their hands with delight, as is the wont of such characters when mayhem is on the horizon. Alas for me, gathered with them – but unseen by me – was my adversary's brother. I should have known that one or more of his big brothers would have to be in the vicinity. The prospect of being allowed to provide a dazzling exhibition before a live audience had also dazzled my perception.

No sooner had I split the surrounding air with a series of textbook straight lefts than the big brother intervened and informed me that he was about to commence my maceration. He was the very antithesis of his fraternal inferior, with a barrel chest, a jaw like a hippopotamus and a right hand about the same size as a leg of mature lamb.

'Come on!' he shouted truculently, as he extended a turnip-sized left hand towards my hitherto unblemished physiognomy.

I did what any intelligent *garsún* would do under the circumstances, especially a *garsún* who aspired to a long and relatively happy life in this vale of tears. I thrust my allegorical tail firmly between my retreating legs and made vague references to a promise I had made my mother whereby I would maintain a peaceful attitude towards all comers whilst on my way from school.

It was a hollow excuse but I had to try something if I was to extricate myself with some modicum of honour. I was indeed made to eat humble pie on that occasion but the digestion thereof stood me in good stead for the remainder of my schoolgoing days. I always looked around for big brothers and other allies when the chips were down.

My final intake of humble pie occurred at a dance some years afterwards. There I was in a new navy-blue suit, in the my twenty-first year, with a legitimate coin of the realm in my trousers pocket and a line of fanciful patter specially designed to woo and ravish consenting females in the vicinity.

Dances came and went and then I saw her sitting on her own in an isolated corner. She was red-haired and vivacious. She was to me what an unexpected oasis is to the parched nomad, what the sight of the sea was to the Greeks of Xenophon when they though they might never see it again, and when they ran towards it shouting 'Thalassa! Thalassa!' I didn't shout thus but I bore down upon the creature like a sheik on an Arabian stallion.

We waltzed to the strains of the 'Blue Danube'. Did I say waltzed? My apologies. We floated but as we were aloft my shoulder was touched by some strange mechanism from the external world. I opened my eyes to find myself confronted by a burly Lothario with a thin moustache so delicately represented it might have been drawn by a single stroke of a ballpoint pen.

'What's the idea?' I asked.

'The idea,' said he, 'is that this is an excuse-me dance – so hand her over.'

I looked to my angelic partner in the hope that she would confirm that it was not an excuse-me, but no sound escaped her cherry-coloured lips. Suddenly they were gone and I was alone. I might have eaten humble pie on that occasion but I learned from the experience and ever after when an external object touched me on the shoulder during a dance, I whisked my partner to the furthest extremities of the dance hall, where I looked into her eyes and overcame her protestations with flurries of exquisitely executed quicksteps.

POTATO-CAKES

Lest there be any doubt about it let me make it clear that nobody has bribed me to take up the pen in praise of potato-cakes.

I do so because, not so long ago, I came across two marriageable girls who had never heard of potato-cakes. They were authorities on rum omelette and loganberry jelly. One had devised an original recipe for meringue crumb pudding and the other blandly announced that her Polish tarts had taken second prize at a metropolitan agricultural show. Neither showed any contrition for not having heard of potato-cakes. One may draw one's own conclusion but I am of the opinion that the pair are destined to remain unmarried permanently unless they lift themselves out of the lethargy which has made them ignorant of the role of the griddle.

A hot potato-cake is like an Indian summer. It soothes and refreshes. It has a strong taste, which is more than one can say for vegetable dumplings. It may be spliced in two halves so that the steam rises from its interior in a mist of surpassing fragrance. It can be smeared on the inside of both parts with melting butter or it needn't be sliced at all because it is just as attractive with a bit of butter on top.

One of the reasons why potato-cakes are so little in evidence at this present time is that they are too easy to make. All that one needs is a griddle or an outsize frying-pan, a little flour and butter and a few leftover potatoes. If the ingredients were difficult to come by and of foreign extraction there would be no scarcity but the surest way to confuse a modern miss is to ask her boil an egg or bake a few potato-cakes.

The perfect potato-cake is not made overnight. Like everything else there must be trial and error, even a little heartbreak, when the mixture turns out dumpy and damp or lumpy and indigestible but there should be no despondency because of early failures. It took a conscientious woman of my acquaintance several years before she perfected her potato-cakes. Overdoing it a bit, one might say, but not when one considers the net result. Her husband, an intractable and unpredictable delinquent in the early years of marriage, is now her devoted slave. He, who once had an alcoholic tremor in both hands, is now her corn-parer in chief, her ware-dryer and hair-dryer and, last but not least, an almost insufferable boaster of her inimitable culinary techniques.

Opinion is divided as to whether the child of today can watch television and do his lessons at the same time. The child holds that he can. The parent holds otherwise. There is merit on both sides. A man can cut his fingernails without taking his eyes from the screen and a woman can do her knitting. I know a bright young man who can read a book and watch television without strain but there is one task which defies them all. You will not eat potato-cakes and watch television at the same time. You will not – because your attention will be wholly focused on the plate and you will regard with suspicion the least movement of those who share the table. Potato-cakes have a knack of disappearing which deceives the distracted eye and the only way to assure oneself of a full share is to trust nobody until the appetite is sated. Friendship and family loyalty are virtues to which all should aspire but to rely upon the restraints of others when potato-cakes are on the menu is pushing friendship a bit too far and asking too much of loyalty.

I haven't eaten a potato-cake now in six months. Maybe this will serve to remind those whose fault it is. Maybe a certain conscience will be disturbed when leftover spuds are dumped without ceremony into rubbish-cans. Maybe there will be others like myself who, by subtle suggestion and innuendo, will drive the salient point home that six months without potato-cakes is carrying the game a bit too far.

Far-seeing mothers, who are adept at making potato-cakes, should instruct their daughters well. Honours in Algebra is not to be scoffed at but, I ask you, which will pay the better dividend – Honours in Algebra or a pass in making potato-cakes? I know, and you know, but does the bride of tomorrow know? I am not saying that potato-cakes will resolve all the problems that arise in the early years of marriage but you can be certain that they will go a long way towards eliminating impulsive departures to momma. They may not be the answer to the in-law problem but in-laws tend to become secondary tribulations when the palate is under the influence of potato-cakes.

Cold weather is the best weather for potato-cakes and the best time to eat them is after returning from long walks, when the air is brisk and days tend to grow shorter. They are an ac-credited repast and constitute a full meal in themselves when fortified by butter, especially farmers' butter. They are essentially, as I said, a winter diet because young or early potatoes lack the body that is required.

I don't want any potato-cake mixture in packages nor in-stant potato-cakes in tins. You must use leftover potatoes and not freshly boiled ones. It's logic in itself, isn't it? If there are potatoes left over after the dinner then by all the powers that be a full dinner was not eaten and if a full dinner was not eaten a full tea is imperative and how better can you have a full tea than by having potato-cakes.

The Drinking Fields

Men who grow anxious for intoxicating drink for reasons which cannot easily be analysed are very often the victims of intolerance and misunderstanding. When I was younger people were more tolerant and when neighbours over drank you would hear remarks like the following:

'Wisha the poor man is plagued by drought', or 'God help him he's cursed with a terrible tooth for porter'. Those charitable souls of yesteryear never inflicted the hard word when a soft one was admissible.

It must be conceded, however, in these days of affluence, wantonness, permissiveness, etc., that drinking is a more serious problem than ever before and that we should look above and beyond the accepted norms for the root causes of this much-abused practice.

Recent disclosures in the national press about the drinking habits of the Irish people will not have escaped the notice of my readers. That they are true is near enough to fact but a very heavy reduction on the per capita consumption must be allowed on the grounds that we have a large tourist intake, not to mention all those buck navvies (of whom I was once a proud member) who come home annually and biannually and whose recreation time is spent, in the main, in public houses. For reasons unknown these navvies have never been regarded as tourists. A probable reason could well be that they spend too much to be looked upon as such. I have known many who spent several hundred pounds in the few weeks available to them, not always on themselves alone but on the many short-term admirers that a flaithiúil hand can attract.

I will not go into the reasons given for the Irish obsession with intoxicating liquor in the most recent published analyses. I have my own theory about these and I have drawn the conclusion, from long practical experience, that our heavy drinking has to do with landscape. Do I hear sniggers?

Let there be sniggers but it should be remembered that I have as much right to put forward my theories about the causes behind the national pastime as anybody. Recently I took a break from the booze. I decided to forego my nightly indulgence to honour the memory of a departed parent. I endured the martyrdom for a month which, when you make allowance for the willpower of the subject, is a reasonable period of abstention. I might not have gone back on the stuff for a much longer period if it had not been for a certain incident which dampened my fortitude.

I am in the habit most evenings of taking a walk through a number of boggy fields outside the town. I intrude upon nobody save the occasional snipe who must only benefit from these incursions of mine if he is to be fully alert for the day when fowlers will threaten his very existence.

On this particular afternoon I stopped for a moment or two to savour a few lungfuls of country air. Between breaths I thought I heard a whisper, a sort of subdued, caressing sibilance from somewhere behind me. I looked around but could see nothing. The whispering persisted and then I learned that it was coming from everywhere. It was the earth itself and it wasn't whispering. It was drinking. Earlier in the day there had been a number of heavy showers and the noise which sounded so like whispering was the squelchy earth swallowing copious draughts of refreshing rainwater. In short the soggy fields were soaking it up goodo. It was an unmistakable sound and it brought back happy memories of intoxicating beverages which I had so often quaffed myself.

To make a long story short there arose inside me an irre-pressible longing for a long and a strong drink of bodied beer in rich quantity to freshen my exhausted fibres and restore to them their old pulpy satiety.

I place the blame fair and squarely on the drinking fields, and had it not been for the convivial whispers under the grasses I might have passed on and inflicted further needless tyranny upon my rapidly dehydrating body.

These particular fields are always drinking. Morning, noon and night they absorb moisture. Even in the height of summer they absorb the dews of night and morning, and dry as the weather may be they lap up the leftover dampness deep down where the sun can't get at it.

To hear them at their best you would want to pay them a visit after three or four days of heavy rain. Then the noise is almost deafening, provided you are prepared to give it your undivided attention. I always say Sláinte when I hear these fields indulging thus.

This then could well be one of the undisclosed causes which might explain our predilection for alcoholic beverages to the degree which makes us stand out above other nations. Shake-speare had the same thing to say about Denmark. Correct me if I'm wrong:

This heavy-headed revel East and West
Which makes us traduced and taxed by other nations.

I hope that what I have unfolded will be taken seriously. To those who are forever seeking messages I would say that it would be wiser for an alcoholically inclined person to steer clear of drinking fields and confine himself to the public highway.

LING

In the days when baker's bread was a luxury and our grandmothers sat in carts holding their donkeys in terror of steamrollers, there were men whose likes will never walk the earth again.

Long before rainbow trout usurped the rights of innocent and familiar tenants in our inland waters and before the first pony shied at the blast of a microphone, there were men in Kerry whose big hands could pull a currach to safety or play a tune on a fiddle that would put a mountain lark to shame, men who caught balls in Croke Park with one hand and with the other made ample room for a clearance as dignified as it was stylish, men who when they kicked a ball would turn around and start a conversation with the goalkeeper, resting assured that the affairs of the world would be put in order before the leather had landed safely behind the white lines of the foe.

To hell with devilled eggs, where they belong, and preserve us from marmalade on toast. We have nothing against boloni and spaghetti, but we resent imposition. Put a couple of pounds of ling steeping in common water and we will give no trouble, because ling is the stuff that gave the backbone to our fathers and inured them against the buffetings of wind and rain. Sit down, if you want to, and make a fool of yourself over grilled salmon and the knick-knacks that make it palatable, but do not preach a gospel to us for we are sick to the gills of innovation.

Volumes could be written about ling and odes composed to it but you need to have it in front of you smothered in its own sauce with well-bred potatoes and a good skelp of fresh butter dissolving delightfully while you say a short prayer in thanksgiving for the good things in life that come for next to nothing.

Life, as the song says, is 'a weary puzzle', but there is no problem with ling so long as there is enough to go round, and the year has been a good one for potatoes. Ling is the food of men whose stomachs have not been found wanting, whose digestive tracts are the envy of anatomists, whose hearts are the hearts of giants and whose strength is the fathomless strength of men who regard noodle-soup as baby-food.

Sausages and mash and fish and chips have played their part in assuaging the pangs of hunger and only a churl would deny the claims of onion-dip and potato-cakes but man must go deeper if he is to find the answer to honest hunger and the rewards of honest toil. Rashers have played giddy tunes on countless frying pans and kettles have whistled melodies that would leave the Top Twenty in the shade but there is a richer music with a deeper meaning and you get it only when you lift the cover from the pot where ling is boiling. Here is the depth of the ocean itself and in the throaty gurgle of the bubbling sauce is the history of mariners who scorned the Atlantic when Columbus was teething and Amerigo Vespucci playing marbles in the alleyways of Italy. Here is all the sibilance of salt-laden breezes and the malicious chuckling of eddying water in pools where the devil-fish lurk and here is an aroma that could transform an articulate man, the essence of composure and sobriety, into a gibbering fool who will be appeased by nothing unless it is ling and ling sauce on his plate. We read of the Spartan boy whose stomach was eaten away by a fox-cub, safe in the knowledge that it could never happen to a youth fortified and hardened by ling, for no fox could penetrate the muscle that it forms.

Ah, but tragically today there is an element, a class that will have nothing to do with ling. I have seen them pass by the doorways where the flitches hang invitingly, cocking their noses into the air. I have seen them passing in their two-toned motor cars and what harm but they're never very far away from ling and who knows but one day they might haggle like fishwives over its purchase and be glad to sit down where ling is the order of the day. I have seen them with suede coats and hairdos executed by imported contortionists and I have listened to them deploring the absence of brill and turbot and baby-beef and I would like to ask them – what is the matter with ling. I would appreciate a definitive defence of their sad preferences.

The rafters in the thatched houses of your grandfathers were never without a flitch of it and when your Auntie Mary came back from America 'twas the first thing she asked for. Bishops and Monsignors were reared on it and it was responsible for the pointing of more fifties than sirloin steak and raw eggs put together.

A word to mothers! Give them ling when they're growing and they'll never lose the tooth for it and maybe they'll never be ashamed of the country that gave them birth or the sagas of their ancestors. But a word of warning! Ling is not for the immature or the uninitiated. Don't give it to Teddy boys or Kerrymen with affected accents for if you do the hair will stand erect on their heads and all the hair oil in the world won't flatten it again but if you have a lad with a likely pair of hands and the indelicate instinct of a full-back give him ling when he's young and maybe one day that is the terrible man you'll see in Croke Park coming out of a swarm of forwards with the ball in his hands and a horrible expression on his face.

You don't need a cookery book for ling because there is only one method of cooking it. Put enough of it down and that way nobody will be disappointed when distribution takes place. Forwards were never discouraged or kept at bay by banana sandwiches and last-minute goals were never scored by men whose mothers were slaves of the frying-pan. You don't see penalties stopped by hands that were moulded by biscuits and sweet cake. Ling is the thing that brought the crowd to its feet and swelled the hearts of supporters when the day seemed lost. Hardy hats and hobnailed boots may be disappearing but there is still hope for the family that is not ashamed of ling. Let its enemies say what they will and let dieticians have the last word but when the shouting is over we'll go home to our dinners and we won't be swayed by the opinions of those who think they know what is good for us. The best judge of the food fittest for our development is the stomach that has to digest it and the pocket that has to pay for it. When our emigrants boarded the suicide craft that took them across the Atlantic, it wasn't tomatoes or tinned pears they took with them. Only the improvident embarked without a few flitches of ling. Tomatoes are all very fine for vegetable soup but when there was a wind from the northeast and ice in the spume a man with tomatoes had as much chance of survival as the old grey mare at the battle of Balaclava.

Let the Russians boast of a better way of life and let the Chinese send their rice in showers around the world but let it be remembered that there was ling before them and there will be ling after them. Let the big powers debate the likelihood of the world's end and measure the force of their bombs but a man with dry turf and a couple of flitches of ling on his ceiling has little to fear from the vanity of demagogues or the threats of dictators.

Ling needs no aperitif but if there's buttermilk handy, a mug or two is recommended before and during the meal. As an after-course you may dispense with the habitual jellies and puddings because ling leaves room for nothing more but I have been told on reliable authority that a few pints of well-conditioned stout a few hours later is acceptable, after which a man may retire for the night and sleep the sleep of the just.

I have been told that the best way to steep ling is in a gallon of sour milk where it should be left for twenty-four hours. I have never tried it and would not recommend it for it is too valuable a commodity to be subjected to dubious experiment.

In conclusion I can only say that if we are not careful to foster a love of ling among the youth of the country, one of our great national dishes will disappear, banned forever from the tables where it held sway since the first small boat was manned and men looked for their dinners in the ocean.

Bringing Home the Drunk

There is no understanding so fraught with danger to the escort as the simple conveying home of a drunken man. Let the escort be a paragon of virtue, a pillar of the church, a most respected member of the community, it matters not a whit when he arrives at the home of the drunken man. The spouse of the incapacitated party, in such situations, cannot and will not see beyond her nose.

Upon beholding the innocent escort, nearly always a good Samaritan within the true meaning of the word, the wife of the drunken man is instantly transformed into a raging she-devil, hell-bent on the destruction of the party who, out of the goodness of his heart, undertook to guide the alcoholically disabled man to his home.

My advice to you would-be benefactors in this respect is to convey the misfit to the vicinity of his home. Mark well the word vicinity. Under no circumstances convey him to the door itself. Dislodge him at least one door away from the one which is his. Prop him against the wall or, better still, seat him gently on his posterior with his back to a solid surface where he can come to no harm. Then draw breath as the man said and knock upon the fellow's door. Having executed a substantial knock withdraw as though you had deposited a lost lion cub at the entrance to its mother's den. In other words, run for your life.

I am not saying that all the spouses of deposited drunkards will turn upon the benefactor but it is an unfortunate fact of life that a substantial number will. This is why it is wise to take no chances. After the knock has been executed, vamoose.

If the first knock is not answered keep making forays to the door, always making sure to remove yourself post haste after the door has been opened.

There are spouses who will invite the benefactor into the house, who will even offer him tea or other forms of liquid refreshment. I have encountered many such females myself and I have been overwhelmed with expressions of boundless gratitude. Indeed very often prayers and promises of prayers were showered upon me by the grateful spouse and I was deeply touched that my good deed was acknowledged.

However, it is definitely not worth the gamble. For every thankful spouse there is an unbeholden one as I have found out to my cost. Perilous as it is to convey home your drunken man it is tantamount to self-destruction to convey home a drunken woman. Men are more suspicious than women. They have less trust in their fellow men. Therefore if you are ever obliged to convey a drunken woman to her doorstep make sure you have another woman with you, drunken or otherwise.

Secondly, it is well to remember that when you deposit your cargo it is vitally necessary to deposit the second woman as well. The minute the husband opens the door the sensible thing to do is to land him with both women. Let him, if the wretch has any conscience at all, convey the other woman home in return for your kindness to his spouse.

There are some other rules which should be observed in the conveying home of drunken men. Firstly, make sure that the drunken man is able to walk or, at least, partially walk. Secondly, never attempt to convey a drunken man home on your own. Thirdly, make certain that his tie is loosened lest he choke himself. Fourthly, make sure he pukes before he reaches his own door. Drunken men have a nasty habit of depositing the contents of their stomachs on their doorsteps the moment the door is opened. Don't ask me why. Some observers have noted that a blast of heat from the warm interior of the house induces the puke in the drunken party. Others maintain that it is the sight of the wife often with hair curlers and without make-up. Whatever the reason it happens frequently.

Try to remember these elementary precepts and you will be well served. Finally, the conveying home of drunken men is the responsibility of the companions with whom he has been drinking or, failing this, the function of the final publican on his drunken itinerary.

WATCHING DINERS

One of the better-known pastimes of my boyhood was watching people eating. In those days there were no sliced pans, and very often great feats of grinding were necessary especially where the slices, cut by hand, were thicker than usual. Remember too that false teeth were still a luxury and the average male, especially from the poorer sections of the community, was rarely possessed of the teeth he started out with. He would be lucky to have half or even less.

Watching a man with poorly deployed teeth chewing crusts was as intriguing and entertaining as watching an aged lion eating donkey-meat in the menageries of the many circuses which came to town in those days. The facial grimaces involved were enough to frighten the life out of the unwary onlooker who stumbled upon the mastication process by accident. Also there were grunts and groans, so great was the physical and mental effort involved.

Our favourite vantage point was outside the large glass window of a pie shop at the bottom of the street, and our favourite subject was a fat man who ate his pie with one hand while he kept his face covered with the other. Like the ostrich he believed that nobody could see him if he kept his hand over his face. He was a shy sort and always managed to find a place as far away from the window as possible. Other times he would face into a corner and look furtively around him between mouthfuls as though he had no right to be there. He had no teeth that could be seen but they were there all right at the sides of his mouth, about four or five in number. Because of this he would be obliged to move the food to either the left or the right side of the mouth. The result was that much of his pie wound up on the table where he unfailingly recovered it when he had finished the plate. He lapped it up as though it were an aftercourse.

I once saw him eating sausages. He put them into his mouth sideways and broke them out with the side teeth. Then he returned them to the centre of the mouth, where he savoured them fully before swallowing.

There was another with false teeth. The bother was that he used to take them out while he was eating. So ignorant were we *garsúns* at the time that we would press our curious faces to the glass the better to study his facial antics as he strove manfully to chew his food aided by nothing more than his naked gums. In those days there was quite a lot of fat meat in the mutton pies which were the standard fare in most of the restaurants in the town. Fat was supposed to be good for a person in those benighted times.

'Look at the Eskimos,' my mother used to say. 'Look at how fat they are and all they eat is blubber.'

'And candles,' my father would add in his helpful way, although he would never say it again after a younger sister swallowed half a candle – a mission candle at that, which had been specially blessed for the renouncing of the devil.

'Eat your fat or you'll fall away to nothing' was a common admonishment by neighbouring mothers.

'Wouldn't they love to have that now in China,' they would say. At the time there was nearly always a famine in some part of China. The communist countries might not be much use at granting civil liberties but I'll say one thing for them: They knew how to starve people.

In Ballybunion the main front window of the then Castle Hotel was a great spot from which to view the diners. We would press our faces to the window and pretend we were starving but it didn't have the slightest effect on the diners. They were far more sophisticated than the men who dined at the pie shop down our street. They tucked napkins under their chins and sat straight upon their chairs. The only weapon the pieman had was a spoon, but these had knives and forks, dessert- and soup-spoons and fish-knives. How many innocent Irishmen were baffled by fish-knives! For years I tried in vain to cut fish with a fish-knife but I had to give it up and return to the normal knife. My Uncle Jack was right. 'There's something fishy about those danged fish-knives,' he used always say.

The only use I could ever find for fish-knives as a *garsún* was for pinking peas across the dining room whenever we paid a rare visit to a hotel. I tried mashed potatoes once but caught a priest accidentally on the face with a spatter that temporarily blinded him. My father nearly murdered me on that occasion. It was no doubt a sacrilege.

We were guilty of causing great discomfiture to innocent country people in the pie shops of the period. Three or four of us would select the most harmless-looking type in the dining area and stare at him remorselessly as he spooned his pie and soup to his mouth. What common blackguards we were and how we glared at him whenever he looked apprehensively in our direction! There was a mixture of fear and guilt on his face as he ground his food in the chamber of his gob. The soup would dribble down the sides of his chin whenever he opened his mouth to rebuke us. He, poor fellow, was being troubled by his conscience, believing that we were homeless urchins on the brink of dying from starvation.

There was another chap of advanced years who used to pull his overcoat over his head to shut out nosy onlookers. This man was the noisiest feeder we ever came across. He reminded me of Moran's dog farther up the street. Moran's dog didn't really eat. He slobbered and sometimes he moaned as if the chore of sustaining himself with food was altogether too much for him.

The man who pulled the coat over his head used also sigh and moan and even grunt while he downed his mutton pie. I remember well that he used to be totally exhausted when his repast was finished. He was hardly able to wipe his mouth with the sleeve of his coat. I'll say one thing for him. There was no grandeur about him. He always blew his nose into his palm and rubbed it to his trousers seat and he never used anything but his coat sleeve to clean his face.

I still wonder why one of our victims didn't rush out of the shop and implant a boot on our backsides. They would have been entitled to do so. Sometimes the woman who owned the shop would send out the girl who assisted her and she would shoo us off, swinging a wet dishcloth.

Those were the days. Everybody has false teeth now – or at least those who haven't have their natural teeth. Signs by people do not grind their food any more and fat or gristle are now regarded as deadly enemies. How things have changed! Now they say 'Eat that fat at your peril', whereas when we were *garsúns* they would say 'Get that fat inside o' you and you'll pulverise Joe Louis.'

PUBOLOGY

Since I spoke recently on public houses and the wisdom to be found therein I have received numerous letters of congratulations for highlighting these hitherto-undisclosed aspects of pubology. One letter deserves my immediate attention, however. It comes from a city reader who says that he has been in our pub here in Listowel several times but he has never seen me. That is quite possible since I cannot spend all my time in the pub. However, it could also be that he is looking in the wrong direction for, as well as looking for me inside the counter, he should look for me outside the counter. The latter is my stamping ground during my hours of recreation. Here I may be seen with glass in hand by those who are sober.

The other letters offer contributions drawn from their own experiences of pub life. A woman from Drumcollogher who supplies her name and address and who used to work in a pub one time recalls a customer who slipped his domestic moorings whenever he sighted visitors in the vicinity of his home.

'He was what you might call a philosopher,' the Drumcollogher woman remembers. 'He had one saying for which I will personally remember him – "For the protection of its inmates, if nothing else, every house should have its visiting hours."'

I couldn't agree more. For some reason totally beyond my ken whenever I sit down to a meal I am besieged by visitors. The phone-caller too always rings at mealtimes for he knows you must eat and are likely to be seated at your own table when he lifts the phone to harass you.

I mentioned cures when talking about pub lore. On Sunday

night last as we were about to close for the night a farmer from an outlying townland arrived offering as an excuse for his lateness the fact that he was a martyr to arthritis. While he sipped his whiskey he was offered several cures. One man in particular had a most unusual remedy. To cure his own arthritis he regularly singes his bare bottom with burning newspapers as they once did to clear recalcitrant feathers from the carcasses of hastily plucked geese. The treatment, if it left a few blisters itself, always worked. I mean, where else would you hear it but in a public house. I have heard of cures that would make the hair stand on your head. Now there's a real cure, especially if your head is bare.

I often wonder why nobody has written a book about pub lore or pub sayings or pub medicine. Could be, as the old saying would have us believe, that the jokes of the night before are not nearly so funny in the morning. I was often tempted to write a book about my experiences in the pub trade and nothing else but I never got around to doing it. Maybe I'm doing it now through this medium.

I once had a customer who consumed all his meals early in the day, ending with his dinner which he devoured at three o'clock in the afternoon so that he could go to the pub early and remain there until closing time. He lived a happy life. So did his wife who, as long as she was permitted to indulge in bingo every night of the week, never objected to his drinking habits. She managed their pensions. She presented him with the price of two pints each afternoon before his departure and with his natural charm, guile and cunning he always managed to have rounds stood to him by those he praised for their courage and generosity. Pubs are filled with men who need recognition for unrecognised talents.

Pubs and poets go together and one of the better verses

I have heard over the years was composed by a drunken man after he had been introduced to a female from the townland of Ballybrohawlinam.

'Where in God's name,' said he, 'is Ballybrohawlinam?'

'Spell it,' called an onlooker.

'No,' said a third, 'get something to rhyme with it.'

The drunken man provided the following without a moment's hesitation:

Beautiful are the bottoms of the women of Ballybrohawlinam
With their chaste eyes heavenwards as though they'd no
   bottoms at all on 'em.

The Taking of Umbrellas

My umbrella was taken last week. I saw it happen but, before I could get to my feet and replace my pint glass on the pub counter, the umbrella and its new proprietor had disappeared through the front door and presumably round a convenient corner because when I eventually got to the same door the street outside was empty save for a dog half-drowned from the rain. I could be wrong but I thought I saw a smile on the dog's face.

Notice I said that my umbrella was taken, not stolen. I would not regard the unauthorised change of ownership as an act of stealing. Neither would I call it an act of misappropriation. To illegally take a pound of sausages or a loaf of bread is, in my opinion, a far greater offence than stealing an umbrella, especially if the misappropriator is not as hungry as he or she should be. In other words, it is all right to steal bread or sausages if one is very hungry but not so when one is not.

The unauthorised taking of umbrellas cannot, of course, be totally condoned but neither can it be condemned for, in the taking of umbrellas there are always extenuating circumstances. The man who stole my umbrella was entitled to do so for the good reason that he did not have an umbrella of his own and, in my book, everybody in this world is entitled to an umbrella, especially those without caps, hats or any other form of headgear. Having made this clear we may feel free to proceed.

I must concede at this point that there will be readers who may not look favourably on my somewhat liberal attitude towards umbrella-lifting. I personally know several clergymen whose views are diametrically opposed to mine. In the course of their ecclesiastical duties clergymen tend to hand their umbrellas for safe-keeping to whoever happens to be standing next to them. The same applies to bishops but whereas the latter would have a secretary or administrator in attendance your ordinary clergyman would be obliged to depend on a layman.

Laymen, with a few notable exceptions, are a weak-willed, dishonest lot and, more often than not, will not return the clergyman's umbrella. Neither will they pass by an umbrella left behind by chance in a church. There are some who will but these would be the more devout and conscientious types. Normal laymen, or Joe Soaps as they are sometimes called, look disparagingly on laymen of the aforementioned kind but this is surely because they are incapable of maintaining the high moral codes which are the hallmarks of those they would deride.

The umbrella which was stolen from me was a brolly of inferior quality because I am of the belief that an investment in a quality umbrella is tantamount to lunacy. The better the quality of the umbrella the greater the likelihood that it will be lifted. Nearly all umbrellas which are found on streets or roadways are of inferior quality or tattered or battered or whatever. That's the reason they are left on streets and roadways, where they eventually disintegrate. You'll never see a high-class umbrella in a public place unless it has an owner with it. Let us return to my own umbrella. It was run-of-the-mill but it was serviceable and would just about accommodate the heads and shoulders of two medium-sized adults. The man who took my umbrella was about thirty-five years of age, a pretty tough period in the life of most men, particularly married men because it is the time that bills multiply at an unprecedented rate, especially if there are children.

The loss of such a man cannot be reckoned. Apart from the grief which his loss would occasion there is the fact that his family will not have been provided for properly. They never are except in the rarest of cases. They just about manage to make ends meet and rarely invest in luxuries like umbrellas.

I was glad, therefore, that it was my umbrella he took and not the umbrella of some begrudging wretch who cared not whether the fellow lived or died. Suppose he had not taken my umbrella and suppose that he incurred a cold followed by pneumonia followed by expiry – would not I feel guilty if he had not taken my umbrella!

Why then, the gentle reader will ask, did I follow him to the door? Instinct and nothing more. If I had caught up with him I would not have asked for the return of my umbrella: I would have been annoyed but that's all. Later, when my feelings would have cooled, I would have been happy to have served my fellow man in some small way.

The gentle reader is sure to ask at this stage if I ever stole an umbrella myself. Of course I did and if I hadn't I wouldn't be alive to tell the tale. I stole an umbrella on a night when torrents of rain deluged the streets and burst the mains. If I hadn't taken the umbrella I would not have survived. But what of the owner of the umbrella? Was not he entitled to some consideration? Of course he was and I'm sure he did the right thing, as I did, and took another umbrella from the plentiful supply which hung in the hallway of the tavern.

If I might be permitted to parody the late Lord Macaulay, I would like to submit the following brief quatrain:

For how can man die better
When facing fearful rain
Than give up his umbrella
And perish earthly gain.
Than give up his umbrella
When every road's a pond
To either a slender, drenched brunette
Or else a dripping blonde.

WHISKEY BUM

To dispel any suggestion of elitism let us now look at a type of career which most people will reject out of hand. I refer to the little-known calling of whiskey bum. Whilst I have personally dabbled in whitewashing, direction-giving and matchmaking, to mention but a few, I have no experience whatsoever of bumming for alcoholic beverages. What I propose to do, therefore, is to present a portrait of a whiskey bum drawn from experience.

In Ballybunion I was recently accosted by a total stranger whose breath reeked of alcohol, whose weak eyes probed my features from beneath a film of water and whose sweaty hand seized mine as though it were clutching a lifebelt in a final attempt to survive a watery grave. As he held my hand he endeavoured to garb his muddled thoughts in appropriate words but all that emerged from his porter-stained mouth was an explosive belch which sent him awkwardly reeling backwards. I hastily leaned sideways lest the full force of the spume-spattered explosion overpower me and force me to the ground.

While he was engaged in the mammoth task of focusing his vision on my face I was presented with the opportunity of making a further study of my tormentor. His intoxication was at that advanced stage where it seemed that every move might well be his last.

His hair stood on his head in a mound of filthy off-red curls. Hair and face and neck and all that part of his hacked anatomy which was visible to the eye were unwashed and had been unwashed for a considerable time. He sported a florid facial colour but this was not due to drink alone. Exposure to the elements was mostly the cause. I had no idea, however, as to the fellow's identity, but it was becoming apparent that he was a wanderer of some kind and that he was determined to convey some message to me, also of an undisclosed nature.

I was reminded of the ancient mariner and the man he detained while on his way to a wedding feast. Was there to be as lengthy and as mournful a disclosure from this besotted traveller?

Again the porter-stained mouth opened. The expression on the face was one of immense sorrow. I waited as he tried to formulate the words that would bring us both the relief we desired and deserved. The mouth opened to its fullest, revealing an uneven mixture of teeth ranging in colour from off-white to dun, to dark and finally to a darkness that was as black as the ace of spades.

Readers who have been apprehended or simply waylaid by inarticulate, drunken men will understand when I say that I was sorely tempted to kick the fellow on the shin. Rather than resort to violence, however, I prayed for patience. His mouth was opening and closing now with unfailing regularity but no word had as yet emerged.

Fair dues to the fellow, he was making heroic efforts to make himself heard. Then came a lull. The mouth went slack but as it did the face purpled and he was seized by a mighty spasm which rattled him to his very foundations.

He still held on to my hand while varied and multiple contortions crossed and recrossed his face. I should have known better. The whole exercise was merely the prelude to a second gigantic belch which sent a pair of low-flying seagulls heavenwards in frantic alarm and which, if it had been discharged in one of the nearby caves, would surely have engineered the collapse of the historic cliffs of Doon.

He slackened his grip on my hand, such was the force of the explosion but I dared not release his. If I released him he would have fallen down fifty feet of the steep, grassy slope to the jagged rocks below. I held on while he fought to regain his balance. To the gentle reader it must by this time seem that he had a hold of my hand for an hour or more but no, all that had passed by way of time was a period of about two minutes. So fraught, however, with tension was that short passage that it seemed like ages.

It suddenly occurred to me that on my keyring was a safety pin. Don't ask me why I carry a safety pin because I don't honestly know. I hung it from the keyring years ago and it has remained there since, waiting for its moment of glory.

Into my left-hand trousers pocket I thrust my hand and fiddled about among the fistful of keys. I located the pin handily enough and quickly set about dislocating it. I smiled inwardly, if such a thing is really possible, at the thought of the shock the ruffian would get when I gave him a dart of the pin in the back of the hand. Suddenly, my imprisoned hand was free. Had he guessed my intent? Of course not. How could he possibly know that I carried a safety pin on my keyring?

His attitude was now completely changed. His tongue hung out and an ample tongue it was. He slobbered like a hound as I withdrew my hand from the pocket. He extended the hand which had imprisoned mine. Its palm was upward. So that was it. He thought I had visited the pocket for change. It became clear at once that all the blackguard wanted from the outset was money for drink.

As the circulation returned to the hand which had been imprisoned I massaged it with the hand which I had withdrawn from my pocket. The wanderer growled and scowled when he saw that the withdrawn hand brought no money with it.

Promptly he seized the hand which had been free. A look of impassioned entreaty filled his eyes. His mouth opened and, fearing that he was about to unleash the third belch, I located a pound in my fob pocket and handed it to him.

He snatched it from my hand and made a brave bid to express his thanks with words. None were forthcoming. Not even a whisper crossed his lips. Clutching the pound he stumbled instinctively to the nearest tavern. My ordeal was over. I had been, not for the first time, the victim of a whiskey bum. It is not a vocation which I would encourage but it must be said in its defence that there are men born into this world who are fit for nothing else.

BEEF TEA

I am certain that there are many people who have never heard of beef tea, much less drunk it. When I was a *garsún* there was a famous greyhound in my native town who was once backed off the boards at Tralee track. He was well trained for the occasion and specially fed as the following couplet will show:

We gave him raw eggs and we gave him beef tea
But last in the field he wound up in Tralee.

Beef tea in those days was a national panacea as well as being famed for bringing out the best in athletes and racing dogs. Whenever it was diagnosed by the vigilant females of our household that one of us was suffering from growing pains we were copiously dosed with beef tea until the pains passed on. The only thing I remember in its favour was that it tasted better than senna or castor oil.

I remember once my mother enquiring of a neighbour how his wife was faring. Apparently the poor creature had been confined to bed for several weeks suffering from some unknown but malicious infirmity.

'Ah,' said the husband sadly, 'all she's able to take now is a drop of beef tea.'

She cannot have been too bad for I had frequently heard of invalids of whom it was said that they couldn't even keep down beef tea. When you couldn't even keep down beef tea it meant that you were bound for the inevitable sojourn in the bourne of no return.

Of course it was also a great boast for a woman to be able to say that all she was able to stomach was beef tea. It meant that she was deserving of every sympathy because it was widely believed that if a patient did not respond to beef tea it was waste of time spending good money on other restoratives. It was also a great excuse for lazy people who wished to avoid work. All they had to say was that they were on beef tea and they were excused. No employer would have it on his conscience that he imposed work on people believed to be on their last legs.

On another occasion as I was coming from school I saw a crowd gathered outside the door of a woman who had apparently fainted a few moments before.

'How is she?' I overheard one neighbour ask of another.

'They're trying her with beef tea now,' came the dejected response. The woman who had asked the question made the sign of the cross and wiped a tear from her eye.

There was another man in the street at the time, a notorious rogue albeit a likeable enough fellow. He was greatly addicted to all forms of intoxicating drink and, as is the case with such people, he frequently found himself with an insatiable desire for meat. He would insist, upon arriving home from the public house, that his wife did not look at all well. As it so happened she was something of a hypochondriac and liked to hear such things.

'I haven't been feeling well all day,' she would agree.

'What you need,' he would say, 'is a nice mug of beef tea. If you have a shilling or two handy I'll go down and knock up the butcher and get a pound of the finest round.'

All beef tea consisted of by the way was the water in which the beef was boiled. As soon as she started to partake of the tea our friend would start to partake of the beef. It was a good ruse and it kept both of them in good health for many a year.

Nowadays there is no talk of beef tea – and more's the pity because I might not be here at all only for it. There were occasions when it was supposed to have brought people back from the very mouth of the grave. Under no circumstances was the fat of the beef to be used. A nice lean cut off the round was the very man for the job.

People may look askance at it now but in my boyhood it was held in reserve to the very end, much like a crack battalion in time of battle. Then when all seemed lost the beef tea, like the battalion, was successfully unleashed upon the enemy: the battalion upon the opposing army and the beef tea upon the harbingers of human extinction.

MEN AND OTHER ANIMALS

Cuckoo, Cuckoo

The summertime is coming
And the birds are sweetly singing . . .

So runs the evergreen chorus. Summer's PRO, to wit the bark-brown cuckoo, freshly arrived from Morocco, has already made several pronouncements in places as far apart as Knockanure and Newcastle West. The gist of his revelations is that the season is legitimately underway now that he has established himself in a ready-made nest, manufactured to measure by a brace of innocent and well-meaning blackbirds whose offspring he simply heaved over the side to make way for his ample African posterior. For thirty years or so now, since I first started to write for money, I have unfailingly made mention of the cuckoo's arrival.

I have published every report I ever received, devoting lengthy paragraphs to the more meritorious. Yet there are people who regularly come along and ask me why I never write about the cuckoo. These people know very well I write about the cuckoo. What they are really asking is why I do not write about their own special cuckoos or rather the individual cuckoo which only they have heard. How true the old saying that there is no cuckoo like your own cuckoo. On reflection I must honestly add that maybe there is no such old saying. If this is so then I hereby sponsor it for inclusion in the next anthology of old sayings.

By summertime many of my readers will have heard a particular cuckoo. It is possible that substantial numbers may have heard the same cuckoo. If this is so, console yourself with the fact that just as surely as no two cuckoos are alike so also are no two notes from any one cuckoo alike. The cuckoo's voice changes from day to day and fades away altogether after a few weeks' residence in his summer home.

Recently I read a very distressing story concerning the decline in the numbers of cuckoos visiting this country during the summer. The fact that the same applies to featherless visitors from Scandinavia and England should not make our concern for the cuckoo any the less. While man multiplies all over the globe the number of birds, particularly cuckoos, tends to decrease. The chief reason for this is that man requires more room and sacred retreats where cuckoos once advertised themselves are now housing estates and factories. I am not arguing against these. What I am trying to do is warn readers against a time when we will hear fewer and fewer cuckoos. A time will come when certain luckless individuals will wait in vain for that magical call which is part of the fabric of every summer. This is sure to give rise to shock and distress among the more susceptible of readers and it is only fair that they should be warned against the likelihood of summers without cuckoos. Personally I dread the thought but I have long since insured against it and I would strongly advise others that they should do the same.

In the event of failure in the not-too-distant future we should be on the lookout for other signs of summer.

It takes a long time for summer to establish itself. For the first week or so it's no different from its predecessor. Gradually, however, it takes hold. More flowers appear and birds grow excited. The sting dies in the wind and all the cows are calved. There are many manifestations and each of us has his own special means of confirming that the season is well and truly launched.

For me summer comes with the arrival of a balding sixty-year-old Clare man, a chap of roving eye and rosy cheek. For many years now he has presented himself at my bar counter at this precise time. He is as constant as the cuckoo or, if you're that way inclined, the Northern Star.

On each visit he brings a female companion of far tenderer years than he. Yesterday, which was Sunday, he presented himself for inspection at 12.30 p.m. He had with him a stout lady who might have been twenty-five or thirty. He seated her and called for a drink. Two brandies with the barest tint of port wine in each if you please and where would we get a good lunch, not too exotic.

I shake hands with him and he introduces me to his girl of the moment. This is pure exhibitionism. He wants to show me what a randy womaniser he is. The girl smiles demurely, adjusts her buttocks on the seat and pulls an inadequate tweed skirt affectedly over fat red knees.

After this covert exercise our man winks lewdly at me as if to suggest that although a pornographic display has been publicly averted there was every likelihood of a comprehensive sexual debauch before the night grew pale and yielded to the dawn. Nobody believes this. Here is as prime an example of a frustrated cock virgin as one could wish to behold. I am reminded of *Titus Andronicus*: 'This is the monstrosity in love, lady, that the will is infinite and the execution confined,' which is merely another way of saying that bullocks' notions will avail you nought.

But let me describe this man who arrives unfailingly every summer. His chariot is an ancient Morris Minor. His women are invariably serious-faced. His scant hair, dyed titian, is so cleverly combed that no part of the crown or poll of his head is without a diverting rib or two.

He has the best in false teeth, upper and lower. Two biros and a fountain pen adorn his breast pocket. He belongs in another decade. You might say the man is dead but he won't lie down.

He was weaned in dance halls where paraffin lamps hung from the rafters and grated candles mixed with dance crystals glazed the uneven floor. Yet here he was publicly acknowledging the arrival of another summer.

His chances of courting a woman are slim, of carnally knowing a woman slimmer, of outright possession slimmest of all. Still he would subscribe to the Shakespearean theory, again to be found in *Titus Andronicus*:

> *She is a woman, therefore may be woo'd;*
> *She is a woman, therefore may be won.*

Outside in the street the people are coming from Mass. The fancies of boys and girls lightly turn to thoughts of love. The serious-faced girl becomes restive. Her thoughts are far from love. A trickle of saliva emerges from a corner of her mouth. Our man is pensive now, noting the other customers, particularly two good-looking girls who are seated opposite him. They are not, as yet, aware of his existence, yet he alone of all the people in the pub has paid his tribute to summer. Now that he has, however, he is mute. He has become a spent force. He is a smolt who will never again return to the clear and sparkling waters of the upriver reeds.

But he has accomplished his mission and this, for me, is the important thing. He has reminded me that it's high time I went into the kitchen and took the wife in my arms to tell her that summer is here and that love doesn't really change or grow grey. It's time to go some place, to get out and away into other places where we can be free for a while.

You can have your daffodils and your primroses. I don't begrudge them to you. Summer's representative has come from Clare. I return to the pub. I address him: 'You'll have a drink in honour of your visit.' His face lights up. Hope sparkles in his eyes. He nudges his girlfriend when I turn my back. His worth has been recognised. His day is made.

In acknowledging his visit I am also acknowledging or saluting the arrival of summer. I am making much of its representative, treating him with the courtesy and respect that I would normally reserve for accredited ambassadors.

UNLICENSED BULLS

Lately I met a small farmer who was summoned and fined for possession of an unlicensed bull.

'You're an educated man,' he said to me, 'so maybe you can tell me something.'

'I'm at your disposal,' I assured him.

'Does bulls take it to heart the way we does?' he asked. What he meant was this. Is the sense of loss experienced by the unlicensed bull who has been apprehended by the bull inspector on a par with human loss of the same kind? A hypothetical question perhaps but one which deserves to be carefully considered nevertheless. The answer of course is that there is a greater sense of loss because man has other outlets for his pent-up energy. The bull is equipped for one function and one function only and that is the simple siring of cows and heifers. Imagine the sense of deprivation felt by the unlicensed bull when the meadows start to bloom and the yellow brilliance of buttercups brightens the hills and valleys. Imagine the indescribable frustration when giddy heifers scamper by to a change of pasture on highways visible to the incarcerated bull whose only role, now that he has been found deficient by the Department, is to fatten himself for the butcher's block.

Imagine the unutterable sense of unfulfilment when a lone cow browsing the roadside grasses peers through the hedge where the victim is confined. Their eyes meet and for a long while they stand, separated by the hedge, contemplating what might have been. Then the cow, as is the wont of cows, resumes her grazing while the baffled bull bawls his heart out in desperation.

Small wonder that bulls have savage tempers. Nature is never easily thwarted but, when it is, agony replaces ecstasy. Does not even the stupefied bullock simulate the actions of his uncut brothers when he recalls his rightful function from the recesses of his clover-dimmed memory? Imagine then, dear reader, how much worse it is for the unlicensed bull possessed, I need hardly add, of all his faculties. He does not savour the perfumed hedgerows which surround him. To him these are the stiflers of his natural talents. Imagine his murderous wrath at the indignity which has been so unfairly forced upon him.

On the brambles small birds are chirping to each other their sweet notes of love while all around rabbits and hares are blissfully preoccupied with the age-old, delightful rites of propagation. Even the lowly insect drones out his love and is requited. Every creature of the field and thicket is free to pursue his lustful instincts without fear of being thwarted.

Alone of all these the unlicensed bull must suffer the humility of enforced loneliness while worse bulls with the departmental seal are allowing themselves to be petted and ogled by a super-fluity of love-hungry heifers. I mentioned before how a friend of mine with a long neck, for which defect the unlicensed bull is struck off, was free to marry twice and nobody objected. Let us return for a moment to this friend. During the Emergency he joined the Irish army and was accepted without question.

They never even measured his neck when they allotted him his uniform. Nobody from corporal to major-general even once mentioned his neck during his lengthy service with the defence forces. Yet our friend the unlicensed bull who only wants to play the role of lover and father is denied these basic rights and consigned to a life of ineffectuality because of whimsical preferences which presently prevail in the Department of Agriculture.

A most interesting question arises from all this, of little consequence admittedly to those who are lacking in concern, and it is this: Which suffers most? Is it the bull who is whipped away when he has grown accustomed to the joys of love and the bliss of bovine companionship or is it the unfortunate virgin bull who has never experienced the ecstasies or satisfaction of cow and heifer-mating?

Certainly it must seem like a difficult question but those of us who are settled down in life will heartily concur with the viewpoint that a bull who has experienced the joys of love suffers most. There are those who will come down heavily in favour of the virgin bull but against this it must be submitted that what he has never had he will never miss. Others may argue that it is worse to be left in a permanent state of surmise and frustration, that all this leads to is a very befuddled bull fit for nothing but the humane killer but I would argue that the bull who has grown used to consistent copulation with cows and heifers suffers beyond all comprehension when he is ruthlessly cut off from his seemingly bottomless reservoir of romance.

The one true conclusion which we may draw from all this is that unlicensed bulls, excepting those who are not apprehended, suffer more than their share in this world. The next time, therefore, you see a bull on his way to market during the early summer, ponder well his fate and thank your stars that those unjust laws do not apply to you or yours.

CRUELTY TO GREYHOUNDS!

Three people were recently involved in a dispute on these here licensed premises. As well as being licensed to sell beer, wines, spirits and tobacco we are also licensed to engage in non-violent disputes from time to time.

The subject of the most recent dispute was coursing, that kind of coursing where two dogs chase a hare with a view to tearing him asunder.

'Coursing is so cruel,' said a mild-mannered old lady as she made gentle conversation with two local coursing men, one of them her brother-in-law, the other a farmer.

'Coursing is cruel,' the latter agreed while the brother-in-law nodded his head emphatically.

'Do you remember that brindled bitch I had that could pick up a hare on the trot not to mind a gallop?' the farmer reminisced.

'Yerra why wouldn't I remember her,' said the brother-in-law, 'didn't the same lady win a bitch trial stake in Glin about twenty years ago.'

'But coursing is so cruel,' the old lady shook her head at the injustice of it all.

'Isn't that what we're after saying,' said her brother-in-law. 'Didn't this poor man have to put down that bitch after she breaking her two legs going after a hare. What could be crueller than that?'

The sister-in-law's mouth opened but she was obliged to open it again for the want of something appropriate to say. 'I had a black dog myself,' said the brother-in-law, 'that took a tumble in a no-course duffer in Clare and she broke her back. I had to shoot her. Don't talk to me about cruelty. I had another dog. She was a bitch and she rose a hare one day and we walking through a meadow at the back of the house. What did my hoor of a hare do only dodge under a fence of thorny wire and let my unfortunate dog run into it. He destroyed himself. He was never any good after that.'

'What about the hare?' said the sister-in-law, the astonishment showing clearly on her face.

'Don't mind the hare,' said the farmer, 'you'll see hares turning on children soon since they started doing away with all the coursing meetings. When the cat is out!'

'I can't understand why people go to coursing meetings at all,' said the old lady.

'Neither can I,' said her brother-in-law, 'there's no money in it and if you have a good dog you're risking his career if he meets a tough hare. It's not the gain that carries us to coursing but the pure love of it.'

The old lady sat holding her heart, unable to believe her ears.

'There's nothing crueller than coursing,' said the brother-in-law. 'I don't know why we follow it at all. A good coursing dog often broke his owner.'

'And his owner's heart,' his friend added.

'But!' the old lady protested, 'but what about the poor unfortunate hares. Look at what they have to go through.'

Her listeners looked at her in perplexity. It was the perplexity of the misunderstood.

'I often cursed hares,' said her brother-in-law, 'two dogs and a bitch I lost over 'em. A dog will follow coursing rules but a hare, the hoor, won't!'

'That's right,' said his crony, 'a strong hare will destroy the best of dogs and there's no resorting to law.'

Both men shook their heads at the injustice of it all.

'You should never course a quality dog,' said the farmer. 'Safer to keep him for the track. That's where the money is. There's too much of a risk in coursing.'

'I'll tell you something now,' said the brother-in-law, and he laid a confidential hand on the old lady's shoulder. 'You take it from me that a game hare, a strong hare now, will do for the best of dogs. A greyhound has no chance at all against a game hare!'

A Song with No Air

There is a quiet man who has, on rare occasions, adorned the corner of the street opposite this place where I calefact my treatises. He is so quiet that even when the dogs piddle with disgusting frequency around the area where he stands he takes no notice, allowing the ill-mannered creatures to indulge themselves without fear of rebuke.

He is not a corner-boy, not even a part-time or temporary one. He is too self-effacing, too mild-mannered, too humble and too gentle by far to fill this most demanding of roles.

He calls to the corner once a week, bends his head deferentially if there is a resident corner boy and meekly allows his ample posterior to rest against the house front that forms part of the corner. Here he will remain for half an hour or so and the following is true. Witnesses will come forward to verify what I say if they are required by doubting Thomases to do so.

From the moment of his arrival to his departure the dogs which frequent the area, as I have already indicated, piddle without restraint all around his legs and sometimes on his shoes. Why the canines of my native town should select this humble representative of the human species for such outstanding honours is something I cannot explain. Is it his meekness and quietness that attracts them? He never shoos them away nor does he even take notice when they begin their relief work.

A neighbour told me lately that certain dogs are like that. They will retain their canine water until they find the right place to let it go. They will spend the morning foraging and fighting, growling and chasing motor cars but the moment our man arrives they slink in his direction, survey him well and survey the scene thoroughly before raising legs aloft to indulge in their varying cascades.

Many are called, says the Good Book, but few are chosen. This man, however, has been chosen by the dogs of Listowel. These dogs are already notorious for soiling our streets and backways. The fruits of their labours are nearly always visible to strangers who stroll around the town. They are mystified. One German woman approached me one afternoon and asked me the following question: 'Deece are sacrit dogs no?'

'No!' I told her, 'they are very ordinary dogs.'

She expressed surprise and explained to some friends in her company that the dogs were not sacred. They also expressed surprise.

'Honely hin Hindia,' said she, 'haf I sin animals that soils de strits and deece are sacrit cows.' She departed after she had taken some photographs of the dogs and their droppings.

Let us return, however, to our quiet friend. Our friend is a man with a split personality – but then who isn't when he has enough booze put away. Booze to the quiet man is what flood waters are to the stranded fish, what the starting pistol is to the straining athlete, what the sound of the whistle is to the waiting midfielder.

The other day I had the privilege of beholding our meek friend in another role. There he stood outside my front door, his arms stretched wide, his head aloft and him singing a song to no particular tune. Granted he was sozzled to the very gills but I have seen other sozzled gentlemen who go home quietly and others still who kick doors, break windows and deliberately bump against offensive passers-by.

Despite the fact that the song had no air, it was not without words. These were of his own creation and I swear that I have never heard anything so complicated and so filled with long, hitherto-unheard phrases. It would take a Joycean scholar to unscramble the message contained therein.

What a change from the mild-mannered chap we saw standing at the corner less than twenty-four hours earlier with dogs piddling left, right and centre and him, half-asleep, indifferent to their defilements.

His singing, if I may call it such, did not grate. Neither was it aggressive. It was soft and sweet as a summer breeze among the sallies of the river bank. He had his coat off and he sang to the passing cars. Some slowed to have a better look at him while others drove by lest he stumble across them. Let me say here that there wasn't a solitary dog in sight. A dog can always tell when a man is drunk. They have cause to know the difference between a sober master and a drunken master.

Our friend had now taken a break. He was holding up the front of my house and doing it admirably. His eyes had a faraway look and he slept for a period, opening bleary peepers occasionally in order to make sure that the world he knew so well was still to the good.

It was after the sleep that he proffered the *pièce de résistance* of the evening. From his open mouth came a faint, high-pitched ululation the like of which you'd hear from an immature banshee. I have never heard an angel sing so I cannot make a comparison but I will say that our friend sang from the very depths of his soul. No sober man could sing the way he sang. The fact that he was drunk must not take away from the quality of his rendition. It was truly magnificent. It attracted the unstinted admiration of two small girls who, for a while, turned away from the cones they were licking to show their appreciation for the unearthly sounds which assailed their young ears.

This was the cream, the essence of this drunken man's

spirit, the very distillation of his purer being. I wished I had a recording device to record it for posterity. I was reminded of a country saying: You'll always meet the biggest bird the day you haven't got the gun.

Then the singing stopped and he wandered upwards, wiping his mouth with the back of his hand. There were different sounds now. He was crying. I left him to his grief and went indoors to tell my wife about the song I had heard. But how would I describe it? I would have to be a Shakespeare. It's there in *A Midsummer Night's Dream*:

> *Since once I sat upon a promontory*
> *And heard a mermaid on a dolphin's back*
> *Uttering such dulcet and harmonious breath*
> *That the rude sea grew civil at her song*
> *And certain stars shot madly from their spheres*
> *To hear the sea-maid's music.*

English Words . . .
But the Accent is Irish

'G'out you waggabone!' The order was directed to a drunken wrenboy who came without flute, banjo or bodhrán and who smelled so strongly of stale porter that he could well be described as a walking brewery.

A lesser man might have termed him a drunken wretch or an alcoholic hoor but I feel that a waggabone was fairest under the circumstances. That time, which was fifty years ago of a snowy St Stephen's Day in the Stacks Mountains, the letter 'V' was rarely used by country folk. Hence the expression 'G'out you waggabone!' which was simply a minor corruption of 'Get out you vagabond!'

The people of that time and clime would hardly know what a vagabond was but everybody knew that a waggabone was a harmless, useless fellow always on the make.

When the waggabone was told to get out he sidled sheepishly and drunkenly up to the fire and awaited the bottle of stout which he knew to be his right as soon as the civilities were disposed of. When he was asked after a while if he would care for a bottle of stout he simply answered, 'very well'.

It is still the same in the Stacks Mountains, all through Renagown, Glounamucmae and Tubbernanoon as well as Dromadomore and Knockadirreen. The Irish accent remains, and you cannot but fail to hear it should you care to sojourn in Carrigcannon or Knocknagoshel. It's alive and well and beautiful, this language with the English words and the Irish accent. It's as though the accent was waiting for the Irish language to return.

Another time; it could have been 1933 or 1934 or 1935. Anyway it was at the height of the exotic lunacy known as the Economic War which lasted from 1932 to 1938 and which almost totally impoverished the unfortunate Irish farmer who had geared himself to beef production with a view to entering the British Market. I won't go into the ins and outs of the 'War,' but it was declared by De Valera who argued that no money should be paid to British landlords for land which they had stolen in the first place.

Dev had a point but the British imposed huge tariffs on Irish imports and vice versa, so that the upshot of the entire ruction was that Ireland found itself with a surplus of calves. They had to be disposed of and soon: According to opposition members of Dáil Éireann their corpses were blocking the eyes of bridges in the villages and townlands of rural Ireland. But what has all this to do with our story, the rapidly tiring reader will be sure to ask. I'm coming to it. In Lyreacrompane proper I was a guest one day at dinner in the home of a small farmer who happened to be a distant relation of my late, lamented father.

There was, steaming on a large dish in the centre of the table, a hind quarter of roast veal. Now roast veal is not the real thing unless it is well basted with bacon lard during its cooking. Also the proper gravy to accompany this delightful dish is best made when chopped onions are added to the fat after the veal has been removed from the roasting pot. Add some water and some thickening and allow the chopped onions to simmer.

There may be tastier dishes in the world but if there are I have neither heard of them nor tasted them. Anyway, just as we were about to dive in, the boy, as he was called, stood up and announced that he would not be partaking of the fare in front of him.

'Pray why not?' his employer asked with great annoyance.

'Because,' said the boy, 'wale makes me womit!'

It was a curt retort, curt as you will find in the long litany of excuses which have been tended by farmers' boys down through the ages when they found themselves unwilling to indulge in the ordinary fare of the kitchen table.

Translated into townie language what he was saying was: 'Veal makes me vomit', which was a fabrication to put it mildly for there was a totally inexplicable aversion to roast veal in rural Ireland throughout the Economic War and for several years afterwards.

'Well,' said the farmer, 'wale don't make me womit.' Then he addressed himself to me: 'Do it make you?' he asked.

Entering into the spirit of the thing I answered, 'No, wale don't make me womit nayther.'

'Shut up you wiper,' said the farmer's boy, 'or I'll wulcanise you.'

As things turned out he did not vulcanise me for, like all braggarts who make outrageous threats, he was quite incapable of carrying one out. Later in the afternoon, when the hunger caught him, he consumed the wale and it did not make him womit! He also ate the wegetables and in no time at all he made large quantities of both wale and wegetables to wanish.

Once in Dirha bog while partaking of lunch with some other bog-workers one came out with the observation: 'These wittles is wile.'

Nobody agreed with him for, like many a man at the time, he did not like fat. He would eat nothing but lean whereas the reasonable man would eat both fat and lean and do himself more good than harm.

The man who intimated that the wittles were wile made objection in the first place because there were no buns on offer after the main repast had been consumed. Neither was there a small pot of black or red jam which was often included with the general fare.

He refused to eat but later in the day he announced to another bogman that his stomach was beginning to wibrate. There is only one known cure for wibrations of the stomach and that is to fill the stomach in question with food. Alas and alack, however, all the food had been consumed so the wibrations intensified until at last relief arrived in the shape of a thunderous belch which his fellow bogmen believed had uprooted all the evil gases which had lurked in the depths of this man's interior for years and years. They said this to console him and to make atonement for their having eaten his share of the rations and for having enjoyed them no end.

'Werily,' said one who had spent several weeks studying for the priesthood before being kicked out on his ear for totally depleting a year's stock of altar wine, 'you'll be wisited by peace and werily your stomach will be wiolent no more and your woice will be the woice of the lark!'

So when you hear a man, dear reader, who submerges the 'V' and emerges with a 'W', remember that you are not listening to a rustic who is not distorting words or letters. Rather are you listening to a man who is being absolutely faithful to his Gaelic heritage and who has said to himself in turmoil and anguish: 'To V or not to V. That is the question,' and who, at the end of the day, decided not to V but to W!

THE ASS AND CART

The other day I was intrigued by a notice which appeared in a provincial newspaper: 'Wanted: a donkey's cart, complete with seat and guards, condition immaterial.'

I put it down to the work of a hopeful sentimentalist for he might have more profitably advertised for 'A young man to handle lions and tigers; no experience necessary.' I am left wondering if he received an answer but, frankly, I doubt if he did. There are still plenty of donkey carts but the 'sate and guard' is a thing of the past. Those of us whose grandmothers sat airily on those thronelike seats will never forget the dignity of a shawled old lady and the status she could give to this most humble and most ancient of conveyances. Invariably the donkey was a rogue but his every idiosyncrasy was known to his aged charioteer who possessed an insight into the antics of pampered asses which was nothing short of a revelation.

The ass and cart is still used to carry milk to the creamery, and the ass and rail is without peer when the turf is stranded in squelchy bogs, but, as a means of transport, the woman of today will have nothing to do with it. Only the old-age pensioner will sit astride the rickety perch or plonk herself bravely between the shaft and the body of the car. She and her conveyance are more sought-after than celebrities by camera-laden tourists and in many a Boston drawing room she hangs, aloof and serene, between outsize prints of Pope John and John Kennedy. She is not camera-shy and neither is her donkey and if a dollar bill comes her way now and then, it is only her due. After all, isn't she a relic of the old days when emigration was a respectable profession and homecoming a highlight of the parochial year?

The donkey and cart offers a livelihood of another kind in the butterfly days of summer. A clever mother will dress her young in patched trousers and scrub their faces until they are spotless, put them into an ass cart and send them up and down a road which leads to a tourist resort. No better tourist bait exists unless we are to credit the presence of leprechauns. A cute youngster with an appropriate expression of angelic innocence will earn more than his father in the round of a day and, if he is experienced, he will not be forgotten by departed holidaymakers when Christmas comes around. A good combination of cart, donkey and youngster is as big an attraction as a round tower or a Celtic cross and I have often seen as many as three carloads of tourists at a time surrounding a single cart with cameras clicking like mowing-machines. An interested onlooker will hear expressions like: 'Well did you ever see anything so quaint!' or 'Gee, he's a real cute burro!' I know of many cases where the ass is retired when the season is over and the cart is carefully oiled and kept in cold storage until the grass grows long and the white dust is on the roads of summer. Sometimes when I sit in a speeding motor car, I secretly long for an ass and cart. I do not mention this to the driver because he might well slow down and tell me that he has no objection and wholeheartedly approves of the change. I am cheered by the unhurried progress and safe consistency of plopping hooves. I am cheered as Xenophon's mercenaries were cheered when they encountered the hoofmarks of asses on their way back from the Persian campaign. These asses were wild asses but the hoofmarks, no doubt, brought back memories to those weary men; memories of shawled mothers in carts on their way to the crossroads in some mountainy corner of Greece. I can see Xenophon, now exhausted. He sits on a stone and wishes he were at home tackling the ass to take his grandfather to the Olympics.

Should you see three ass and carts together in this day and age it does not mean that a chariot race is about to begin. It means that the day is Friday and that the weekly trek for the old-age pension is under way.

There is no safer means of travel, and I have lost count of the number of times I met a drowsy old man or woman who had a half-whiskey too many. The reins hung loosely over the donkey's neck but the ass clung religiously to his appointed portion of the roadway, surely a classic example of teamwork. In the cart his charge slept soundly and the only instructions passed on to the donkey were the occasional indecipherable snores. Home was always reached safely and will you tell me who remembers a fatal accident involving a donkey and cart? If there are such accidents they are never the fault of the donkey. More than likely they are the fault of the two-legged donkey in charge of the motor car. The two-legged donkey is an astonishing animal. Put him behind the wheel of a car and his powers of reasoning desert him. He lacks the patience of his four-footed brother, who always gets where he wants to go without mishap or disaster.

Should there be a fine week this summer I would recommend a leisurely trip through the little-known roads of the country in a donkey and cart. The donkey is not a choosy feeder and will fend for himself among the roadside grasses. Don't carry a stick or a whip. Give him his head and in his own good time he will go places. A quarter stone of oats, now and then, will rise a gallop without urging. An ass's gallop is as smooth as aeroplane travel and as unpredictable. The difference is that, when the donkey stops unexpectedly, you will be still seated in the cart.

Inevitably, a tourist in an ass and cart will be regarded as a curiosity, and many well-meaning souls will mistake it for a publicity stunt. Rest assured that the ass will not be ruffled by comment or curiosity. His job is to pull the cart as his father and mother before him did and his indifferent assurance can be heart-warming when a horn hoots outrageously as if it were sole proprietor of the public road.

HEIFER COURSING

I would like to see employment created where none existed before which brings me to the metier of the sports organiser, on a professional basis, I need hardly add. Since cities, towns and other built-up areas are well catered for in this respect we must look to the countryside. There are many lucrative openings in this field and a young man with energy to spare and a modest amount of capital to invest can look forward confidently to success.

Let me, therefore, endeavour to establish my aspirant in his chosen career. Here is how he might begin. First let him invest in a score of mountainy heifers, the leaner and wilder the better. Isolate these temporarily in an out-of-the-way pasture and, at his leisure, prepare an advertisement for the newspapers. Let it state that there is to be a heifer-coursing contest for thirty-two farmers in the heavyweight class. Light or agile farmers would not serve our purpose, as you shall see.

Let there be an entrance fee of, say, £100 per farmer, which would give him purse and expenses money of £3,200. Let him present £1,500 to the winner, £500 to the runner-up and to the beaten semi-finalists £250 each. This leaves £1,200 for advertising, insurance and the salaries of the organiser and his assistant or assistants. Allowing that there would be an admission fee of a pound or two, the aforementioned sum would more than pay for the hire of the venue and for the remuneration of the judges.

First let there be an open draw to select sixteen pairs of farmers. When this is done the heifers should be brought down from the hills or wherever to the venue.

Let the coursing then commence – two farmers to chase one heifer, which would have roughly a hundred yards start. The idea would be to award points to the farmer who succeeded in roping the heifer, taking into account first, second and third turns, as in greyhound coursing. After the first round we would be left with sixteen fitter and faster, less weighty farmers. There would be no public outcry as in greyhound coursing. Indeed the organiser would be more likely to be commended for providing the district with fitter farmers. Abulia, inertia and obesity would soon disappear from the face of the countryside and there would be a greater interest in fitness on the farmlands in general.

However, let me return to the second round of the heifer coursing. By this time the lazier and fatter farmers would be weeded out but amongst them there would be a resolve to do better in the next heifer-coursing contest. Indeed there might be a consolation stake for sixteen no-course duffers.

The main contest, however, would go on until all had been eliminated save the two finalists. Imagine the excitement as the fastest of the heifers, specially confined for the final, is released. The last two farmers are slipped, and off they go after the heifer amid wild cheering from the crowd. They swing their ropes and emit ancient and traditional cattle-calls as they endeavour to capture the heifer. Afterwards the cup is filled and the loser congratulates the winner in a sporting fashion.

The sports organiser then moves on to the next venue, where a similar event would take place. The winners of local contests would go forward to compete in regional contests and from there to the national final.

The most attractive aspect of heifer coursing is that anybody can enter. As well as that an essential service is being provided. Overweight sons of the soil who cannot be induced into Turkish baths or weight-losing establishments have at last been presented with a means of losing weight, and not only can they lose weight but they can win glory.

Heifer coursing need not necessarily be confined to farmers. City people, however, who might be frightened of cattle, might avail themselves of cats or even dogs which could be pursued over specially laid-out courses which might have obstacles like water trenches or hurdles.

You can see, therefore, that there are immense possibilities in heifer coursing for heavy farmers. People might abandon their armchairs for a while to spend some time in the healthy outdoors and heaven knows how many new jobs would be created. Government aid from the Department of Health should readily be forthcoming. A fit farmer must, of necessity, produce more than an unfit farmer. A government subsidy, therefore, would be a wise investment and would yield a fine harvest in time.

There are, of course, numerous other forms of sport which might be utilised for the good of the country. In selecting heifer coursing we have shown that new jobs can be provided without affecting other job sources. We have shown that the most vital ingredient of all for creating new employment is the imagination. Indeed the imagination, because it is not fettered by strictures, should be used more and more by industrialists, politicians and job-planners in general.

If heifer coursing does not appeal to you, you will always find something that will if you put your mind to it, by simply using the imagination the good God has given you.

Dogs

Now I'd like to mention dogs. However, let me say that this treatise is not addressed merely to dog-lovers or dog-fanciers. It is addressed to all manner of people, from those who cannot abide dogs to those who prefer cats or budgies and even to lion-tamers and their wives and families. Dog-lovers and dog-fanciers are free to read it if they so wish, but only as long as they remember that it is not addressed exclusively to them. Having made this clear we are now free to proceed.

My dog, if I had one, would be a wire-haired terrier of set ways and agreeable disposition. The reason I don't keep a dog at this present time is that my last two, both innocent pups, were stolen from me by dog thieves. The last fully grown dog I owned was what we who are not experts loosely call a sheep dog. He was afraid of rats and mice but, great as was his fear of these, he was even more afraid of other dogs.

'Don't get him going,' said the man who sold him to me, 'because there's no tiger his master.'

He sat outside our door for a good many contented, untroubled years with a reputation for ferocity that grew with his age. He would look dreamily up and down the street, and when cross dogs approached with suspicious sniffs and provocative snarls he would immediately close his eyes and pretend to be asleep. Aggressive dogs who invaded his territory got the impression that he just couldn't be bothered, that he didn't have to prove himself, that he was a dog to be avoided.

Luckily for him he had a fighter's face, scarred and bruised from investigating empty canisters and broken jam pots. This alone was often sufficient to intimidate those dogs who are forever on the lookout for a good fight.

He died young, as dogs go, but I was led to believe that this was due to lack of exercise because, while other dogs barked in anticipatory delight whenever their master appeared equipped for a stroll in the countryside, my dog was nowhere to be found.

Still, I like dogs because all dogs, like human beings, are bluffers, and no two are alike. I always salute dogs with whom I am acquainted, that is to say the dogs of neighbours and the dogs of friends. None of these has ever saluted me back. Some I have saluted sidled away self-consciously while others followed me for long distances as if the salute were a command to accompany me.

I have a brother who was followed by dogs all his life and during his first visit to the city he was followed aboard a bus by two common curs who could not possibly have known him because he had never been in the city before. When he found a permanent position in the capital he would go for long walks on fine evenings. Always he would be followed home to the door of his lodgings by one or more dogs. There was something in his make-up which held a special appeal for dogs. Cross dogs never barked at him and would follow him instead, respectfully, to the farthest boundaries of their bailiwicks, assuring his well-being and privacy as it were until he passed into some other canine's domain.

When he started to do a bit of a line with a good-looking girl who worked in the same building the dogs became an embarrassment. Whenever he took her for a walk he was followed by a dog or two. There was a particular mongrel of heterogeneous breeding, predominantly Alsatian and greyhound, who used to lie in wait for him in doorways near his place of employment. In the end he was forced to leave the building by a rear exit.

At the back entrance there would always be others to take the place of the one at the front.

Once while strolling in Stephen's Green, where he frequently went to admire the ducks and find a measure of peace from the turmoil of the metropolis, some instinct told him to look to his rear. At the time he was in the company of a new girl having long before broken off negotiations with the first one. Close on his heels there was a small, sad-looking terrier who persisted in dogging him no matter what direction he might take. He became justifiably annoyed and started to fling stones at his pursuer but the dog refused to go away. Again and again the same sort of situation arose. There he would be walking in some pleasant place with a girl when a dog would appear at his heels and remain there till he reached the safety of his lodgings.

Then one evening a friend told him how the problem might be overcome.

'Get a dog of your own,' he suggested. He then explained that those dogs who were in the habit of following him did so in the hope that he might adopt one of them. 'When they see you with a dog of your own,' his friend assured him, 'they will leave you at peace.'

So he got himself a dog, a genuine 'five-eights'. A five-eights is a dog with five parts of a true breed and three parts of all sorts. Personally speaking, I know dogs who have as many as ten different breeds apparent in their dispositions and physical characteristics.

I am seriously thinking of getting a dog again. I am in the market for a quiet, efficient fellow who would like to take up employment in a home where prospects are good and where there is every hope of advancement. Canvassing will disqualify.

FARMERS' BOYS

This essay constitutes a farewell to farmers' boys. It does not propose to look at the whole history of the farmer's boy as distinct from the *spailpín*, or seasonal worker. It will examine some aspects of his existence before he was designated an agricultural worker by a more benign form of government than that which existed during the days of the hiring fairs and Spotting Days.

Your true farmer's boy was a part-time poet as well as being a part-time cobbler, tailor and barber. Depending on your point of view he was as odious to his detractors as Free State soldiers, Republicans, blueshirts and Emergency men were to theirs. He was very often blamed for disorders in which he hadn't hand, act or part but this could be because men of property were fond of blaming all kinds of civil strife on men who had no property. It is also a known fact that when men of no property aspire to property they quickly shed their socialistic tendencies. The farmer's boy is the only livelihood with which I am acquainted which offered no promotion or material advancement to those who opted for it or were forced into it as a career.

The hours were long and the pay was small. Worse still, supply exceeded demand, and innocent labourers who dared mention the word 'union' in those benighted days were regarded as out-and-out anarchists with nothing else in their heads but the ultimate destruction of church and state. District justices, upon hearing that the defendant before them was a farmer's boy, would lift their heads and peer hard and long at the unfortunate creature whose only crime might be that he temporarily purloined a bicycle from some street corner in the town lest he be late for the milking of the cows in the morning. I once heard a conservative politician on the eve of a general election make the following remark:

'This country,' said he, 'is full of farmers' boys and low-down latchikoes that has to be kept in their proper place. Jail isn't good enough for them,' he went on, 'but if we gets in we'll work them to the marrow of the bone.' No wonder the emigrant ships were full.

I remember a court case at which I was a spectator. In my youth I was fond of spending long periods in court. It was a good way to pass the time and there was always the promise of drama. One afternoon the case in question was called. A farmer's boy was suing his employer for extra wages for the simple reason that the food promised by the farmer in the original agreement between the two had not been forthcoming. When the farmer's boy's name was called out the judge quipped, 'Bring him up so that we can have a look at him.'

The farmer's boy, whose name was Tom, entered the dock, where he was examined closely by the justice who peered out over his spectacles in a most inquisitorial manner.

'You look a hardy fellow,' said the judge.

'Oh he's a prime buck, your honour,' said the solicitor who was defending the farmer. The solicitor for the farmer's boy objected strenuously and cited grievances for his client. The chief of these was that the farmer had promised three square meals a day, the midday meal, being the chief one, to consist of bacon and cabbage or, as was more commonly known, mate and cabbage. The farmer swore on oath that his wife had always given the boy mate and cabbage enough.

'Yes,' interjected the boy, 'mate and cabbage enough but never cabbage and mate enough.'

It was a good point but in the justice's view enough was enough, be it cabbage and mate or mate and cabbage.

The case was lost. I'll concede that there were instances when your farmer's boy was not above setting fire to a haystack rather than take his grievances into court. These were honest hard-working men, underpaid and underfed. How true the old Latin quotation: *Probitas laudatur et alget*, which means in English: 'Honesty is praised and starves.'

References were never asked of a farmer's boy. If he was big and strong, prepared to work long hours, seven days in the week, to draw back from the table early and not be looking for tasty diet, this was the best possible reference. As I said earlier, they were also part-time poets, and they often rhymed out of pure hunger. Take the case of the farmer who presented the four men he had working for him with fat, lardy bacon for dinner. One composed the following on the spot:

Oh Lord on high who rules the sky
Look down upon us four
And give us mate that we can ate
And take away the boar.

THE LARGE WHITE DUCK

Old soldiers like the leg of a duck

(Song)

Since the arrival of the white turkey much fuss has been created concerning the qualities of this pampered bird. Much undeserved publicity has resulted from its outlandish activities, while others of no less consequence have suffered from this unfair projectivity. In the barnyard he swaggers and struts like an emperor, forgetting that he is mere fowl the same as his contemporaries. The large white table duck waddles but this does not detract from his stature for when necks are stretched and feathers plucked it is performance at dinnertime that counts.

I have a profound respect for painters, for those who flick magic from palette to canvas and who capture forever an aspect or feature of a face. Yet when the covers of bastable ovens are lifted and the doors of cookers thrown open upon the golden rotundity of the large white table duck, one can hardly expect them to harness the thousand elements of pungency or vivify with mere paints and brushes the superb disinterestedness of tongue-tickling plumpness which glistens and crackles magnificent and alone.

There is something I always forget to do when glasses are full and friends are thrown together in conviviality in public houses, and that is to uplift my beaker and propose a toast to rosy-faced old men who wore gaiters, at whose insistence flocks of specially fed ducks were nurtured to table-ripeness and who had such a preference for ducks that they frequently called the more endearing specimens by their Christian names.

We often hear the expression 'as hoarse as a duck' and, lest this be interpreted as a reflection, it should be remembered that neither Micawber nor Sam Weller were endowed with gifted voices and that what might seem like hoarseness to us could well be the musical mating call of a handsome drake, beloved of many and as fiercely proud of his rendition as the grossest of barrel-chested operatic singers.

The large white table duck is no ordinary duck. Socially he is several flights above the common duck but you would never know it from his behaviour in the farmyard as compared with the hauteur of individuals like Rhode Island Red cocks and obstreperous ganders. His behaviour, to say the least, is gentlemanly. His temper, while perverse and uncertain at intrusion, is nevertheless even and fairly well-balanced most of the time. If there would seem to be bouts of occasional hysteria in the presence of marauding dogs he is merely bluffing his way out with as much bustle and commotion as possible. He is a friendly fellow and responds well to favour, and I have known several instances where particular ducks have been adopted by small boys who succeeded in turning them into likeable pets, and there are cited cases where they have been known to be as possessive and protective of their charges as dogs or even nannies.

The large white duck does not know the meaning of the word cowardice. He will charge a foe ten times his size when he has to. He will not vacate a chosen seat upon the roadway no matter how suicidal his actions may seem. He will not be rushed, and if his quacks are annoying at times who knows what strange duckland lyricism is emanating from his brangling bill?

The large white duck, unlike his mongrel brethren, carries enough weight to do battle with well-peopled tables. The common duck has his work cut out for him to cope with a pair of appetites but the large white is deceptively wealthy in the matter of meat and has material enough to satisfy several. His crisp hide, soothed by a spoon of apple sauce, is chewing matter as provocative as tobacco, and his breast meat is beyond compare. Duck liver needs no introduction to those with sensitive tastes, and the soup of duck's giblets is as nourishing as new milk. Boiled duck is somewhat uncommon but it is true to say that the white duck boils better than most fowl.

The old soldier is a man of few preferences and the world has taught him a considerable amount for in his profession experience is dearly come by. But it will be noted, as we are told in the song, that he liked the leg of a duck and many of those old songs which have survived more than a few wars are ingrained with truth. He may have liked Bologna pudding or sardines but the song does not say so. We only know that he liked the leg of a duck. It was Shakespeare who said that *'foul deeds will rise, 'though all the earth o'erwhelm them to men's eyes.'* If this is so, they are slow enough in rising, and the proof lies in the answers to these questions. How many of you have eaten a duck this year, a duck, mark you, not to mention the white duck? What is the frequency of white ducks on menu cards? How many by persistent implication have fostered duck dinners? The truth is that none of you have, and ducks are now almost always reserved for the late dinners of tourists.

I can't speak for my readers but for myself I can most certainly say that on at least three occasions between now and Christmas my Sunday table will be enriched by the presence of the large white duck.

A HORSECHESTRA

'I'd swear if I was asked,' said Henry, 'I 'eard a horsechestra.' Henry was my English landlord and he made the remark as we walked through the park in Northampton. Sure enough, after we had listened a while, there came the strains of a brass band, and in no time at all it was upon us with drum, cymbal and French horn.

'Hoi was right,' said Henry. 'Hit was a horsechestra.' There chanced to be a third party with us at the time, and he nudged me rather forcibly, winking conspiratorially as he did at Henry's mention of the horsechestra.

Later in the pub he told me in an aside that he thought Henry first meant there were some horses in the vicinity.

'Not so,' I informed the fellow as curtly as I could without offending him, 'for if Henry had meant that there were horses neighing or whatever in the vicinity he would have said "I 'ear 'orses neighin'."'

Another day we were leaving the church after a particularly gruelling sermon from an elderly priest who covered the same ground several times over the space of thirty-five minutes. We tended to be critical as we moved away from the church in the general direction of the neighbourhood's hostelries.

'Naw, naw!' said Henry emphatically, ''im be all right, 'im be upliftin' in 'is way.'

''Ymn!' said the same man who had spoken in the pub after the horsechestra's appearance, 'what hymn! I didn't hear any hymn.'

'Neither did I,' I returned bitingly.

'Wot's he on about now?' Henry asked.

'He says he didn't hear any hymn,' I informed Henry.

"E didn't 'ear no 'ymn,' said Henry dismissively, "cos there werrint no 'ymn.'

Henry was not of our persuasion, but he came along on Sundays out of respect. Since we shared the same pub in the church's vicinity he decided that it couldn't do any harm if we shared the same church. Feeling that he might have been a trifle abrupt with our friend he placed a hand on his shoulder and asked him gently, 'Wot 'ymns you like then, lad?'

Mystified, the young man addressed himself to me. He spoke in a whisper.

'Will you tell him,' said he, 'that I am not a hymn-lover, that if I was asked to sing a hymn to save my life I couldn't do so.'

"Im that don't 'ave no 'ymn,' said Henry, at his most apocalyptic now, 'be askin' for it.'

'Asking for what?' my friend asked, as mystified as ever.

'Look at it like this mate.' Henry laid a paternal hand on his shoulder for the second time. 'Suppose the life rafts was all agone. Wot was we gonna do if we didn't 'ave no 'ymn? Answer me that mate!'

No answer was forthcoming. It would be some time before our friend accepted the fact that Henry had his way of saying things and that all one had to do was come to terms with this.

'If I 'ad a rum for every 'ymn I sung at sea,' Henry shook his head, 'I reckon as 'ow I'd fill a fair-sized pond.'

Then there was the time of the ham. Henry's wife, Beryl, had gone for her annual weekend to her only remaining relative in Hull. We were left to fend for ourselves. We consumed only half the food we normally would but we balanced the books as it were by consuming twice the amount of beer or in 'Enry's case three times the amount.

We decided to forego lunches over the weekend. We had sizable reserves of fat built up over the spring and early summer, and anyway, as Henry was fond of pointing out, it was "an 'orrible waste of drinkin' time.'

'Oose 'avin' 'am?' Henry asked as he proceeded to cover our plates with cold meat at Sunday supper.

'That isn't ham but I'll have some,' said my friend. Now we all knew it wasn't ham. Meat was rationed at the time but it was as near to ham as one could get in the post-war period.

'It's more 'am than not,' Henry countered and slapped several slices on to each of our plates.

'Hoime hunhappy.' Henry paused with a forkful of the artificial ham an inch from his mouth.

What he was really trying to intimate was that he missed Beryl.

"Ere!' He turned on my friend, "ave my 'am,' and with that he placed two untouched slices on my friend's plate.

'You're sure?' asked my friend.

'Hoi ham. Hoi ham,' Henry assured him.

We finished the meal in silence as Henry's eyes moistened with memories of Beryl.

'She'll be home tomorrow,' we consoled him.

He cheered up at once.

"Ome tomorrow!' he clapped his hands. "Am today!' and so saying he recovered his ham from my friend's plate and gobbled it down like a hound for he had no breakfast and he had no lunch. He had only beer.

"Im be awright!' He pointed at my friend.

'Oh go on then,' said he, 'sing a hymn if you must.'

Henry needed no second bidding. It could be said that he was ripe for song. He had a broken baritone with a nice froth on it:

Nearer, my God to thee
Nearer to thee!
E'en though it be a cross
That raises me.

We succeeded in stopping him eventually when we managed to get it through to him that the pubs would be in danger of closing.

'Bloody 'ell!' he said. 'Bloody 'ell an' all!' A horrified look appeared on his good-natured face. He lifted his cap from its peg. We followed him out on to the bright street, lit by a full moon. He sang:

Rock of ages, cleft for me,
Let me hide myself in Thee.

Then and only then did he notice the moon.

"Im be awright,' he said, "im be awright.'

HATCHING

I remember once there was a somewhat contrary hatching hen appointed to sit on a clutch of eggs which weren't her own. She was a Sussex Blue and the eggs were laid by a Rhode Island Red. Maybe this was why she was so reluctant to stay sitting on the eggs. Did hens have a way of knowing one egg from another? I suspect they did.

Certain hens will hatch anything from pheasant to duck eggs, but there are no two birds alike as the cock said to the drake. Let us return, however, to our own bird and her reluctance to hatch the eggs of a stranger. There she would settle, trancelike, as only hens can when suddenly for no apparent reason, she would make for the door. She would be recaptured instantly and reminded firmly of her obligations but no sooner would she be reseated than she would desert once more. She exasperated the entire household whose every member took a turn keeping an eye on her.

'There's only one cure for the hoor,' announced an old woman who chanced to call one evening for the loan of a cup of sugar.

'What's that?' we all asked.

'The bottle,' said she. We waited for elaboration but none came. We asked again.

'What bottle,' said she, 'but the hot stuff.'

Of course we all knew what the hot stuff was. Weren't the man of the house and his cronies greatly addicted to it without any great harm!

'It will rest the creature,' said the old woman, 'and it will keep her off her feet.'

Up in the 'Room' was a bottle of the very hot stuff in question, as hot, according to himself, as ever was brewed.

'Mix it,' said the old woman, 'with a saucer of Indian meal
and you'll end up with a nice paste that she'll find palatable.'

The reluctant hatcher was presented with a saucer of hooch-
paste but showed no interest at first. It didn't look very appetising so the woman of the house spoon-fed her till she began to
cluck appreciatively and cock her head high for more. I never
saw any creature of the female gender take so quickly to booze.
In less than three minutes the saucer was empty and she was
sleeping as soundly as a drunken apostate during a long sermon.

'She'll die surely,' said the woman of the house.

'She won't nor die,' said himself who knew from long experience that a person could be dead drunk without being dead.
How right he was! She slept for several hours without moving,
contributing throughout every moment of her repose to the
hatching process beneath her craw. When she awakened she tried
to rise but failed. She fell asleep again. The next awakening was
different. She staggered around the kitchen until she arrived at
the door, where she was assailed by the arch-enemy of all forms
of drunkenness, fresh air. It revived her instantly but a second
saucer of hoochmeal was prepared and presented to her before
she could sober up. Afterwards she fell asleep for a whole day.

After a fortnight the eggs were hatched and there emerged
twelve of the handsomest chicks you ever saw.

The hatcher died soon afterwards of liver disease but she had
nobly served her purpose, and if some may crib about forcing
her into alcoholism I say to these to come and have a gander
at the lovely chicks she hatched. They grew up into outstanding
specimens of their breed, seven hens and five cocks. One hen
who wandered too far from the fowl-run was carried off by a
fox but the other eleven survived, and I know for a gospel fact

that not a solitary one of that fine clutch ever put a taste of booze to their beaks to the day they departed for that heavenly hen house in the sky. So we see some more of the good uses to which whiskey may be put – as if there weren't enough already.

Shake Hands with the Devil

There was a man in Ballybunion once who used to catch rabbits by means of snares. He would attach a loop of light copper wire to a small stake and as soon as the rabbit was ensnared there was no escape. The more he struggled the tighter became the snare. The rabbit-snarer was an agreeable fellow and for some strange reason he was never accused of cruelty to animals. In fact I never heard or read of a rabbit-snarer who was so maybe it's only the rabbit who thinks it's cruel. Rabbits, like hares, can be unreasonable like that.

Anyway to proceed with our tale, the rabbit-snarer was a chap much addicted to strong drink, particularly Jamaican rum and bottled beer, a disintegrating diet for all save the strongest stomachs. As soon as he disposed of his rabbits he would entrench himself in his favourite pub and spend his earnings on the aforementioned intake.

When the rabbit money would be spent he would make himself so agreeable to the visiting strangers for which Ballybunion is notorious that they considered it a favour if they were allowed to buy him a drink. Other of his victims would have been local drunkards who found it impossible to hold audiences when they became maudlin. The rabbit-snarer would listen attentively to all sorts of raimeish and even encourage the drunkards to continue, remarking from time to time how sagacious were their comments. Out of appreciation for his perspicacity they would buy him drinks and he would listen enthralled while they made the most pedestrian of outpourings.

He would hang on until the flow of drink was staunched by

self-inflicted impoverishment, after which he would cast about him for other sources. The result of this prodigious consumption often left him with shaking hands and trembling eyelids when he woke up in the morning. His judgment was also impaired which left him in no condition for the confrontation of his life, which took place on the early morning of 16 August in a graveyard contiguous to Ballybunion. In those days Ballybunion was noted for its mushrooms as well as its rabbits. The rabbit-snarer, in fact, became a mushroom-gatherer during the mushroom season. He would rise with dawn and head for the golf links where the mushrooms abounded. The earnings from the mushrooms went the same road as the earnings from the rabbits.

One sunny morning on the date cited our friend happened to be passing through the graveyard with two buckets of mushrooms when all of a sudden he was seized by the leg. His heart stopped but fortunately for him it started again. His immediate thought was that someone had risen from the dead and was determined to bring him under. He tried to scream but no sound came. The more he tried to escape the tighter became the grip by the unseen underground hand. Finally he found his voice and there followed a series of roars which would do justice to a three-year-old bull. Alas and alack it was early in the morning. There was nobody abroad. Terrified to look around at the ghastly visage of the creature who held him fast, he fainted. He recovered and again he roared for all he was worth.

All in all he spent some two and a half hours in the grip of the underground demon. At last his weakening cries were heard by a winkle-picker on her way to the shore. She entered the graveyard with considerable trepidation and called from a distance to find out what the matter was.

''Tis the devil,' he called back. 'He has me by the leg.'

'Devil the devil do I see,' said the winkle-picker as she

approached. She examined the leg which was held fast and discovered that he thrust his leg in one of his own forgotten rabbit loops. It was a well-made loop. After a while she managed to release him but to her horror discovered that his hair had turned white.

The moral of this story is that you should never set traps unless you are prepared to fall into one some time. As they say in French: *Cela va sans dire.*

CANAVAN'S DOG

It must be five or six years now since I last made mention of Canavan's talking dog, Banana the Sixth. In response to numerous letters from readers over this period I am happy to assure them that all is well with this remarkable canine. Banana is now in his tenth year and from time to time is give to those priceless utterances which have made him justly famous. The other night as he and Canavan sat by the fire the dog's attention was caught by a report which appeared on the back page of a paper which Canavan happened to be reading. He placed one of his paws on the column and indicated to Canavan that he would appreciate it if the contents of the report were read out to him. Canavan obliged. The dog, as everybody knows, is illiterate, although he is a fluent speaker in both Irish and English. At the head of the column was a photograph of a man and a dog and this was what claimed Banana's interest.

It transpired that the report was an obituary notice on the famous American conman Joseph Yellow-Kid Weill. The dog was one of Weill's internationally known talking dogs although people who purchased the dogs claimed that immediately afterwards the mutts were permanently stricken with laryngitis. This may have been true to some extent since Weill was a competent ventriloquist.

Canavan's dog nodded his head and wagged his tail when his master concluded, a sure sign that he was about to make a major pronouncement, which he promptly did.

'That dog,' said he, indicating the one with Weill, 'is a cousin of mine.'

'How can that be?' Canavan asked, 'when none of your seed or breed was ever in America?'

'My dear man,' said the dog, 'my late ancestor, Banana the First, had a sister called Spot who was press-ganged aboard a rat-infested coffin-ship for the sole purpose of disposing of the rats in question. She never returned to her native Lyreacrompane because nobody would give her a passage home to the Land of Slugs and Dossers. Instead of dying of a broken heart which any ordinary bitch would have done, she instead mated herself to a one-eyed Yukonian watchdog who was three-eighths wolf, one-eighth Alsatian, one-eighth elk-hound and three-eighths Kerry blue. Of issue there was but one male who went on to father the only known American family of talking dogs. This dog, therefore, which you see before you is a blood cousin of mine. Need I say more?'

'Fair enough,' said Canavan, knowing that it was useless arguing with the dog when he struck a vein like this. The pair sat silently in front of the fire watching the flames as they flickered in the ancient hearth. Outside a curlew called and in the distance a dog barked. Deep in the bog a lost ass brayed long and low and a mating bittern bleated romantically.

'You referred there,' said Canavan, 'to the land of Slugs and Dossers when you must have meant the land of Saints and Scholars.'

'Slugs and Dossers is what I said,' Banana the Sixth announced firmly, 'and Slugs and Dossers is what I meant. Is it a country where men who won't work and who were used only to asses and carts ten years ago have now fine motor cars? Is it a country where men earning twenty to thirty thousand pounds a year are looking for more when old-age pensioners are expected to live on a fraction of that? Looking for more, imagine, and they having plenty already. Is it a country where they won't show up for work and where doctors' certs are as common as bogwater?'

'Now, now,' said Canavan, 'you'll give us a pain so you will.' 'Don't mind your now, now,' said Banana the Sixth, 'don't you see them yourself resting in their motor cars and they reading papers when they should be working? Don't you see them at everything except the job they're getting paid to do? There is no work being done in this country at the present time. Don't I see them going down that very road outside to the bog and they wearing low shoes and collars and ties? What country could stick that kind of carry-on? It couldn't last. No country could carry so many dodgers and survive for long. A nation of Slugs and Dossers is what I said and a nation of Slugs and Dossers is what I meant.'

So saying, the dog rose and went out into the haggard, where he addressed himself to the moon which was in the last quarter. He howled high and clear until a band of ragged clouds came from the direction of Ballybunion and hid Diana in their midst. The dog went indoors and sat in his favourite place near the hearth. Canavan put out the lights and went to bed.

KEYS TO THE KINGDOM

THE COLOUR OF KERRY

I could introduce the Kingdom of Kerry with a description of its incomparable physical attributes from Cahirciveen to Bally-bunion but a few well-taken photographs would eclipse my most passionate prosopography.

I might also write about Kerry football and outline for you a particularly well-taken point from boot to crossbar but I would much prefer to write about the living lingo of the greater, hard-necked, Atlantical warbler known as the Kerryman, who quests individually and in flocks for all forms of diversion and is to be found, high and low, winter and summer, wherever there is the remotest prospect of drink, sex, confusion or commotion!

Plain, everyday language is of no use to your genuine Ker-ryman. I remember to have been involved only last year in the purchase of a trailer of turf for my winter fires. A countryman friend, in order to bring down the price, spoke disparagingly of the trailer's size. Said he, dismissively, 'A young blackbird would bring more in its beak'.

On another occasion the same gentleman was breakfasting with some friends on the morning of an All-Ireland final. The fare consisted of the usual rashers, egg and sausage but, alas, the rashers were of the fatty variety and were possessed of no meat whatsoever. He put the rashers on his side plate and proceeded with the demolition of sausages and egg.

'Why,' asked the companion at the opposite end of the table, 'are you not eating your rashers?'

'Because,' said our friend, 'they are too fat.'

'Is there any taste of lean meat at all in them?' asked the other.

'No,' said our friend, 'not as much as you'd draw with a single stroke of a red biro!'

However, for all his wanton but worthwhile diffuseness our friend would regard himself as a rather inferior sort of Kerryman. 'A bit of a country boy,' as he says himself. He reminds me of the Kerryman who thought he had an inferiority complex: 'I am only the same as everybody else,' said he.

There is no such entity as a conventional Kerryman. If you try to analyse him he changes his pace in order to generate confusion. He will not be pinned down and you have as much chance of getting a straight answer out of him as you would a goose egg out of an Arctic tern.

He loves words, however, and that's the only way you'll get him going. Snare him with well-chosen words and craftily calefacted phrases and he will respond with sempiternal sentences, sonorous and even supernatural.

On the other hand, he also has the capacity for long, perplexing silences. It is when he seems to be speechless, however, that he is at his most dangerous. He is weighing up the opposition, waiting for an opening so that he can demoralise you.

He never talks in ordinary terms, and why should he when he can aspire otherwise?

Once, on our way back from a football game in Dublin, a party of us stopped at a pub in West Limerick but we were refused admission on the grounds that there was more morning than night in the hour that was in it.

'Be not forgetful,' said the oldest of our party, remembering Saint Paul, 'to entertain strangers, for thereby some have entertained angels unawares!'

'Let them in don't we be damned,' said the woman of the house, who happened to be a Kerrywoman too.

An old man once told me that Kerrymen were uniquely

articulate because the elements were their mentors.

'They can patter like rain,' said he, 'roar like thunder, foam like the sea, sting like the frost, sigh like the wind, and on top of all that you'll never catch them boasting.'

No Chairs

I fondly recall an old lady who lived a few doors down the street from the house where I was born. At the front of the house was a small shop which her husband tended all day long. Behind the shop was a small kitchen. There was no other room downstairs. She had a great method of dealing with unwanted visitors.

She would remove all the chairs in the kitchen to the backyard at the sight of known interlopers. All were welcome to call but she had been held hostage all too often in the past by those who overstayed their leave.

I was often party to her subterfuges and once when a large party of rustic relations appeared in the shop we lifted the kitchen table which had just been laid for supper out into the backyard. This was followed by the chairs and by a small stool. These would have been the total seating arrangements of the kitchen.

When unwelcome squatters arrived, the first thing they did was to try and find a place where they could sit down. Upon finding none they were generally too polite to comment on the absence of chairs. When somebody did ask a direct question about them she had stock replies at the ready.

'Oh,' she would say, 'I'm after washing them and they won't be dry for a while.'

Other times she would say that they were being painted and if certain more resolute arrivals intimated they were going to hang around anyway she would point out that the chairs had been removed to facilitate washing of the kitchen floor. There is absolutely no comfort to be found in a kitchen where the floor is being scrubbed.

One would think that these actions altogether would deter the unwelcome visitor. Far from it. They would endeavour to surprise her by suddenly seeking entry but, as always, the kitchen door was bolted and could only be opened from the inside. She had, of course, a few chosen friends. I was one of these and could sit at will, although, to tell the truth, young chaps of my age and gender rarely spent more than a few minutes in the same place.

The idea often occurred to me that long tedious meetings might easily be subverted by having all chairs removed beforehand. All the participants would be forced to stand, regardless of their sex or size, and in this way the meeting would come to an end at a reasonable hour. In my early days or nights at meetings there were no distractions on offer. There was no television and very few had motor cars. There was no free travel and there were no community centres so what could be more inviting, I ask you, than a nice warm room with plenty of chairs where one could pass the night in non-contributory comatoseness. The longer the meeting the better, for it cost the members nothing and there was no cheaper way of passing a long, winter's night.

In the rural Ireland of the time the annual general meeting was a diversion second only to the annual visit of the missionaries but while the missionary confinement lasted only an hour the proceedings at the general meeting could, and did, go on all night.

I would respectfully suggest to people who are obliged to tend meetings to ensure early termination by the simple expedient of removing all the chairs beforehand. It's the only known method of circumventing large, ponderous bores and there's no better antidote for curbing compulsive talkers. Inevitably, somebody is bound to ask why there are no chairs but this can be neatly included under Any Other Business, or, if the chairman is tough enough he can rule the question is out of order.

Bohareens

Oh, I do like to wander down the old bohareen
When the hawthorn blossoms are in bloom . . .

(Song)

One of the great tragedies of this modern age is that people do not go walking down bohareens any more.

They don't walk up bohareens either, because one must go down to come up.

The dictionary has words for those who explore caves and collect coins but there is no word for the bohareen-walker. All around us are little roads and grass-covered, rutted tracks that lead to nowhere. There should be a society for the preservation of bohareens or, if this is not possible, each of us who has an interest in what is simple and good in life should adopt a bohareen. Nothing could be less expensive for all that has to be done is to repulse takeover bids from companies like Briars and Nettles and Thistles and Docks and to encourage small businesses like the Wild Rose and the Buttercup.

Walking down bohareens is a must for those who find members of the opposite sex endearing and a man who hasn't walked down a bohareen with his best girl has missed much. Those couples who haven't held hands and skipped a bit between high whitethorn hedges had better do so at once, not for my sake but for their own. Who knows what woes will taint the winds of coming summers and, after all, we're only young once. Now is the time and who knows better than those of us who dallied with sweethearts of yesterday that we are travelling on

a one-way ticket in this topsy-turvy world, and truly the man
who has paid his dues to bohareens can say, when his hair, if
any, is grey: For me the past has no regrets for I am one who
has honoured the little roads that lead to nowhere.

I myself have not given up bohareen-walking and I know a
few good ones where children can be nurtured to appreciation,
where the only traffic is the annual haycart and the only life
the occasional donkey without portfolio. The bohareen is the
last sanctuary of overworked ponies absent without leave, rogue
nanny goats, hare-shy greyhounds, indisposed hedgehogs and
other unseen creatures who prefer the cloistered quiet of grassy
ways to the tumult of terror-laden thoroughfares.

The bohareen is a refuge, a haven for harried souls who
like to amble along safe from the noisome jarring of car horns
and the sudden death that their absence precipitates. This is
the age of racing because people are always in a hurry these
days and I doubt if many know where they are really going.
They're burning it up and those of you who speed like luna-
tics through the fear-filled countryside would be well advised
to slow down when you're passing the hallowed entrance to
a bohareen. You would be wise to stop and stroll down. The
heady scents and peaceful surroundings might steady you down
and, who knows, the half-hour you should spend there might
not be the cause of saving your life but it could be the cause
of saving somebody else's.

I don't know what put bonnets into my head but the setting
for a flowery bonnet is a bohareen, a background of browsing
cows and woodbine wild.

Nobody thinks more of the bohareen than he who has no
access to it. Many a man in New York, Durban or London would
give his right hand to saunter down the distant bohareens of
his boyhood, and the woman who wrote the 'Old Bog Road'

was one whose heart was in the right place or, if you like, in her native bohareen.

The bohareen is the byway of the uncommercial traveller. It is absolutely rustic and the man who pollutes its purity with the exhaust-fumes of an obstreperous motorbike is guilty of sacrilege, to say the least. Even bicycles should be barred and nothing but what is truly pedestrian admitted to its protective windings. A small chuckling stream may accompany it but this is not really necessary either so long as there is no scarcity of sheltering whitethorns and an adequate disorder of all that is wild in flowers. Nowhere does the bee buzz so soothingly and even the bandit wasp is respectful in such sacred precincts.

Blackberries and elderberries thrive and it is a poor bohareen that doesn't lead to shining sloe groves and mushroom-dotted pastures. Instead of a gin and tonic I would be inclined to saunter down a bohareen to assuage the pangs of hangovers and sick heads. I have never visited a psychiatrist. Why should I when I can go to a bohareen for nothing and figure myself out at my ease?

You don't need an umbrella or a plastic coat if your choice of walk favours the bohareen. You can stretch yourself back against a mattress-like hedge and relax under a canopy of mixed leaves. The fragrance of crushed herbs will delight you while the rain hammers the open roads and drenches the green fields.

It is rather strange that those who mass-produce attractive picture postcards should show a somewhat prejudiced prefe-rence for ungainly cliffs and unsporting seas. I have never seen a picture postcard depicting a genuine Irish bohareen but still, despite all forms of neglect and the absence of any sort of National Bohareen Protective Society, the tiny uncharted lanes of tousled greenery have lost none of their charm and still remain unspoiled and unobtrusive.

Some time, if you have little else to do when you visit a great city, you may see a prosperous elderly man leaning across the parapet of a bridge. Do not disturb him if you are looking for the nearest way to the theatre. He is remembering evenings of long, long ago and wishing that he was back again walking the bohareens of his green years.

Had I my chance to journey back, or own a King's abode
'Tis soon I'd see the hawthorn tree down the Old Bog Road.

Matchmaker

Recently a young man came to me in search of a job, any kind of job, his own words. Alas there were no jobs available, as I found out when I tried to help him. To be more accurate I should say that there were no orthodox jobs available. I suggest, therefore, to today's crop of unemployed that they create their own openings. For instance there is no matchmaker operating in Kerry at the time of writing.

There certainly is a need for one. I can testify to this. There's no week I don't receive a visitor questing a long-term partner and there's hardly a day I don't receive a letter asking me to intervene in man's constant struggle with loneliness. Unfortunately, I have neither the time nor the talent to be of genuine assistance but I would be prepared to forward correspondence on the subject to a genuine matchmaker.

Dan Paddy Andy O'Sullivan was the last matchmaker to operate in Kerry. From his modest home in Renagown, Lyreacrompane, he conducted a flourishing trade and was responsible for directing four hundred couples to the altar of God. He had only one failure out of the four hundred and that was when the female member of one particular contract decided she was prepared to fulfil every role required to her save that of bed-mate. No marriage can survive under such conditions so the couple separated. It wasn't really Dan's fault but he accepted responsibility nevertheless.

So where does all this preamble leave us? It leaves us with a vacancy for a matchmaker. To any man willing to fill the role I can guarantee success. The secret is to charge enough. The demand is there, as anyone in the Kingdom of Kerry will tell you, as indeed anyone will tell you from Malin Head to Cape Clear, from Canberra to Newfoundland.

Dan Paddy Andy made many a wise and many a prophetic statement during his sojourn in this vale of tears. The most memorable and prophetic that I recall is the following, and it has particular reference to what I said earlier about young men making their own openings.

'You may make hay,' said Dan, 'while the sun shines and you may stook your turf when the wind blows but as sure as there's mate on the shin of a wren there's more to be made working the head at the shady side of a ditch on a wet day.'

Ah what foresight is here, what astuteness! In the tersest of terms Dan tells us that the obvious way is not always the right way. While ordinary men laboured at ordinary chores Dan examined unexplored territory.

As he once said to a television producer during the shooting of a film about matchmaking when asked if he felt nervous about appearing on television: 'No,' said Dan, 'for I'm a man who would knock on every door to earn a bob.'

And Dan did knock on every door. He even built a dance hall in the wilds. No doubt he plotted this one out at the shady side of his beloved ditch while the rain drove relentlessly through the glens and ravines of the Stack Mountains. Remember that the only alternative for Dan was emigration. I can see him as though it were yesterday, fingering the rigid stubble in his resolute jaw as he devised ways and means to support his family. I dare say it was out of sheer desperation that the idea of becoming a matchmaker came to him. A man without a shilling in his pocket or the filling of his pipe will resort to quare measures, and while Dan's certainly were not quare they were unorthodox.

Dan's great achievement was staying at home in his own countryside with the wife and family he cherished. All around him men and women were packing up and leaving, bolting and nailing their doors and windows and departing for England or America, most of them never to return. Dan stuck it out. His methods of earning the requisite bobs for survival met with criticism from laity and clergy alike but there must have been a lot of truth in the old saying that God loves a trier. Dan survived. You might say, in fact, that he succeeded.

This is why it is so important for young men to repair to the shady side of the ditch or the privacy of their own rooms, or indeed to the toilet. The late Robert Leslie Boland in his fine poem 'Ode to a Lavatory' describes that little, snug spot as 'the throne room of soliloquy', which indeed it is.

In these unlikely, out-of-the-way places, a man may contemplate upon his future with the coolness and detachment which that unknown quantity so richly deserves. It was in such a place that the great matchmaker Dan Paddy Andy O'Sullivan, after much self-examination, made up his mind to be a matchmaker. It was a historic decision. He left his mark upon the countryside. Indeed I wrote a book about him in Irish entitled *Dan Pheaidí Aindí* which turned out to be a best seller. The matchmaking supplemented the income from his small farm and from his tiny dance hall.

I would ask those who are jobless to consider the life and times of Dan Paddy Andy. Never was there likelier fodder for the emigrant ship. Remember too that he was nearly blind. If you cannot find an orthodox job look around you the way Dan Paddy Andy did. Create you own opening. I know for a fact that there is no full-time matchmaker operating in this country just now so why not be a matchmaker and guarantee yourself fame and fortune.

GREAT GOALKEEPERS OF OUR TIME

Monuments are never erected to the type of man I have in mind. His words are never quoted and his opinion rarely sought. His greatest quality is his abundance. He forms the majority. He is ninety-nine per cent of any crowd and you can almost be certain that he will never be interviewed on a television programme. When he dies only a few will mourn him but that is hardly the point, for this man has made his contribution, and that, in itself, is worthy of mention.

But perhaps my picture is not too easily recognisable so I will try to draw the man accurately – and the only way to do that is to create a situation.

First of all, take any given Sunday in summertime. He gets out of bed. He shaves. He dons his sportscoat, flannel pants, and sandals and goes downstairs to a breakfast which inevitably consists of a rasher, an egg and a sausage. He is not feeling too well but he puts the breakfast where it belongs all the same. He glances through the papers and goes to Mass. He doesn't go too far up the church but he doesn't stand at the door either. After Mass he stands at the nearest corner for a few minutes. He meets a man just like himself. There may be certain physical differences but they are two of a kind. A stranger looking on would be at pains to observe any sort of communication between the two but, by some colossal instinct which defies analysis, they enter a nearby public house together.

In the public house the customers are talking about a football match. The local team are playing in a challenge game in a village several miles away. Our man goes home to his dinner of roast beef, peas and potatoes. He has a good stroke with a knife and fork and is no joke when it comes to making the spuds disappear. After dinner he is between two minds – whether to go to bed or take out his bicycle and go to the football match. The porter and the heavy meal have made him drowsy but the instinct of the sportsman is strong within him. An uncle of his was once a substitute for the North Kerry Juniors and a cousin of his mother's was suspended for abusing a referee.

Our hero duly arrives at the football pitch. The crowd is small as this is a game of little consequence. He parks his bicycle and pays a shilling admission fee. The teams are taking the field. His interest is aroused. He gives vent to a spirited yell in support of his own team. The familiar jerseys have brought his loyalty to the surface but he notices a discrepancy in the side. He counts only fourteen men and then, suddenly, he hears his name being called. The first faint suspicion dawns on him but he pretends he doesn't hear. Casually he begins to saunter to the other end of the field but the voice, pursuing him, grows louder. He increases his gait but the unmistakable call arrests him:

'Hi Patcheen! Will you stand in goals?'

He can run away now and be forever disgraced in the eyes of his neighbours or he can stand and be disgraced anyway. His coat is whipped off and, before he knows it, there is a jersey being pulled over his head. He hears a disparaging comment from some onlookers on the sideline:

'Good God! Look what they have in goals?'

His blood is up. He thrusts his trousers inside his socks and tightens his shoelaces. He takes up his position and the game is on.

He is not called upon to do anything during the first half or during the second half either. There is little between the teams but what little there is stands in favour of our man's team. A high lobbing ball drops into the square. The backs keep the forwards at bay and our man goes for the ball. He gets it – only barely but the important thing is that he gets it. The forwards are in on top of him. He's down. He holds on to the ball like a drowning man and for the excellent reason that he has nothing else to hold on to. He hears a rending sound. His flannel trousers are torn. One of the shoes is pulled off his foot. Someone has a hold on his tie and is trying to choke him. He is kicked in the shin and he receives a treacherous wallop in the eye. There must be a hundred men on top of him!

Then the whistle sounds and he is able to breathe freely. He is safe now and here, at last, is the great opportunity. He rises with the ball in his hands. He hops it defiantly and then, in one of those great moments which only happen once in a lifetime, he goes soloing down the field. The whistle blows again but he pretends not to hear it. Then he stops and turns and with a tremendous kick aims the ball straight at the referee. Dignified, he returns to his goals with his torn flannels flapping behind him and his tie sticking out from the back of his neck like a pennant on the lance of a crusader.

Nobody offers him a lift after the game. He cycles home to his supper of cold beef and bread and butter. He changes his clothes and makes no attempt to conceal the black eye. He combs his hair and walks down to the corner. He meets his pal and they stroll leisurely towards the public house.

Our man calls for two pints and, settling himself comfortably on his stool, launches into a detailed account of the save. If he adds a little it is understandable – and if he had been wearing togs and boots heaven only knows what would have happened. The important thing is that he wasn't found wanting when his time came. He made no headlines but he didn't disgrace himself either. The football scribes will not mention him when the annals of the great are being compiled but in the eyes of his compeers and in consideration of the porter he had drunk and of the dinner he had eaten I think he must surely be reckoned among the great goalkeepers of our time.

Is Cork Sinking?

This summer a man I had never seen before entered the premises and declared to all and sundry that Cork was sinking. Having made the announcement he called for a small Paddy and a pint of stout.

There was no immediate reaction to this outrageous revelation. You must wait a while for an appropriate response when you suddenly tell a bar full of Kerrymen that Cork is sinking. It isn't that they don't care, it is simply that they are slow to react to news, be that news good or bad.

Those with poor hearing endeavoured to ascertain if the intruder had really said that Cork was sinking.

'About time,' said one old gentleman when it was confirmed for him that Ireland's largest county was soon to be submerged for all time.

'And I'll tell you something else,' said the stranger who made the announcement, 'when Cork sinks Kerry will sink with it because the larger county will drag it down.'

'That means so,' said a bespectacled *garsún* who happened to be in the company of his parents, 'that all the other counties will sink as well because Kerry and Cork together are so heavy that they will bring down Limerick. That's three counties down and the weight of the three will bring down Clare and Tipperary.'

'Exactly,' said the Corkman, 'and Waterford and Kilkenny, then Carlow, Wexford and Wicklow.'

'Dublin, Meath and Westmeath,' added the bespectacled *garsún*, warming to his task.

'Offaly, Cavan and Monaghan,' the Corkman continued, 'till

the entire country is completely covered by the sea.'

To give the Corkman his due he sounded so convincing that some patrons were already feeling sorry for themselves. There was an unprecedented demand for fresh drinks. The Corkman executed a delightful swallow which landed him half-way down his pint. He spoke like a man who believed every word he was saying.

'What about the Aran Islands and the Blaskets and the rest?' I asked of this man who was either a prodigious liar or had very special information available to him. He did not answer immediately. He looked into his glass as though it were a crystal ball. He sloshed the stout about and looked me right in the eye.

'The backwash will bring 'em down,' he said cheerfully, 'there won't be a rock or a sandbank to be seen, not to mind an island. All the birds will emigrate to England or America,' he spoke the last piece with baleful finality.

'The country lasted a long time,' said a small farmer from the Stacks Mountains.

'It made a great battle surely,' said another.

The conversation took another turn when someone suggested that Ireland would sink anyway because of the great weight of water from the unprecedented rains.

'We're after some of the wettest years in the history of Ireland,' said a gloomy man who made immediately for the door lest his pronouncement provoke physical retaliation. Time passed and relevant matters such as corn, hay and turf came up for discussion. The conversation was turning pedestrian, banal in fact. The commonplace was being trotted out.

'How do you make out Cork is sinking?' I asked the stranger, who I suspected of being a Corkman. At least he had a Cork accent and his hair was combed outwards from a central crease which ran in a straight line from his forehead to his poll. Only Corkmen retain this hairstyle, so popular from the 1920s to the 1960s.

'How do I know Cork is sinking?' He repeated my question to ensure the widest possible audience.

'I'll tell you how I know,' he said, 'and I tell you too my friend that it's no mystery. Cork is sinking because of all the gas they're taking out of Kinsale. What do you think has kept Cork afloat for so long? Did you think there was lifebelts on to it or what?'

No one made an answer. It was apparent to me that this particular Corkman was on his way to Ballybunion to join his wife and family who had either a lodge or a caravan rented there. He was merely amusing himself while taking a respite from the rigours of the road, popping back a base for the session of beer-drinking and singing that would take place later that night at an appointed hostelry.

He was, however, more than a mere bird of passage. An ordinary person would have taken no more than a single drink and made no more than a single statement before heading for the door and freedom. Here was a man who was prepared to take on a barful of Kerrymen at the ancient game of balderdash.

Some might think him brash. Others might think him forward. Whatever anyone might think, it was apparent that he was a man committed to the art of living during all his waking hours. He reached for his drink and would have swallowed what was left had not a mild-mannered patron invited him to partake of another half-whiskey. I was more than surprised. I had never seen this particular patron offer to buy a drink for anyone up until this time.

The Corkman declined on the grounds that he had to drive to Ballybunion and was dangerously near the alcoholic limit under which all travellers must remain if they are to drive with impunity. Although he declined the offer of a drink he showed his thanks by returning to the subject of the sinking of Cork. He shook his head dolefully before his next pronouncement.

'It might not happen in my time,' he said, 'and it might not happen in yours but happen it will when sufficient gas is taken out.'

'What a story you have for us,' said a surly individual who had earlier been refused a drink on the grounds that he was already drunk.

'It's not my story,' said the Corkman. 'I am merely stating the facts. Cork is sinking while we sit here arguing.'

'And can anything be done?' The question came from the patron who had offered to buy him a drink.

'There's only one thing to be done and that is to pump all the hot air out of Dáil Éireann into storage tanks and according as the gas is withdrawn from Kinsale let this air be piped underground in its stead.'

There were murmurs of approval from the majority of the patrons who must often have wondered if the superabundance of hot air in the Dáil would ever be utilised for the benefit of the Irish people.

Some readers will ask if it is strictly necessary to devote so much space to the visit of an unknown Corkman when other more relevant and more important matters might more profitably be aired. I respectfully submit that it is. He was different from the general run. He had something unusual to say for himself. If there were more like him the public houses of Ireland would be brighter and better places. God preserve us from churlishness, from lack of common civility and from thuggery and send us more men with cheerful dispositions and outrageous revelations like that vanished Corkman.

A Personal Tramp

I'm a lucky man in that I have my own personal tramp. He has, more or less, adopted me. I am beginning to understand what the ascendancy classes meant when they spoke or, indeed, boasted about old retainers.

'I am your personal tramp,' he informed me in a rare fit of indulgence some time ago, 'and I am here to see that no other tramp annoys you. If you are to be annoyed I am the man who's going to do it. Who has a better right! I am, after all, your tramp. Therefore, thou shalt not have false tramps before you.'

I decided to keep my mouth firmly closed. He is a tramp who uses any and all things I say for his own ends. He can, as the poet said, cite scripture for all his purpose.

There is one great advantage about having one's own personal tramp. Tramps have their own code, a code that is rigidly observed by themselves.

'Never mind what Fentiles think,' he said righteously, 'it is what we, the brotherhood, think that matters.'

No, I didn't mean to say Gentiles. Fentiles is what I said and Fentiles is what I'll stick to. Let me explain about Fentiles. It is the name given by our friend the tramp to all those who are not tramps. It is a corruption of Infantiles. Fentiles, therefore, in his eyes are what you and I are, gentle reader. Personally I am extremely grateful since I know this man's capacity for heaping abuse on people and for all his skill at labelling people, labelling them so that the label sticks and cannot be washed away by time or by detergent, often quite unfairly, just because the label would not buy him drinks or listen to his ideas.

The reader may interject here with the suggestion that customers should be protected from this sort of treatment but I would point out that it is not my function to do so unless they are incapacitated and cannot move of their own accord. The customers under attack are free to move away to another area. However, let us suppose that our friend pursues them to the second area which I regard as an area of refuge then their liberties have been challenged and it is my duty to insist that the gentleman responsible behaves himself.

Generally speaking, customers in public houses are well able to look after themselves. That is why they venture into public houses in the first place. There is always a gamble attached to sojourning in public houses. One is never totally safe, regardless of the high standards of the establishments one visits. One blackguard can disrupt the peace and harmony of any given public house and feel free to do so until the law arrives to remove him. We publicans may not ourselves remove blackguards even if we were able.

This again is what attracts law-abiding people to the public house, the element of risk, the prospect of being abused, castigated, interfered with or assaulted. Some customers go so far as to wear public-house clothes lest drink be spilled on their Sunday bests. There is the prospect of being savaged, ravaged and contaminated. Few as they are who are left, the last remaining breeds of fleas still prefer public houses to cinemas, theatres and bingo halls.

Let us return to our friend the tramp. There is no such thing as a resident tramp. His very calling militates totally against permanency of tenure. There is one great advantage though in having one's own tramp, and it is that all other tramps are discouraged while he is around.

Just as commercial travellers defer gracefully to each other when they meet in shops and other business houses, so does the tramp stop at the entrance when he beholds another tramp in residence. It is all part of the code of the tramp. There is no handbook for the behaviour of tramps. There is no need. Tramps observe their own rules, and woe betide the member who breaks it.

I look forward to the temporary return of my own personal tramp now that he is safely elsewhere. I need him from time to time to ward off worse. I also need him to provoke me. One of the great fears of all writers, and this one in particular, is the awful prospect of becoming sedentary. My personal tramp is sometimes so annoying that he occasionally sets me fuming and, therefore, on my toes. A fuming writer will take on anything but a sedentary writer is a danger to himself and others. By others I mean those who are likely to be bored by him.

Provocation is to me what the raindrop is to the parched flower, what the scalding droplet is to the unfortunate cat.

We were arguing one night about pishogues and the evil effects they are likely to have upon innocent people. The subject of magpies came up. You know the rhyme: one for sorrow, two for joy, three to get married, four to die, five for silver, six for gold and seven for a story that was never told. My friend the tramp had been listening respectfully up to this. Then he put in his spoke.

'A magpie,' said he, 'has no more to do with bad luck than a meat pie.'

This audacious comment succeeded in infuriating the scholarly gentleman who had been holding forth for over thirty-five uncontradicted years on the subject of magpies and pishogues. Blows were avoided when the tramp made his way under the scholar's legs and out the door.

One night as we stood talking in the street the rain came

down, sparing nobody. An important man from the business sector of the town was hurrying by when our friend forestalled him.

'Quick,' said the tramp, 'go after April and tell her she forgot her rain.' Give the businessman his due he seemed to enjoy this allusive direction.

'So she's gone off without it again,' he said as he stroked his chin. He looked up and down the street and shook his head.

'Too late,' he said, 'she's gone.'

I wonder when this personal tramp of mine will show up again. He disappeared last year for the entire summer. Then my wife and I spotted him in Galway. He was a different man. When we hailed him he was self-conscious and nervous. I had the awful feeling for a moment that he had sold out and become somebody's tramp. I knew, however, that this was not strictly true.

I discovered the truth the following night after the races. There he was in another pub annoying several customers at the same time. So that was it. I was his by winter and another publican's by summer. I decided not to interfere. My wife and I left quickly lest he spot us. He was dressed as usual: a peaked cap, a shabby raincoat and a high-class umbrella hanging from his arm. Could that man carry an umbrella! He carried it as though it had never been stolen, as though he had been born with an umbrella on his arm.

A Warm Bed on a Cold Night

Many years ago, when I was a *garsún*, I was friendly with an aged bachelor who had a unique method of heating his bed on a cold night. He did not require permanent heating, just something to start him off. He was opposed to artificial heating, as he called it, and would have no truck with hot-water bottles or electric blankets.

He lived in the countryside, a mere stone's throw from the tar road so that he was never short of callers. These varied from people who had lost their way to wandering tramps and outcast itinerants as well as journeymen, tradesmen and unapproved evangelists.

Anyway, when nights were frosty or when the snow blanketed the countryside, our friend would admit one of the aforementioned and provide him with shelter for the night. It was the custom in those distant days to allow a wanderer a place beside the fire until daybreak when he would be given a mug of tea, a few slices of bread and butter and a boiled egg or two and would be sent upon his way to prey upon somebody else.

Upon being informed by our bachelor friend that he would be granted shelter for the night, the wanderer would be profuse in his thanks, calling down all God's blessings in the most colourful fashion on his benefactor.

'Spare your thanks,' my elderly bachelor friend would inform him, 'but go up instead to my bedroom. Then strip to the pelt and proceed to warm my bed. Let that be your thanks. When the bed has been fully warmed, you may come downstairs and take your place on this settle bed beside the hearth.'

Willingly the wanderer would disrobe in the dark bedroom and stay in the cold bed until it was warmed. Sometimes a wearier wanderer than most would fall asleep and would have to be forcibly removed. However, most did what was expected of them.

Our ancient friend would then disrobe and take his place in the warm hollow between the sheets. Sometimes the bed would be very warm and other times not so warm. It depended upon the age, size and health of the would-be warmer.

It was a good system from which both sides benefited. He was, I must concede, a trifle choosy about the type of person he would allow into his bed.

If there was any sort of whiffiness off the candidate he would not be dispatched upstairs to begin the bed-warming process. If he looked overly fragile or anaemic he would be considered incapable of bed warming. There were exceptions, however, and he fondly spoke of a skeletal-type traveller who literally burned up the sheets, such was the heat he radiated.

The most welcome type was a large, well-fleshed, middle-aged male. Because of his proportions, this type of warmer flushed the cold out of every corner of the bed, thereby providing the legitimate owner of the bed with considerable leeway without the danger of cold, out-of-the-way corners. He could lie on back, belly and sides and stretch his toes to the utmost and be certain of natural warmth wherever he turned.

It was a fair exchange and my friend attributed his great age to this unique heating system. Women who do not share their husband's beds take note. Send him first to warm your bed before entering it.

I also remember a family in our street. One of the children was always sent upstairs at night to warm his grandmother's bed.

In the end, for all that may be said in favour of electric

blankets and hot-water bottles, there is nothing to equal the blissful heat of a partner's body after coming in from the cold of a winter night.

RACECOURSE TIPSTER

I believe that there are people born into this world for no other purpose than to be deceived. They themselves accept the role as if it was theirs by right. They are, as it were, the fodder on which conmen sustain themselves. They have long been easy meat for clairvoyants, astrologers and palmists, to mention but a few of the prophets of the modern world. Americans have a name for them. They call them suckers.

A worthwhile if somewhat frowned-upon career can be built from simply preying on these all-too-plentiful gulls. Now, therefore, we will deal with the little-known occupation of tipster as distinct from the more highly regarded profession of racing correspondent.

I must confess here and now that I have not encountered a racecourse tipster for twenty or more years which should encourage aspiring candidates to the position. I can't imagine why this is so because it was a lucrative trade as well as being colourful and sporting.

I was once acquainted with a racecourse tipster. He was the father of a large family, several of whom entered holy orders and remained in holy orders, much to the betterment and general edification of themselves and their communities. One became a doctor, another a teacher and the youngest a black sheep. Black sheep, I might add, flourish only where there are large and highly successful families. An only son rarely turns out to be one. Let me return, however, to our friend the tipster. A successful member of the tipping fraternity once told me that the cream of his clients consisted of middle-aged women who purchased his tips out of charity rather than out of any hope of backing a winner. Other customers were drawn from all walks of life while a hard corps was made up of patrons to whom he had previously peddled winners and placed horses.

Racecourse tipping calls for little or no skill. A peaked cap and well-worn raincoat is the usual attire and while a pinched face is an asset it is not an absolute necessity. An air of confidentiality also helps. The first practising tipster I knew managed to give the impression that he singled out only certain people for his favours. Before attempting to make a sale he would first look all about to make sure that nobody would know what was happening, thereby convincing the customer that if too many people knew the identity of the horse the odds would not be worthwhile. He might also hint that he was a drop-out from a racing stable and was possessed, as a result, of inside information. Throwaways like: 'He was nobbled last time out,' or 'He likes it yielding,' or 'He's off today' never fail to impress prospective customers.

Now let us look at the trade's accoutrements. These are simple and few, I am happy to be able to report. First one must be able to read and write. Secondly, a large stock of notepaper and envelopes is essential.

Now let us suppose that there are nine horses in the first race. Let the tipster write the name of each horse on a single sheet of notepaper and indicate whether it should be backed for a win, a place or each way. Obviously hot favourites should be backed only for a win. Outsiders should, of course, be backed for places and each way. Place each sheet of notepaper in its own envelops and seal the envelope. Place the nine sealed envelopes in a larger envelope and indicate clearly that it contains the entrants for the first race. Follow the same procedure for the remaining races. Tips should be sold for roughly a pound apiece.

When all are not sold, the unsold envelopes should be given away for nothing since it is absolutely vital that all the envelopes be distributed. This guarantees a winner and three placed horses in every race which has sufficient runners for place betting. Let us presume that there is place betting in the six races on the card. This means that you will have tipped six winners and twelve placed horses. It also means that there will be a substantial number of satisfied customers.

During the races the tipster might repair to the bar and partake of a few bottles of stout and a ham sandwich. He should always vacate the bar before the last race and place himself in a conspicuous position near the main exist. There are certain risks involved. A punter who may have plumped on a loser recommended by the tipster might well seek physical redress. There is also bound to be heaps of abuse, as naturally he will have tipped far more losers than winners but these are the hazards of the trade and who wants a trade without hazards.

On the credit side, there is a good chance that those who have backed winners will not be unmindful of the man who provided them. Those who back winners celebrate as a rule through the medium of intoxicating liquor and it is widely held that intoxication breeds generosity. Racecourse tipping is open to both sexes. In fact it is a calling at which a presentable female might excel more than her male counterpart.

The Nine Rules for Corner Boys

Over the years I have been invited by as many as twenty readers to visit some of the corners in their native towns and villages to view the many fine specimens of corner boys on view there. I have always declined for I believe that while it is all right to write about one's own corner boys it is improper to intrude upon the domains of others.

If, for instance, I were to spend say six months or a year in the vicinity of an authenticated corner boy pitch then I might very well sit down and turn out a thousand words on the denizen or denizens therein but even then I would not be happy that I had produced any more than superficial conclusions. No. It is best to concentrate on one's very own corner. One is then aware of the terrain and one may relate the arrival of a new corner boy to his surroundings without too much difficulty.

The letters I receive begin something like this: 'You must come and see our corner boy.' This opening would be followed by a colourful description of the corner boy in question. They believe that by spending an afternoon looking at and speaking to a candidate for the position of corner boy all will be revealed, so to speak. The truth is that I would require several months of the most acute observation under a massive set of varying circumstances to deduce whether or not the boy at any given corner was really a corner boy.

Corner girls do not exist. If they did I would be the first to write about them. For obvious reasons girls may not stand at corners all day long. Prurient and ignorant minds have seen to that. The corner, therefore, is the exclusive property of boys.

For boys you may take men.

To tell the truth I find it difficult to pass through a strange town without inspecting the corner boys on view. I would find myself quite accidentally in the vicinity of the corner in a distant town and would recall that the very same corner had been recommended to me by a reader.

Without seeming to do so I would observe the resident corner boy and after a while might even ask him the location of the post office. If he chanced to be a communicative corner boy I might very well draw down the state of the weather and if he were a very well-disposed corner boy I might even share his corner for a while. Sometimes I would just sidle up to the corner as if I had been acquainted with it for years and pretend to draw a sigh of relief at having met up with it once more.

Then there are readers who write and ask if it's really true that I can tell a corner boy at a glance. The answer is no. My advice to those who wish to know whether their corners are playing host to bogus or genuine corner boys is to look to the following guidelines:

First make sure that your corner is a regulation corner i.e. a substantial street on either side.

Secondly make sure your corner boy is fully clothed i.e. shortcoat, trousers, shirt, shoes, etcetera. A true corner boy will never be seen at a corner without his shortcoat, not even in sweltering heat.

Thirdly if your corner boy is drunk he is bogus. A real corner boy uses his corner as an observation post and not a support for drunkenness.

Fourthly a true corner boy will never queer his own pitch i.e. crush his cigarette butt, puke, piddle or whatever at any hour of the day or night. Neither will he spit or finger-blow his nose. He will remove himself to another area for all the foregoing purposes.

Fifthly he never stands with his hands into his trouser-pockets. He always keeps his hands behind his back.

Sixthly he never calls a visitor to the corner by his name although the identity of the caller may be well known to him. This is to discourage permanency of residence.

The corner boy is a past master of the withering look. He knows that his claim to sole proprietorship of any corner will not stand up in court. He must therefore resort to other non-violent means in order to preserve his claim. The withering look will discourage all pretenders if it is properly brought to bear. I have seen outsize, accredited thugs wilt before it. The dog may be the master of the nerve-shattering bark and the lion the paralyser of his prey with his mighty roar but when it comes to withering looks we have to hand it to the corner boy.

Seventh, your fully-qualified corner boy will not be influenced by weather. Hail, rain or shine he will stick to his difficult task by the simple expedient of removing himself to the other side of the corner when one side is besieged by the elements. But what if the rain is not driven by the wind? What if it falls straight down from the skies overhead? What then? The corner boy will simply pull his shortcoat up over his head and conceal himself as best he can in the corner doorway. Every corner has at least one doorway a few steps away from where the corner boy normally stands.

Eighth and this is most important. If he is the genuine article he will always touch his forelock in the presence of a member of the Garda Síochána. Whatever else he might be, the genuine corner boy is no fool. He knows that the garda is the only authority with the power to remove him. All the guard has to say is 'Move along there!' and the jig is up.

We all know the corner boy is no loiterer but you try proving that in court and you're in for a big suck-in. We all know that he is no obstructionist but proving it on a busy day with hundreds of people passing could well be beyond the scope of the most skilful advocate.

Ninth and finally, your true corner boy is like a Greek chorus. He watches life go on around him but never permits himself to become involved. That is why he is always so reluctant to answer questions. It is not that he is churlish. It is that he does not wish to fall out of character. But what is the role of the corner boy? It is to be there, to witness, to play his part, however fragile, in the ongoing turmoil without complaint or observation. When he stands at a corner he is marking himself present and on Judgement Day will be able to say: 'I held my corner. I could do no more.'

THE KINGDOM OF KERRY

Addressing the Old House of Parliament in Dublin in 1793, the great Irish advocate, John Philpot Curran, commented adversely that the magistracy of the county of Kerry were so opposed to the laws of the land that they were a 'law unto themselves, a Kingdom apart'. The name stuck and at balls and banquets thereafter the Kingdom was toasted roundly. In fact there are many Kerrymen who say there are only two real Kingdoms, the Kingdom of God and the Kingdom of Kerry.

Among other things this Kingdom contains the next European parish to America which is Ballinaskelligs in the southwest. Then there is Killarney of the Lakes, Tralee of the Roses and Listowel of the Writers. The county is distinguished by a gossamer-like lunacy, which is addictive but not damaging. Tralee is its capital, and a worthy one it is, often called the gateway to Kerry. It hosts annually the great Festival of Kerry, which is without equal anywhere in the world.

Kerry contains dell and crag and mountain and a thousand vistas of unbelievable beauty. There is hardly a roadside where the ever-changing chortling of a fishful stream cannot be heard. Then there is the towering, chattering, sometimes silent Atlantic, which washes the shores of Kerry from Ballybunion golf links, beloved of Tom Watson, to Kenmare.

Ballybunion is beautiful beyond compare. What does one say about the champagne air and the daunting cliffs that has not already been said! Perhaps a tale from the past will serve better than an avalanche of laudatory adjectives from the present. Let us go back to the time of the Fianna, pre-Christian guardians of Ireland's shores.

Imagine young Oisin the poet, his chieftain father Fionn and a few more of the Fianna indulging in one of their less-favourite pursuits, i.e. assisting in the saving of hay for one of the local farmers. The meadow in question lies halfway between Listowel and Ballybunion. Overhead there is a clear sky, and a balmy breeze blows inland from the nearby Atlantic. The time would be the end of June.

Suddenly out of the distance comes the thunder of hooves. The Fianna, no less fond of diversion than any other voluntary labourers, lean on their wooden hay rakes and wait for the horse and, hopefully, rider to come within their ken. They have not long to wait, for immediately they are confronted by the comeliest of maidens astride a snorting white charger.

No cap or cloak, as the song says, does this maiden wear but her long flowing tresses of burnished gold cover the sensitive areas of her beautifully shaped body. Standing erect on her steed she surveys the menfolk all around, and a doughty bunch they are, each man more robust and more handsome than the next. No interest does she evince as her blue eyes drift from face to face. Then her gaze alights on Oisin, poet, philosopher, charmer and athlete. She surveys him for a long time before she gives him the come-hither. He hesitates.

'Come on,' she says.

'Where?' asks Oisin.

'Tír na nÓg,' says she.

'Go on, man,' urge the Fianna in unison. No grudge do they bear him, for such was the code of the Fianna.

He hesitates no longer but throws his rake to one side and, with a mighty bound, lands himself behind her on the back of the magnificent white steed.

'Gup outa that,' says she, and the next thing you know they

have gone from view.

'Where did she say they were going?' old Fionn asks anxiously.

'Tír na nÓg,' the others answer, 'the land of the ever-young.'

Then one day, fifty years later, at that part of the Listowel–Ballybunion road known as Gortnaskeha the white horse re-appeared, bearing upon its back the handsome Oisin and the beautiful blonde. They came upon a number of men trying to move a large boulder from one side of the road to the other. All their efforts were in vain. Oisin leaned down from the horse and with his little finger moved the great stone to one side but, in so doing, fell to the ground.

As he lay there he changed from a lusty youth to a withered old man in a matter of moments. The blonde flicked the reins and was never seen again in that part of the world although other blondes would surface in Ballybunion with unfailing regularity year after year down to this very day, and every one of them as lovely and dangerous as Niamh of the Golden Hair, which was the name of Oisin's partner.

Finding himself unable to rise, Oisin placed a hand on the shoulder of one of the Gortnaskeha men.

'I've been in Tir na nÓg,' he said.

'Tir na nÓg!' they exclaimed in wonder for all had heard of it.

'Tir na nÓg, my tail,' said an old man with a pipe in his mouth. 'Ballybunion he's been to!'

'But how did he age so much?' the others asked.

'Listen my friend,' said the old man, 'if you spent a weekend in Ballybunion with a blonde like that you'd look fifty years older too and you'd have wrinkles galore.'

Which all goes to prove that a long weekend in Ballybunion can knock more out of a man than a score of years anywhere else.

Nearby is my native, beautiful Listowel, serenaded night and day by the gentle waters of the River Feale, Listowel where it is easier to write than not to write, where life is leisurely, where first love never dies and the tall streets hide the loveliness, the heartbreak and the moods, great and small, of all the gentle souls of a great and good community. Sweet, incomparable home town that shaped and made me.

Killarney is the gateway to the southwest of the Kingdom, and so beauteous and captivating are the vistas thereafter that one is lost without a loving companion to share the pain and the hurt that great beauty induces. Without the love of my heart beside me I, personally, am lost here.

In 1842, at the age of thirty-two, Tennyson wrote about this enchanted region:

The splendour falls on castle walls,
And snowy summits old in story.
The long light shakes across the lakes
And the wild cataract leaps in glory.

Tennyson knew and loved Kerry. Kerry, however, is as much its people as anything else. Once, years ago, in my native town of Listowel, I listened to an overheated preacher as he ranted and raved about the declining morals of Kerry folk. On my way from church I asked an elderly friend what he thought of the sermon.

'His fulminations will have the same effect on the morals of Kerry people as the droppings of an underfed blackbird on the water levels of the Grand Coulee Dam,' he said.

The Kerry attitude is spiced with sarcasm and humour. There is a jaundiced undertone to all our observations and we have a fine contempt for pomp and vanity. Other counties joke about us but they must not be taken seriously for what is a hypercritical county after all but an organisation that revels in its own imagined supremacy and, to cover its inadequacies, frequently makes up cheap jokes at the expense of its more talented neighbours.

Long, dull sentences, especially religious and political, are anathema to the true Kerryman. The well-made, craftily calefacted comment, the stinging riposte and the verbal arrows of cold truth will always penetrate the armour of cant and hypocrisy in the eyes of Kerry people.

We tend to digress as well but we do so for a purpose. Kerry folk know that there is no such thing as a truly straight furrow or a simple answer. Our digressions are what oases are to desert nomads, what incidental levities are to pressurised, underpaid workers. To a Kerryman, life without digressions is like a thoroughfare without the side streets.

I might write about other aspects of Kerry such as its fishing and its horse racing (over twenty days in all) or I might outline for you the course of a particularly well-taken goal from boot to goalposts but I think it's more important that we concentrate on the living lingo of the Greater, Hard-necked Atlantical Warbler known as the Kerryman who quests individually and in flocks for all forms of diversion and is to be found high and low, winter and summer, wherever there is the remotest prospect of drink, sex, confusion or commotion.

He loves his pub and he loves his pint and he will tell you that the visitor, no matter where he hails from, is always at home in the Kingdom. He is hospitable to a fault but he eschews everyday language.

There is no such entity, by the way, as a conventional Kerryman. If you try to analyse him he generates confusion. He will not be pinned down and you have as much chance of getting a straight answer from a cornered Kerryman as you have of getting a goose egg from an Arctic tern.

Your true Kerryman loves words, however, and that's a sure way to get him going. Snare him with well-chosen words and outrageous phrases and he will respond, especially if he's intoxicated, with sempiternal sentences, sonorous and even supernatural. On the other hand he has the capacity for long, perplexing silences. It is when he is speechless, however, that he is at his most dangerous. He is weighing up the opposition, waiting for an opening, so that he can demoralise you.

One evening last summer as I sat outside a pub in the shadow of Beenatee Mountain in Caherciveen, the old Gaelic teacher with whom I had been drinking for most of the afternoon told me that the reason Kerrymen were so articulate was because the elements were their real mentors. 'They can patter like rain,' said he, 'roar like thunder, foam like the sea, sigh like the wind and on top of all that you'll never catch one of us boasting.'

Kerry's two great peninsulas provide a topographic mix which no guidebook, atlas nor survey map can adequately convey. There are mountain lakes and waterfalls, mysterious inlets, sheer cliffs and golden beaches, breathtaking in their vastness where often I have not encountered another human in the round of a summer's day. The peninsulas of Kerry are only half-discovered. Everywhere along your route are tiny roads leading to secret slips and piers and periwinkle-studded rocks where the bright water laps and laves. The flatlands of the Maharees on the Dingle peninsula boast Fermoyle strand which is overshadowed by Mount Brandon, called after Brendan the Navigator, patron saint of Kerry and discoverer of America, whatever others might say.

Schools of dolphin traverse the adjacent seas and occasionally stand on their tails on the water to execute their own Irish jigs when they spot humans on *terra firma*. If you wish you can make the acquaintance of Dingle's own resident dolphin, Fungi, by simply hiring a boat.

This is a landscape I know and love. Where else could I walk a golden strand for an entire afternoon in my pelt in the certainty that I am safe from prying eyes. As a precaution I carry bathing togs on top of my head but rarely anywhere else! The Ring of Kerry takes in the peninsula of Iveragh as well as other smaller peninsulas – dotted with quaint coves, rock pools and comfortable pubs that specialise in fresh seafood and friendly staff ready to adopt the stranger. From the windows of these amiable establishments one can watch the ebbing and flowing of the tides in comfort.

The towns of Kenmare, Caherciveen, Waterville and Sneem are all on the Ring of Kerry route, and I stay sometimes at the Lansdowne Arms in Kenmare, where the landlord will sing with me and his other customers in the blissful Kerry night. Away from the golden sands are sally-fringed streams, rivers and lakes where one can enjoy a preview of paradise and rare moments of sublime tranquillity.

I recall many such glorious occasions and one in particular, a little way from Dingle town with its fishing fleets and elegant streets, no two of which are alike. It was that time of evening when light resigns itself to half-light, yielding finally to darkness, and it seemed that all nature was aware that stillness was needed if honourable surrender was to take place. Only in Kerry, with its magical retreats, can one experience such peace.

There is an achingly beautiful road between Kenmare and Sneem which takes you along the shore of Kenmare Bay past Templenoe and Parknasilla where Shaw wrote *Saint Joan*.

Being born in Kerry, in my opinion, is the greatest gift that God can bestow on any man. When you belong to Kerry you know you have a head start on the other fellow. You don't boast about it and you never crow abut it. You just know, because of your geographical location, that you are IT. You are the bee's knees. You really don't need any other assets. You need no great talents, no heavy financing.

One thing it doesn't give you is respectability but that's the last thing a true Kerryman wants. Knowing where you belong outweighs respectability any day. In belonging to Kerry you belong to the elements, to the spheres spinning in their heavens. You belong to history and language, romance and ancient song. It's almost unbearable being a Kerrymen and it's an awesome responsibility!

. . . Makes the World Go Round

Young Love

The old believe everything, the middle-aged suspect everything, the young know everything.

(Oscar Wilde)

Sometimes in the pub at night the older members of the clientele bemoan the moral laxity of our time, with special emphasis on the younger generation who would seem to be without inhibitions, scruples, conscience or the grace of God – or at least this is the distinct impression an unbiased visitor might get if he happened to be holding a watching brief. Tales of murder, arson and rape are legion while ordinary misdemeanours such as theft, vandalism and disorderly conduct are no longer taken seriously. Drunkenness, sloth and unpunctuality would seem to be the chief distinguishing features of those who yearly teeter towards the terminations of their wanton teens while virtue of all kinds would no longer seem to be a thing to be sought after as a matter of course.

Others speak out in defence of youth and point out that this is a better generation than the last. The other night, however, an erudite gentleman, properly paunched and past his prime, made a comparison between his time of heyday and now. He spoke, of course, from the entrenched position of age and property. He spoke with authority and with conviction, and one would think to hear him pontificate that he was never a young man himself. As he accounted the wrongs perpetrated by the present generation his body trembled with barely suppressed rage and self-righteousness. According to him there was never a time like the present time and he warned that continued vigilance was the only guarantee against the lot of us being murdered in our beds.

He maintained that nowadays women go around half-naked and, worst of all, wear no clothes at all in bed. A number of grey heads were seen to shake at this monumental revelation.

'You would think,' said he, 'that they would hold on to some stitch and not be making a holy show of themselves. My own wife,' he continued, 'wears her vest, her bloomers and her nightdress in bed, not to mention a woollen cardigan if there's any touch of frost in the air.'

An older man in the company told him he should be truly thankful to have such a modest woman for a spouse.

'Women,' said he, 'that are only half-dressed are agents of the devil and if the law was the law all them that wears bikinis would be arrested.'

'Modern women,' said the properly paunched man, 'couldn't boil an egg for you. But,' said he, 'they would do away with a bottle of vodka while you'd be looking around you. Then they go so far,' said he, 'as to make love with the lights on.'

'Oh, great God entirely,' said the older man, 'can there be luck or grace where you have that sort of carry-on going on.'

In his time, apparently, this was unthinkable, and he went so far as to quote us a classical example of the vast void which separates then from now. An aunt of his, a comely and shy girl in her twenties, married herself to a neighbouring farmer for whom she had a great wish. After the wedding breakfast they did what all sensible couples do. They sought out a hotel in order to consummate the marriage. Mary went to bed first while Jack kept his back turned to her in case he might see anything. When Mary was safely between the sheets she covered her head so that Jack might undress himself. Need I say that

Jack undressed himself in no time at all and made a buck leap into the bed which would put the best efforts of a Thompson's gazelle to shame. For a while they lay side by side not daring to breathe. After a while, however, nature asserted itself and they turned towards each other with affection and abandon.

We will not dwell on the details of the consummation. We will pass them over which is the proper thing to do, and proceed to the morning. When Jack awoke he was astonished to discover that his young bride was nowhere to be seen.

He rose in a panic and was about to raise the alarm when he heard her dulcet voice assuring him that all was well from behind the closed door of the wardrobe. He sat upon the side of the bed cogitating in full earnest. That she was alive and well there seemed to be no doubt whatsoever. What baffled him was why she should have transferred herself from a warm, comfortable bed to the dark and narrow confines of an uncomfortable wardrobe. The ways of country women are strange, he told himself. Patience and understanding were two items which were solely needed here.

'Why are you in the wardrobe?' asked Jack without the slightest shade of annoyance in his tone. At first no answer came so he repeated the question: 'Why are you in the wardrobe, Mary dear?' he asked. After a while the answer came back in a half-whisper:

'I'm here after last night,' said Mary.

'And what was wrong with last night?' Jack asked.

'Oh 'twas fine,' said she, 'but it was dark at the time whereas 'tis light now and I'm ashamed to show myself after what happened.'

Jack was a patient man. He coaxed her out after a while, and when she shyly complained about the light he drew the curtains and darkened the room. Our middle-aged friend was convinced that no modern bride would behave as did modest

Mary. He went on to recount an incident of more recent vintage. It concerned a woman who was sexually assaulted while she was cutting her corns. The guilty party was a lusty man who lived next door. Without a word of warning he came at her while she was paring her small toe. He did the foul deed and left silently by the back door. The first person the victim told was her mother. At first the mother was speechless. She sat on a convenient chair clutching her breast. After a while her composure returned.

'Why didn't you resist?' said the mother.

'How could I?' said the daughter.

'Hadn't you a blade in your hand?' said the mother.

'It fell,' said the daughter, 'the minute he laid hands on me.'

'Why then didn't you screech?' asked the mother.

'Why didn't he screech?' said the daughter.

If we are to believe our middle-aged friend there is a vast moral divide between his time and ours. But wasn't it ever thus and it's a long time now since the first man posed the immortal question: 'What is the world coming to at all?' It's coming to an end, of course, and has been since it was first created. As we debated the rights and wrongs of the situation a newcomer entered and called for a half-whiskey and a pint. He happened to hail from the nearby town of Glin which overlooks the mighty Shannon river as it cruises towards the Atlantic. He told us a refreshing story of youthful innocence. It restored our faith in human nature.

A young man not too far from Glin took a wife unto himself and spent the night of the honeymoon under the roof of his father's house. He did not appear for breakfast in the morning, nor did he appear for lunch. In sensitive matters of this nature people pretend that everything is normal and that nothing untoward is taking place. They go about their business in the normal manner, knowing from experience that sooner or later everything comes to an end. Consequently no comment was made regarding the young couple in bed. However, as the afternoon wore on the father and mother began to exchange apprehensive looks.

At this stage the father decided, somewhat reluctantly, to take action. He smote upon the bedroom door and announced to the son that the ware was on the table for the supper and it was time to rise and shine. Back came the son's answer without a moment's delay: 'Burn my clothes,' said he, 'I'm gettin' up no more.'

Inlaws and Outlaws

'Give me an outlaw any day before an in-law.' I heard the phrase in the pub one night after a football game during which a number of players had been laid out lovingly on the greensward from right crosses, left hooks and common or garden uppercuts. The man who expressed the opinion quoted at the outset fell foul of an elementary straight left delivered by one of his in-laws.

I disputed his contention at once and asked if in-laws were to be denied the basic right of free-for-all brawling. He hummed and hawed and closed with an unprintable selection of swear words which brings me to the nub of this contribution – the rights of in-laws.

There can be no doubt that most people have a surplus of in-laws, with the mother-in-law the main target for revilement, victimisation, misrepresentation and bogus accusations. As an in-law myself I would have to agree that there are in-laws and in-laws and if there is anybody reading this who suffers from a shortage of in-laws let him contact me and I'll gladly supply him with some of mine free of charge. The others I will keep and cherish for the truth is that there is a percentage of blackguards in every denomination under the sun. Police, medics, teachers, even clergy have their fair share of bad apples so that if a few turn up on the in-law front we must not be surprised.

I am a man of many in-laws and I would be obliged to concede that only ten per cent or less are troublesome and less than five per cent are truly perverted. Not a bad ratio at all but then I ask myself how can it be explained that there is more bad blood between in-laws than any other form of human relationship?

I think the reason may well be that we take our in-laws for granted, and unless we have evening classes on how to deal with in-laws in general the situation will go from bad to worse. We never value anything we take for granted and therefore we don't value our in-laws half enough. We should from this moment onward resolve to make amends for the wrongs we have inflicted on our in-laws and I have no doubt that after a decent interval they will do the same unto us for what is an in-law after all but a semi-detached human with only one gable and very shaky foundations!

What is an in-law in the spiritual sense but a one-winged angel the same as ourselves, and what is an in-law in the geographical sense but a victim caught up between two families, neither of his choosing and neither prepared to give in a solitary inch when it matters most!

I remember that the most unfair assessment I ever heard of in-laws as a whole happened one night of Listowel Races many years ago when I wasn't possessed of a solitary grey hair and preferred bull's eyes to beer.

There was a serious row in progress at the entrance to the marketplace. A man lay on the ground bleeding after being struck by a kettle. The female who inflicted the wound swung the kettle in a wide arc in the hope of adding another casualty to her collection. Mayhem is the only word to describe the awful carnage and screaming and roaring and shouting and pulling and tearing and kicking.

'Get the guards quick!' a man called out, 'before someone is killed.' After a while two guards appeared on the scene. One stood with his back to the market wall while the other went to investigate. Both were elderly chaps, ponderous and easygoing.

The guard who went to investigate succeeded in partially breaking up the row. Slowly he returned to his companion.

'What was that all about?' the companion asked.

'Only in-laws,' came back the weary response.

'You had a right to let them at it,' the other said, and with that they disappeared into the night-time together.

GARTERS

I am now about to embark upon a treatise trickier than any I have ever tried before. The subject matter is so potentially explosive and fraught with likely dangers that, in this instance, there may be justification for the use of the Shakespearean adage that 'fools rush in where angels fear to tread'. It was Mark Twain who said that 'man is the only animal who blushes and the only animal with reason to blush'. I hope, however, for another blush, the blush of modesty, when I disclose the nature of the subject, i.e. the common elastic garter.

The garter has been in wide use from earliest times but did not come into prominence until the year 1351, when the English King Edward III rebuked a number of onlookers when he, the king, reclaimed a garter from the ground. It had been dropped by the Countess of Salisbury after a dance and when he stooped to pick it up he was so irritated by the suggestive laughter of his courtiers that he was quoted as saying: 'Shame on him who thinks ill of it.'

This led to the founding of the Order of the Garter, which should clearly indicate that garters were revered even in medieval times.

There is no Irish equivalent of the Order of the Garter. The first reference to garters in Irish history is to be found in the prophecies of the ancient monks of Ballybunion. These particular prophecies, written in Irish, might in fact be referring to the youth of today, and I am sure that the ancient monks had this very time in mind when they wrote, in reference to the youth of the future, *Beidh siad gan giobal, cleite no brístín*. Translated into English this means: 'They shall be without garter, plume or knickers.'

We must wait and see whether the monks were wholly right or only partly right. The way things are going it's odds on that they weren't too far wrong.

The monks resided on the Virgin Rock off the rugged cliffs of Doon, which stand guard over the golden beaches of Ballybunion. Of the Virgin Rock local legend says this: 'A virgin will not be found within an ass's roar of it till all the seas are still and the tides cease to pour.'

All this, however, is getting us nowhere. The subject is garters and I will now endeavour to adhere to them. At the time of writing the only folk wearing garters are hurlers and footballers not to mention the odd lady who refuses to succumb to tights and still wears pairs of stockings maintained by elastic garters. Referees also wear garters although many an irate partisan would prefer to see them round their necks rather than their legs.

When I was a *garsún* garters were all the go and I have lost track of the number of times I was sent to neighbourhood emporiums for yards of black and white elastic ranging from an inch in width to a quarter-inch. Older ladies and dowdier ladies would wear gibbles or *giobals*, i.e. garters without elastic or, if you like, any sort of an old cloth which would hold up a pair of stockings. Gibbles were frowned upon by ladies of fashion and it was also common knowledge that they left deep circular welts around the base of the thigh. The fatter the thigh the deeper the welt. Consequently, a lady who was fond of wearing a bathing costume at opportune times had to be very careful about selecting suitable garters. Wide garters left little or no marking on the thigh whereas a narrow garter often bit into tender flesh and left a red band around this most sensitive of areas. Only two kinds of elastic went into the making of garters in provincial Ireland. White elastic was worn by maids and black elastic was worn only by married women and widows although if certain widows chose to wear white, allowance was always made.

The question which arises here is this: Will there be a return to garters? The answer is, of course, yes. There will be a return to garters when women abandon their slavish habits. The trouble with women is when one wears tights they all wear tights but I say to you, as others have said to me, that garters will be as plentiful in my time and yours as was once the moose on the shores of Lake Huron and the midges that swarm under the bowers near the lakes of Killarney.

Garters also played the part of guardian against incursions above the knee. The garter was the timberline of morality and the Plimsoll line of security. Can the same be said for tights?

REJECTION

To be rejected by a female is merely to be seasoned for a second assault upon the citadel of romance. We've all heard how the stone rejected by the builder became the cornerstone. According to a farmer friend, the same applies to bulls. I know. I know I've written about rejected bulls for years but, this time out, I am writing about rejection generally.

There was a footballer one time who could not get a place in the Knocknagoorley junior football team and he wound up playing for Kerry. We must not blame the Knocknagoorley selection committee for overlooking our friend for he may have been no more than a gangly apprentice at the time. How often does the misshapen sapling turn out to be the regal oak which stands broader and taller than any of its companions! Eh!

How often were my own works rejected for one reason or another and yet at the end of the day they survive! I blame nobody. Rather do I blame the time, the place and the circumstance for by such matters are we governed. Then, if our star is not in the ascendancy, we may be left stranded or, as Shakespeare said: 'All the tides of our lives will be bound in shallows and in miseries.' I may not have it exactly right but then I tend to take liberties with the great bard for, as many of you will know, Shakespeare's mother came from a townland between Tarbert and Listowel and would be, so to speak, a neighbour, and what are neighbours for, I ask you, but to be used as we see fit!

Then look at all the rejected songs and singers. How long did it take for them to truly surface and take their rightful places on the world stage!

Look at the great cooks who couldn't boil an egg when they were young and who, later in the day as it were, watered the mouths of countless monarchies. Then mourn for those who never made it, who never got the breaks. How's that Thomas Gray puts it:

> *Full many a gem of purest ray serene*
> *The dark unfathomed caves of ocean bear.*
> *Full many a flower was born to blush unseen*
> *And waste its sweetness on the desert air.*

Then look at all the good footballers who came on stream during the reign of Kerry's greatest football fifteen. They were good but not good enough. They would have been good enough any other time except the time they appeared. They were destined never to star.

Rejection, my friends, is no joke. It can set a man back upon his heels and leave him in a position from which he'll never recover.

There is only one situation where rejection can be an advantage. I speak, as if you hadn't guessed, about our friend the rejected lover. I have always maintained that only a lover who has been rejected not once but several times will attain to the very highest pinnacle of his profession.

I was first rejected by a red-haired *cailín* in the Pavilion Ballroom in Ballybunion in the year 1945. She would have been three or four years older and it could well be that I did not represent a sound investment for her time and attention. She would be on the lookout for a marriageable chap with a steady job. I was still a schoolboy and a steady job was nowhere on the horizon. My friends told me at the time that I had aimed too high, that I should have gone after somebody of my own age who was less attractive than the beautiful redhead. I refused to lower my sights, however, and went after a second mature partner. I was scoffed at by the object of my desires. A lesser soul would have wilted but I was imbued with a reckless courage which came from my Stacks Mountains ancestors.

Third time lucky. I approached and was warmly received by a brunette of about twenty-four. Of course she would dance with me. Why wouldn't she! We waltzed and we exchanged confidences. When the dance was over she handed me her purse to mind.

'It will only be in my way,' she explained, 'while I'm looking for my future husband. You have an honest face,' she said, 'and you won't run away with it.'

It was total rejection, no matter what way one looks at it. I was consigned to the role of purse-minder rather than woman-minder. Time passed and I would escort many girls home from dances. Other times I would be outdone, outfoxed and outdanced, not by the obvious Casanovas, the loudmouths, the loud dress-ers, the show-off dancers but by the sly ones, the self-effacing chaps who said little or danced little or indeed who did not look like real opposition.

I am reminded of that great writer Malcolm Lowry. How did he put it again: 'How many patterns of life are based on kindred misconceptions. How many wolves do we feel on our heels while our real enemies go in sheepskins by.'

I have often felt that it must be terrible for a man to have never been rejected by a woman, to be always acceptable whilst the ordinary mortal must suffer his share before he matures to manhood or to an age where rejection matters not a whit. To be old and not to have been rejected must surely be an unbear-able situation. Whilst most of us ponder on what might have been, the unrejected man has no cud to chew. How the blazes can you enjoy success if you have never tasted failure! How can you attain to perfection if you haven't gone through the furnaces of rejection!

I knew a man who went to Mass every morning of his life in total thanksgiving for a rejection which changed his life. There he was, infatuated by a beautiful woman in his own street. Not a minute passed that he did not think about her.

'I must whip up,' said he, quoting our friend Shakespeare again, 'my courage to the sticking point.'

Then came a summertime dance. She was there in all her glory, dressed in dark green, which perfectly matched her eyes. He invited her to dance and she gladly accepted. He was a presentable chap with a steady job. It certainly would not be beyond him to maintain a female in the style to which she had become accustomed. Later, after he had danced with her three times in all, he asked her if it would be all right to see her home. She replied in the negative. Not to be outdone, he asked again and, upon being rejected, asked a final time. She made it clear that she was not interested.

Some months later she married a man from out of town. She broke his melt, as the saying goes, and he endured a life of sorrow and suffering throughout their marriage.

Our friend who had been rejected was so delighted that he underwent a change for the better. He married a plain Jane but she made him happy and that's all that matters in the end, that and the grace of God.

Too Serious

It would have been in the mid-1930s. I would have been a *garsún*, a mere nipper. A good-looking girl arrived to work in one of the local boarding houses and was noticed immediately by an agricultural worker employed by an uncle of mine who kept a large number of milch cows. The cows were driven home every morning and evening from the town's outlying fields and were milked in a long shed at the rear of the dwelling house a few doors from where I lived. We shall call the agricultural worker by the name of Rest because he never rested.

'Give her this note,' he said to me one evening, 'and let me know what she says.'

I delivered the note and awaited a reply. She took her time and read the note a second time. I also had a look at the note's contents. There wasn't much to it, just a desire to go with the girl to the exclusion of all others.

'Well!' I asked after a decent interval.

'I won't go with him,' she announced, 'because he's too serious.' It was a fair assessment. He was a serious chap. He never laughed.

Too serious! Well it takes all kinds to make a world but I feel that we have too many serious people. Then it must be said that we are all either too fat or too lean, too tall or too small, too rich or too poor and so forth and so on.

'Let me have men about me who are fat,' says Julius Caesar, 'all lean men are dangerous.'

They may have been dangerous in Caesar's time but fat men have been more dangerous since. Look, for instance, at

Goering, Mussolini and Stalin, and let us not forget Idi Amin, prime bucks all.

The apple of the agricultural worker's eye would not have known of these men. They had not come into prominence and anyway I doubt if she would follow their careers with any great degree of interest because everybody would agree at the time that she was very self-centred and had little interest in anything outside of herself.

I daresay that the opposite of seriousness would be cheerfulness. It is good to be cheerful but the phrase 'cheerful idiot' was not coined by accident, and onlookers could not be blamed if they deduced that a non-stop cheerful man had something the matter with him. The point I am trying to make here is that there is no real difference between a cheerful man and a serious man. All we have to go on is surface cheerfulness and surface seriousness. The girl who turned down our friend John Rest did not take this into account. Indeed most people don't and this is a pity because it means that serious-on-the-surface contenders for the hands of non-discerning females are at a disadvantage.

Then there's the expression 'God loves a cheerful giver.' The truth is that God loves all kinds of givers and I believe that a cheerful giver suffers less when giving than does a serious giver. The cheerful giver gives instinctively and often starves his wife and family whereas the serious giver wrestles with his conscience a good deal before parting or not parting, as the case may be, with his few bob.

Those who teach Shakespeare have a lot to answer for. For several days I had a low image of myself over what Caesar said about lean men. The teacher had agreed with Caesar but then one day as I was eating some boiled mutton and parsley sauce it dawned on me that the teacher in question was the fattest in the school. He would naturally agree with Caesar.

The girl who turned down John Rest did so for superficial reasons. I saw her several times since. She had disimproved with age, God rest her. I often meet John Rest, and he said to me after he heard of her death, 'I hope she don't be turned down by Saint Peter. He seems a serious man to me.'

A BULL IN AUGUST

This morning I met a sourpuss. I hadn't encountered one in years, for the good reason that most of my outings are to places where humans are few and far between. I meet animal sourpusses often enough, especially in the late summer. These in the main would be bulls who have been stretched to their sexual limits by the demands of numerous cows and heifers. These animal sourpusses need to be kept at a distance because your sourpuss bull will attack without provocation, venting his wrath on luckless humans and turning his ponderous posterior to the cows and heifers who left him in such a state of debilitation.

The sourpuss I met this morning was male and in his forties. He scowled, growled and cleared the street in front of him like a tank.

'Watch where you're going!' I heard an old lady say. For a moment I thought he was going to demolish her. I passed him the time of day in cheerful tones but all I received in return was an almighty snort.

'Wrong side of the bed,' the old lady ventured as soon as he was out of earshot.

He entered a supermarket and emerged after a few moments followed by a blonde woman who looked to be half his years. He seemed to be upbraiding her but, to give her no more than her due, she gave as good as she got and went back in.

'That's the second wife,' said the old lady, ' he bullied the first one into her grave and she a great woman entirely that went nowhere, not even the bingo.'

Our friend was now returning the way he had come. I

thought for an awful moment that he was about to bellow before charging. I decided that it might be prudent not to salute him on this occasion. It was he who took it upon himself to address myself and the old lady.

'What are ye f------ looking at?' he asked belligerently.

'Nothing,' the old lady answered, at which he bridled and bristled and barked like a mastiff. He decided not to devour us there and then. Instead he turned on his heel and proceeded to his car. He sat there glumly awaiting the blonde woman who was still in the supermarket.

Eventually she appeared in the doorway and made her way to the car where he still fumed and frothed and manufactured four-letter foulies. His new wife was followed by a supermarket attendant who bore her bags of groceries in her wake. She opened the boot of the car and he deposited the groceries therein. She entered the car but so vehement was the tirade of abuse which greeted her that she re-emerged at once, banging the door behind her.

'Ah sure I have it all now,' said the old lady. I waited for elaboration as she folded her arms and nodded her head.

'The young wan is too much for him. She has the taspy knocked out of him and he's fit for nothing only mischief – the same as a bull in August.'

There it all was. The answer was provided by a gentle old lady who knew the ways of men and bulls. I was tempted at the outset to call this contribution 'Of Bulls and Men' but that might give the game away prematurely.

I resolved there and then to make allowance for all the grumpy, middle-aged men I would be likely to meet thereafter, especially those who might be married to young, demanding spouses.

Unlawful Sex

Illicit sex is bad for the heart. I do not say so personally but it is now widely believed in continental medical circles that sex without a licence will put paid to the beating of the most consistent ticker. It was also accepted in a limited way by certain of the religious who, fair play to them, insisted for starters that it was bad for marriage first and for a number of other things afterwards.

I remember a fiery missioner with whom I often imbibed a few whiskies when he would finish up for the evening. During one of his sermons he described a married man who had left his wife's couch for the couch of another.

'This heinous wretch,' said he, 'was not content with going to hell himself, oh no he had to take another unfortunate soul with him.'

One night, however, it transpired that after a night with his mistress the fellow was seized by an inexplicable pain in the forehead. He fell to the ground, never to rise again. According to the missioner, if he had loved his own woman instead of fornicating with another he would still be in the land of the living.

That night I asked him if the story was true. He swallowed a drop of his whiskey and looked me squarely between the eyes.

'Who's to say?' he said. 'Anyway,' he went on, ''twasn't to tell 'em fairy stories the parish priest brought me all this way. I will tell you this, however,' and he paused to finish his glass, 'a man without the grace of God has no peace of mind and a man with no peace of mind cannot possibly lead a normal life. A man who does not lead a normal life cannot expect to live a long life. Therefore, a man who indulges in unlawful sex should be prepared for a premature departure from the land of the living.'

I remember at the time I found my friend's logic acceptable. More recently I read in a Sunday newspaper where Professor Bernhard Krauland of the University of West Berlin was quoted as saying that 'extra-marital sex is bad for the hearts of middle-aged men.'

According to Krauland, love-making in the marital bed is a healthy exercise whereas the middle-aged man who goes to bed with his secretary could be flirting with death.

I wasn't all that interested in the good professor's claims, for the simple reason that here was another gambit or exercise which was bad for the heart. Almost everything these days from beer to butter and bad thoughts to bingo is blamed for the high incidence of heart disease. There is no day now that some newspaper doesn't carry an account of new cardiac dangers arising from the consumption of too many overfried sausages or tying one's laces too tight.

I must say, however, that I found the professor's revelations intriguing so, on the Wednesday after reading the newspapers, I took myself to the bog of Dirha West. Sonny Canavan was alive and well at the time. How we have all grown to miss that sage and sensible man.

I found him counting his goats near an ass passage. Over our heads curlews wheeled and bleated in the rain-filled skies. The goats grazed happily and one might say that the scene was a truly pastoral one. Background music of a high quality was supplied by a concealed roadside brook. Having concluded his goat-count, Canavan turned his nose directly into the wind. He did not sniff. Rather did he scent the air.

'Rain,' he announced, 'heavy and long without a break.'

We walked along the narrow roadway, picking our steps between the clusters of shining marbles, freshly deposited by the constipation-free goats.

As we savoured the salt-laden, southwesterly wind I conveyed Professor Krauland's findings to Canavan.

'What's he a professor of?' was Canavan's first question.

'Medicine,' I replied.

'With regard to sleeping with secretaries,' said Canavan, 'he may be right and he may be wrong. Who am I to disagree with him that never had a clerk, not to mind a secretary.'

Once more I quoted from Professor Krauland.

'According to this man,' I said, 'a girlfriend is usually more demanding than a wife.'

'That,' said Canavan, 'would depend on the wife.'

'Are you saying the Professor is wrong?'

'What I'm saying is this,' said Canavan, and a frown appeared on his unshaven face, 'a bird in the hand is worth two in the bush. A wife in the bed is worth two outside of it. The wife is where the action is. The others are not.'

Again I quoted from Professor Krauland: 'Most of the lovers who die in their girlfriends' beds are between fifty and fifty-nine.'

Canavan paused. 'There's a man we both know,' said Canavan, 'lives not far from here. He has three wives planted in a grave-yard that you often wrote about. Single, married or widowed, he ramboozled all makes of women as fast as you'd pull 'em out from under him. 'Twas the nature of the poor man. Some men are wild for drink, some for money and more for travel but there's others, like our man, and sex comes as natural to them as it does to the puck or the pony stallion.'

'That man,' said Canavan, 'is past a hundred years of age. He has an appetite like a horse for fresh mate or salty. He has the health of a spring salmon and the same desire for women that he had eighty years ago.'

We walked towards the main road which links Listowel and Ballybunion. Canavan looked at the heavens. His nose twitched, a sure sign of rain. The skies darkened and in the distance beyond the fabled hills of Cnocanore there was the faintest rumble of thunder. From above us there came a long, confidential whisper, and suddenly a vast flock of starlings whirred by over our heads. A fat, shawled woman, a legacy from our far-off yesterdays, rode by in an ass-cart.

'Good morrow men,' she called but flicked her reins rather than tax herself with heeding our replies. She had sufficient on her mind. The ass trotted off briskly at the wrong side of the road. Canavan stopped and tapped me gently on the chest with his index finger.

'Most of those,' said he, 'that tended their wives and their wives alone are presently growing daisies while your man that lifted every skirt in sight is still hale and hearty and there's no one knows him will deny that he gave more time in the beds of others than he gave in his own. The man was a born ramboozler. It came as natural to him as crowing to a cock or braying to a donkey. If this doctor is right the man should be dead fifty years ago whereas he's still alive and kicking as any respectable female around these parts will verify.'

'But,' said I, 'Professor Krauland maintains that sex outside marriage is bad for the heart because it's so much more exciting than lawful sex.'

'Of course it's exciting,' Canavan said, 'only a fool would say otherwise, and I'll grant you while it might be bad for some hearts it's just the job for more hearts. There's no two hearts alike no more than there's two doctors' opinions alike.'

'One more question,' I said.

'Fire away,' said Canavan.

'Professor Krauland says that extramarital sex carries hidden dangers. What have you to say to that?'

'Plum pudding carries hidden dangers,' Canavan replied. 'So does fried bread and so does bottled stout, even gettin' out of bed does whether there's a secretary in or not.'

So saying he turned and faced for his house after raising a hand in silent farewell. The Oracle of Dirha had spoken.

BED HERMITS

One Monday morning a neighbour complained to me that she could not get her daughter out of bed. I cited for her an ancient cure for this now-uncommon malady.

There was a time when every community boasted at least one bed hermit, that is to say a person who took to the bed and stayed there over the years in spite of the fact that no sickness was apparent. These bed hermits are less common nowadays for the good reason that they cannot find people to look after them. This task was usually allotted to elderly spinsters and other timid creatures who lived in constant dread of the great outdoors for reasons best known to themselves.

I personally remember a postman from my early youth. He was wrongfully accused of purloining a sixpenny postal order from one of the letters entrusted to his care. He was dismissed and was allowed to remain in this woeful state of criminal suspension until it accidentally came to light some weeks afterwards that an error had been made. When his superior called to see him he was not admitted to the house. The postman's sister informed the official that her brother had taken to bed the day he was dishonourably discharged and had not left it except for basic purposes in the interim. Others called in an attempt to dissuade him from the bed but all to no avail. Thirty years were to pass before he would again reveal himself in public.

He was one of several bed hermits of my acquaintance. The most notable lived three miles away in the countryside. Some years before, at the age of eighteen, she took to the bed and stoutly refused to budge even when her irate parents threatened to burn the bed upon which she lay. All fruit failed, however, and when all fruit fails we must try haws, the haw in this case being a black doctor who visited Listowel for one week in the year during Listowel races and plied his venerable trade in the market place.

His name was Doctor Curio. I remember him well. He was of Nigerian extraction and was as black as the proverbial ace of spades or blacker than a famine spud as they say in these parts. He wore a tall hat and a swallowtail coat. He operated from a small bamboo table upon which were placed a few dozen of his internationally famous Curio's Cure-All. This incredible mixture sold at the modest price of two shillings a bottle and it differed from conventional doctors' bottles in that it could be used externally as well as internally.

Doctor Curio boasted that it also exterminated fleas. It could be used for the treatment of blisters, craw-sickness and carbuncles as well as for the eradication of warts, welts, vertigo and all female disorders. It was without peer as a liniment and was guaranteed to banish cramps, sprains and strained muscles when properly applied.

Doctor Curio, according to his credentials, was a graduate of the university of Walla Walla which, for undisclosed reasons, was not to be found on any African maps of the time.

When the good doctor was approached by the parents of the female bed hermit he listened carefully to what they had to say. Having digested everything of relevance he asked a most pertinent question. How much was in it for him? After a certain amount of haggling, in which neighbours of the parents, the fattest woman in the world and a pair of three-card tricksters were involved, a fee of five pounds, an enormous sum at the time, was agreed upon.

Duly the black doctor arrived at the abode of the recluse.

A large and curious crowd had gathered to witness the miracle. Doctor Curio first demanded the fiver which was handed over to him at once. He then ordered all the occupants of the house to remove themselves from the vicinity. This they did and, with the neighbours and others, stood at a respectful distance await- ing developments.

When the black doctor entered the bedroom the first thing he did was to remove his hat. He then politely suggested to the lady in the bed that it might be best if she abandoned it. This she refused to do. Instead she pulled the clothes tightly around her and stuck out her tongue at Doctor Curio. He decided to ignore this monstrous irreverence. Without a word he removed his coat and placed it at the foot of the bed. Only then did the first look of alarm cross the bed hermit's face. Calmly the doctor removed his waistcoat, shirt and vest and a string of shark's teeth which happened to be tied around his belly to protect him from evil spirits.

The bed hermit was now sitting up in the bed, a look of absolute panic having replaced the one of alarm. Calmly the black man started to take off his trousers. This was too much for the lady in the bed. With a frightful screech she threw back the clothes and fled through the front door, her nightdress trail- ing behind her. She ran past the astounded audience, shrieking at the top of her voice. Fully dressed, the great Doctor Curio appeared in the doorway. He lifted his hat to his audience and returned to take up his rightful position in the market place.

The lady in question never took to the bed again. Neither did she reveal the methods which the black doctor employed to eject her.

'PLENTY COTTON'

Recently I was asked by one of my sons if I could tell him what was meant by the expression 'Plenty Cotton'. I was happy indeed to be able to answer in the affirmative because I recalled that the expression was in wide use around that time when you could buy a narrow bottle of superfine brilliantine hair oil for tuppence and when a great majority of country people were still suspicious of tomatoes.

The expression 'Plenty Cotton' was first used by the late Dan Paddy Andy O'Sullivan, the famous Lyreacrompane matchmaker, to a group of Irish army privates and noncoms who stood shyly outside the entrance to his famous dance hall one warm Sunday night in 1941.

In those days, several hundred troops were camped in Lyreacrompane. They spent their days cutting and saving turf in the surrounding bogs and their nights in search of women and other simple diversions. Their pay was in the region of a pound a week so it will be seen that it was absolutely necessary to manufacture home-made entertainment if they were to remain mentally stable.

These 'Emergency Men' were nearly all volunteers who supplemented the meagre battalions of regulars when it was felt that Ireland was in danger of invasion. They were young men in their teens drawn in the main from the adjacent counties of Cork and Limerick. They were the cream of the country but they were as green as their uniforms and many of them had never seen the inside of a dance hall before.

As I have already intimated they stood in a circle around the front and only door of the dance hall, their uniforms spick and span, listening with a newly born yearning to the romantic strains of 'South of the Border', which was the rage at the time, or to 'Let Him Go Let Him Tarry', if the three-man orchestra happened to be subscribing to that novelty of novelties, the foxtrot.

Dan Paddy Andy, if business was slack, would come to the door of the hall and call out to the eager-faced troops: 'Come on in lads, plenty cotton here.'

This was to suggest that there were women in plenty inside since simple cotton dresses were the dance frocks that prevailed at the time.

In those days, dress dances were confined to places such as Duhallow and like spots and went under the misleading nomenclature of 'hunt balls'. Be that as it may, it is with the expression 'plenty cotton' that we are now dealing. What nicer method of describing an abundance of the opposite sex? As I recall there were less poetic descriptions at that time. They were known as pieces of skirt, totties, dolls, birds and longhairs, to mention but a few. Dan Paddy Andy, at least, had pride in the feminine produce of the local countryside and was determined that they should not be degraded by ill-becoming names.

This is not to suggest that they wore cotton dresses alone. Far from it. A few of the older girls wore corsets but these were in a minority. The standard apparel was your cotton frock, underneath which was a slip, a chemise, a chastity cord and a doughty pair of long, sensible bloomers designed to withstand any onslaught which, God forbid, might take place in the heat of the moment when a couple might find themselves alone with no company save the sedge and rush and no sound save the base booming of the mating bullfrog. Apart from the bleating of the jack snipe and the distant barking of dogs, these were the only sounds to be heard in the happy countryside.

Inside the hall was a large paraffin lamp, which was ideal for such a situation as its light was weak and consequently more conducive to romance. In fact there was a song of the period which contained the line: 'Don't you know it's more romantic when the lights are low.'

The prevailing odour, if one were to discount the sweet and transient whiffs of 'Outdoor Girl' or 'Pond's Powder', was that of paraffin oil.

Paraffin mixed with dance crystals or grated wax candles was also used to make the floor 'skeety'. In those days boys and girls would dance till they were drenched with sweat and happily exhausted from a score or more of consecutive dances.

From time to time I meet middle-aged men who were soldiers in Lyreacrompane in the early forties. They all speak nostalgically of those halcyon days and nights and they will remind you emphatically that there was no place like Dan Paddy Andy's dance hall and no sport like the sport they had then.

There is one man in particular who ended up a sergeant in that army who lives presently in the city. The last time I met him he told me that he has a recurring dream. There he is, a raw recruit, a mere *garsún*, with his cap perched jauntily on the side of his head and he standing with a crowd of his fellows listening to the music which floated outwards and upwards to enchant him. Always from the past comes the voice of Dan Paddy Andy: 'Come on in lads, plenty cotton here.'

THE GIRLS WHO CAME
WITH THE BAND

Long ago when I first started to dance in country halls I was quite taken by the girls who came with the bands. They would always be dressed more brightly and more fashionably than the local girls and made up to the point of what was regarded as immodest.

Many missioners and priests of the time were death down on paint and powder for reasons best known to themselves but bad as were paint and powder the worst of all was when a girl painted her toenails and wore sandals to flaunt her scarlet toes before the young men of the countryside. Nearly all the girls who came with the bands painted their toes, and they wore high-heeled shoes. They also wore short skirts and they didn't care. They were lovely and stylish and beautiful in the eyes of the young men of the hills and the valleys but who were they, these girls who came with the bands?

They weren't vocalists or instrumentalists or they weren't professional dancers hired by the management to lead the floor with a willing partner drawn from the ranks of the locals. They certainly weren't ladies of easy virtue and they weren't the wives or sweethearts of the members of the band.

I had better tell you who they were. They were big-town girls or city girls who had come along with the band for the drive or for the crack. They had grown tired of the fierce competition in the populous halls of the towns and cities. In their own halls they were nobodies but when they came to the village halls and the crossroads halls, they were somebodies. They came armed with the latest steps, the latest hairstyles, and they had no real competition from the modest and cautious girls of the locality. Knowing this gave them extra confidence and poise, and they took the country hall by storm. In fact any time a really smart girl appeared it was always assumed that she had come with the band.

Only the more daring young men would take them on in the dance – students and lads home from England or soldiers on leave. The girls who came with the bands truly excelled at the tango, their long legs unhindered, freed from all constraints by the excessively long splits in their skirts. The local girls wore the tiniest of splits in their skirts and were inhibited in their movement as a result.

Sometimes the more rustic, the more demure and bashful of the local couples would withdraw from the floor when the lady who came with the band and her partner swept round the hall like a tornado. The newcomers had other important characteristics. They never carried their purses with them when they danced as did the local girls. They left them instead on the stage near the drummer where there was plenty of room and where they were at all times visible although at that time purse-stealing was as rare as the swallowtail coat is now. The fact that they did not carry their purses while they danced meant that they were not available for transportation to areas outside the hall by would-be Romeos. It meant that they had come only to dance and that they had no intention of making up with any male of the area, no matter how handsome or how imposing he might be.

Sometimes when a partner swept them to the back of the hall where stood the shy and the halt and the blackguardly, these last would pinch them in passing to see if they felt the same as the local girls. These pinches hurt like hell. Once I remember a girl complained to the saxophone player that she had been molested. He laid aside his instrument and left the stage. The girl pointed out the molester and the saxophone player kicked him smartly between the thighs. He sat out the remainder of the dances and all were agreed that he deserved what he got. There is no lower form of animal life than he who would molest a girl.

The girls who came with the band vanished forever shortly after the war. The country girls started to cotton on and soon they began to look themselves like girls who came with the bands.

CIRCUS PASSION

This is the story of Antonio Feckawlo, often mentioned in passing but never given the full treatment he so richly deserves. Feckawlo was drowned in the Feale River in 1912. Originally of Italian extraction, he was, in his heyday, a devil-may-care, curly-haired, moustached Lothario who earned his living as a knife-thrower with Hanratty's Circus which used to tour rural Ireland on a regular basis up until the end of the First World War. As a knife-thrower he left a lot to be desired. In straight throws he was quite without peer but in the backhand flip it was rumoured that he wounded several of his human targets.

The reason I am writing about him is that it is over seventy-five years since his body was discovered in the River Feale with a knife clenched between his teeth, his oily hair slicked back without a rib out of place and his dark eyes concentrated in a deathly stare.

Hanratty's Circus consisted of three piebald horses, an aged Shetland pony, a toothless lion who survived on minced donkey meat, a female slackwire walker, the aforementioned Antonio Feckawlo and Hanratty himself, who quadrupled as lion-tamer, clown, juggler and horse-rider. Hanratty's wife saw to the box office.

The trouble started after the night-time performance in Listowel's market place in the year 1910. For some time Hanratty had suspected that his wife had been having a passionate affair with the knife-thrower and in this respect his suspicions were to be proved correct. According to residents of Market Street and Covent Lane, which still front the market place, Mrs Hanratty, Dolly to her friends, was a red-haired, vivacious lady of fifty-odd years, whereas Hanratty was thirty years her senior and it might be supposed that the demands of his numerous roles in the ring seriously militated against his prospects as a lovemaker.

The opposite would seem to have been the case with Antonio Feckawlo. Knife-throwing is an artistic vocation calling for little or no physical input. Consequently Feckawlo found himself with considerable time on his hands. Idleness, we are told, makes a mockery of morals. Idleness too, it might be said, is the chief nourishment of lust. Inevitably the knife-thrower and Dolly Hanratty were thrown together and as time passed they grew careless.

In Abbeyfeale one quiet Sunday afternoon, after a matinée, blows were exchanged between Hanratty and the knife-thrower after the former had surprised his wife and her lover as they paddled among the reeds a mile or so upriver from the town. Feckawlo, who was without his knives at the time, was no match for Hanratty who, despite his years, was still a skilled boxer. Some said he had been a sparring partner with the late Jack Johnson. The upshot of the ruction was that Feckawlo ended up with two black eyes and one broken nose. He fled the scene but, like a true performer, he reappeared for the night performance.

Then came the incident at Listowel, an incident remembered by several octo- and nonagenarians, mostly female, whose eyes still sparkle when they recall the seductive charms of Antonio Feckawlo.

As soon as the later performance ended, the taking down of the canvas commenced. This was an event in which all hands, male and female, participated. Halfway through the proceedings it was discovered that Dolly Hanratty and Antonio Feckawlo were missing. Immediately Hanratty instituted a search and to his astonishment found the lovers in a warm embrace in the lion's cage.

They foolishly presumed they would be safe from prying eyes in such surroundings. The lion, sated with minced donkey meat, slept soundly, as was his wont after late performances.

On this occasion Feckawlo was armed with a wicked-looking knife. Hanratty fled for his life with the Italian at his heels. Hanratty mounted the fleetest of his piebald horses and rode bareback through the streets of the town until he came to the river's edge. Here he dismounted, patted the horse on the rump and hid behind a thorn bush. The horse crossed the swollen river with Feckawlo furiously following.

Thus ends this torrid tale and thus ended the tempestuous career of Antonio Feckawlo at the bottom of the Feale River with his knife still in his mouth. He never knew the river was in flood. As they say in Latin, the language of Feckawlo's ancestors, *nec scire fas est omnia.* It is not permitted to know all things.

SUCCESS WITH WOMEN OR
HOW TO SUCCEED WITH WOMEN

There was, in Ballybunion when I was a youth, a tall, slinky slow-foxtrotter who was frequently forced to fight off women whenever a ladies' choice was announced. Remember that I speak of a time when good foxtrotters were as plentiful as pismires at a picnic, when the strains of Pat Crowley's music brought out the best in otherwise uninspired terpsichoreans, when there were cups for quicksteps and waltzes and dance halls were really for dancing. Our slinky slow-foxtrotter did not stand out on the ballroom floor. There were no flourishes to his finishes and I never once saw him execute a really neat combination of steps.

He was a careless dresser. His shortcoat was never buttoned and his trousers were never pressed. Neither was his hair racked nor his shoes polished. When I was in my heyday a man never combed his hair. He racked it or if you like raked it. In country places in those days a comb was called a hair rake.

The rest of us went to great pains to polish our shoes and maintain knife-edge creases in our trousers. We plastered our hair with tuppenny bottles of superfine brilliantine and we always topped our cigarettes and buttoned our shortcoats before inviting a lady to dance.

Our friend was different. I had better put a name on him, although readers who were part of the Ballybunion scene in those halcyon times will have him tagged from the opening line. He was known as Bango Malone. He was not, strictly speaking, a native of Ballybunion. He spent most of the summer there with an aunt and he came from the Tralee side which could mean anywhere between Tarbert and Ballinskelligs. He had a season ticket for the Pavilion ballroom but little else by way of worldly matters. He is now deceased, as is the aunt who provided his long summer holidays.

He was an easy-going chap, no more than twenty, but he had about him an air of quiet assurance which belied his tender years. We envied him. No woman ever refused him a dance and as I have earlier pointed out he was besieged before the drums rolled for the start of a ladies' choice. Sometimes a damsel with exceptional looks would appear in the Pavilion. When she showed no inclination to accept the countless offers to dance made by some aspiring foxtrotters like myself we looked to Bango to see if he could make any fist of her. There was no need to worry. After a while he would sidle in her general direction and before he was half way to her she would be on her feet waiting for him to sweep her into his arms.

What was it about him, we asked ourselves? He was non-descript enough. He never used superfine brilliantine as we did. He never cracked jokes and the women he chose as partners never laughed during the period of the dance. He wasn't good at quips but he was a consistent and slinky slow-foxtrotter, and this was the only apparent asset of which he could boast.

Oddly enough we didn't envy him. He was never smug and never in the least boastful about his accomplishments in the female field. He never went home alone from a dance. There would be a rush for partners as Joe McGinty announced that the last dance of the night was at hand. The best-looking girls were swept up quickly or rather they allowed themselves to be swept up quickly by those they had earlier chosen to look after compacts or purses. Bango moved late. Joe McGinty would be singing the opening lines of 'Goodbye Sweetheart' when he would drift across the floor to the lady of his choice. She would have refused earlier invitations and gambled all that Bango would select her for the ultimate caper. We marvelled at the ease with which he charmed every make of woman. He never spoke during that drowsy last dance. He held her close but not too close. She would endeavour to look into his eyes as if searching for a secret truth which might reveal the inner thoughts of his heart. Then and only then would he permit himself the very faintest fraction of a smile. As the magical melody wore on and Joe McGinty's sleepy sonorousness drugged us into dreamland, Bango would be seen to be dancing cheek to cheek. When a lady consented to dance cheek to cheek it meant, without question, that she had allowed herself the luxury of an escort to her place of abode or mode of transport. Bango never asked. It just happened. With the rest of us it was different. Only on rare occasions could we induce a lady to leave the hall with us. Occasionally a kind-hearted soul would answer in the affirmative when permission was requested to see her home but for the most part we would be given one of the standard answers such as 'My sister is with me' or 'My brother is waiting for me at the door.'

Another favourite rejection was for a girl to say she had a cold and was afraid to pass it on. Others had to leave immediately after the dance, while more went home in bevies, having been forewarned by anxious mothers to spurn would-be escorts and seek safety in numbers. Hard to blame the mothers for, beyond doubt, there were some unscrupulous rogues at large in Ballybunion at the time. It was the confluence of all romantics, lawful and unlawful, for that place and period.

All this, however, does not help us in our analysis of Bango Malone. Bango is, of course, a *leas-ainm*, or nickname. His real name was Beneficus or Benedicus or some such cumbersome attachment. His friends abbreviated this to Bango. There was none of us at the time who could explain Bango's success with the fair sex. Some, the more impressionable, took to imitating his mannerisms, few and all though they were. We gave up using superfine brilliantine and tried not to be raucous or noisy, as had been our wont. We let the creases escape from our trousers and gave up buttoning our shortcoats before asking a girl to dance. It was all to no avail. If anything we were less successful than before. It was as if the girls knew we were imitators because they refused to take us seriously. With Bango it was the same as always. At the end of their week's or fortnight's holidaying females would go home, heartbroken after Bango. He would promise to write but this alas was something he was incapable of doing, having abandoned school at an early book. Looking back now over the years it is not too difficult to understand his success with women. He never stood out like a sore thumb. He was never noisy. He never did anything brilliant while dancing yet he never did anything foolish. He stayed away from the centre of the ballroom. He was a headlands-dancer, preferring to do his eurhythmics in the quieter areas. I'll grant you there are women who love the limelight, who like the centre of the floor, who like to be in the thick of things whether these situations are embarrassing or not but the truth is that the vast majority of women are content to drift through life with the Bangoes of this world.

Bango succeeded because he was an average man. He never lost because he never gambled. He never made his partner look awkward on the dance floor. He took no chances. He never bored her with idle talk. He let the music and the atmosphere do the work and was happy and, which is more important, was seen to be happy whenever his partner searched for the truth in his eyes. He wasn't great but neither was he mediocre. Women sensed that here was a man who could go through life without rocking the boat and this basically is the chief requirement of a female in the long term.

If he were in the cavalry Bango would never lead a charge. The chances were he'd live to tell the tale. He knew his limitations. He wore his clothes the way he did because he did not want to attract too much attention. He could not cope with it if it came his way. It was Shakespeare who said that 'the apparel oft proclaims the man'. In Bango's case it was true. He was, in short, a man who could lay a spell upon all females great and small.

... INTO THAT GOOD NIGHT

FOUL DEEDS WILL RISE

There's many an honest Irish man and woman down on their knees thanking God for the arrival of the funeral parlour. Where once there was none now there are many.

How deprived now are those hawk-eyed inspectors of the indoor scene who looked upon a death in a neighbour's house as a passport to an uncharted land where new vistas might be examined and the manners and means of the inhabitants taken into account. These avid inquisitors would arrive at the scene before the off and take up their places at the bedside from which vantage point they were at liberty to study the hats, clothes, shoes and general appearances of every mourner who knelt by the deathbed to pray.

I often criticised them and now I'm sorry because I miss them more than I can say. They were part and parcel of the rural scene and they kept us all on our toes. With two rows of these redoubtable matrons ranged at either side of the bed, their hands decorated with massive dangling rosaries, there was no time for frivolity and the corpse was accorded his or her fair modicum of respect.

Once I was present in a wake-room when a sacrilegious act was perpetrated. I was on my knees at the time and so were the others, a fat man who smelled of freshly consumed whiskey and two women whose bodies and visages were covered by black shawls which were in common use at the time. As we were being relentlessly vetted there was an eerie silence which was common only to wake rooms. Suddenly it was broken by a sharp succession of poorly suppressed wind breakages.

The sounds died as quickly as they had come, leaving behind a silence far more devastating than the first. Then came a gasp of horror and outrage from the several females in attendance. It was unequivocal in its condemnation. The kneeling females shook their heads and gazed with sorrow at the fat man who continued with his praying as though no such earth-shaking and sacrilegious outrage had taken place.

He rose, blessed himself, and withdrew to the porter room which was the name given to that area where the alcoholic beverages were being distributed.

He was followed by one of the two women who knelt by my side. Deeply scandalised by the unexpected outburst she retired meekly to the kitchen where tea was being served.

The other woman was next to rise. I slunk out after her but as she exited from the room, just out of earshot of the inquisitors, she unleashed a minor tattoo from the rear, similar in all respects to those to which we had been subjected in the wake-room.

How right was Shakespeare:

Foul deeds will rise
Though all the earth o'erwhelm them to men's eyes.

THE NAME OF MONEY

Men who leave fortunes behind them are rarely remembered for long. When the resources they so carefully husbanded through life are exhausted by the profligate heirs so does the memory of the benefactor also expire. I'm not saying we should not leave our possessions to our heirs. What I am saying is that we should not leave too much behind us. We should endeavour to measure out our possessions with care so that we derive the maximum benefit over our closing days in particular.

If you want to be remembered by your relations the best thing to do is leave a few modest debts behind you. You won't be remembered affectionately but you will be remembered. In fact, every time a payment is made to reduce the debt you left behind, your name will be drawn down by whoever it was that was saddled with it.

In the street where I was born there was an old man who spent his declining years in the houses of several different relations. He had a crumbling, thatched house of his own in the suburbs but it was not fit for human habitation. He was therefore invited to stay with one of his relations. He was not invited out of the goodness of their hearts. He had the name of money, and having the name of money is just as important as having money.

He once owned a farm but what the relations did not know was that he invested the price in liquid assets. A legacy left to him by an aunt also went down his gullet. So addicted to drink was the poor fellow that he once sold a pair of pyjamas to cure a hangover and slept in his shirt for the remainder of his life.

In fact I knew a man who sold his false teeth so that he might satisfy his craving for porter. On a personal basis I was caught on a few occasions to secure people for bicycles, beds and radios. As soon as I signed on the dotted line they promptly sold the articles for which I had secured them and left me holding the baby. They sold them for drink. My problem was that I found it difficult to say no to people, apart altogether from the fact that those I secured would have been far-out relations of mine.

My problem was unexpectedly solved one morning as I sat at breakfast with some total strangers in a south Kerry farmhouse whose proprietors had contracted to supply us with bed and breakfast. Sitting opposite me was a tall, lean, pious-looking man of advanced years. One word borrowed another and the subject of securing people came up. I think I may have casually said that I could afford several holidays if those I secured had honoured their commitments.

The pious-looking man said in the most offhand of manners, 'I was asked recently by a cousin to secure him for a motorcycle. I just told him that civil servants could not secure, that they would be dismissed the moment it came to the attention of their employers.' The ploy worked. I then explained that I was not a civil servant.

'Have you a brother or sister who is a civil servant?' he asked. I told him that I had a brother who was.

'Tell those who want you to secure them,' said he, 'that your brother will be sacked without redress if you secure anybody.'

It worked. The next time I was asked I explained to the female who wished to exploit me, and not for the first time either, that my brother's job would be at risk if I obliged her. 'He's a civil servant,' I informed her emphatically, 'and you know what happens when a family member secures someone.'

Rather than admit ignorance she nodded her head solemnly.

But where is all this leading us and what about the man who came to live with his relations? He lived first with one and then with the others. He would spend a maximum of about three months with each. He made notes of their particular kindnesses in a jotter especially bought for the purpose. He would enter sums of money borrowed and the cost of special foodstuffs like lamb's liver and sausage rolls. All would be revealed in his will and all who maintained him would be well rewarded.

When he died he left not a single penny behind him but he left several relations who would never forget him. They had invested heavily in him and there was one in particular who plied him with expensive cakes after his dinner. She saw him in much the same light as the post office, a good solid investment which would be there for the taking the moment he permanently closed his peepers.

The bother with investing in humans who have the name of money is that there is a high risk factor. You cannot really believe humans when it comes to money so that I would be tempted to advise the investor to stick with the post office or a reliable building society or even the banks. At least your money will be safe whereas with the relation who has the name of money there is no guarantee whatsoever and, remember too, that he will be safely out of reach when the will is read and it is discovered that he has nothing.

Different if the person you invest with has a conscience. He will leave sufficient to meet the requirements of the investors. Alas the party without a conscience will lead the investor all the way to the grave with false promises and nothing to back them up. I have seen cases where bankrupt investors were even saddled with the cost of the funeral. I have even seen investors supply an abundance of drink and food on the strength of a will which had not yet been read.

By all means help out a worse-off relative. Even go so far as to buy him delicacies but do not expect anything in return. You should try to remember that virtue is its own reward and that charity begins at home. 'Whatsoever you do in my name,' saith the Lord, 'it shall be rewarded one hundredfold in heaven.' Alas there are too many who just will not wait for heaven. They want their heaven right here on earth and they want it by way of large fortunes left by relatives. It's all a matter of attitudes. I remember once to hear it said of a friend of my father's that he drank out two farms. The woman who disclosed the poor man's folly shook her head sadly as she spoke, whereas an old man who disclosed the same story in a pub around the same time shook his head in admiration. I'm all for leaving something behind. Don't get me wrong on that score. What I have will go with a good heart to my next of kin. However, to leave them too much would be bad for them, and there is the danger that I would be obliged to neglect myself were I to aim too high on their behalf.

Enough is enough and anything more is merely a surfeit. I would not perform as Tom Daly did. I would not do away with it all before I died. Still his will was a chastening one and should be a reminder to expectant relatives. 'Being of sound mind,' Tom wrote, 'I drank every halfpenny I had before I died'.

OBSTRUCTORS

Recently I spoke to the proprietor of a funeral parlour in the city of Dublin. He had read some pieces of mine about the ups and downs of the undertaking business and he told me that he was impressed. That is why he left the party with whom he was drinking and made his way from one end of the bar to the other in order to compliment me.

I asked him a number of questions about undertaking. Firstly I asked him why they were called undertakers in this country. He smiled.

'I suppose,' said he, 'it's because we takes 'em under.'

The bane of his life, he informed me, were queue-breakers who line up to sympathise with the relatives and then break ranks when the queue doesn't move fast enough for them. I informed him that we had transgressors of the same nature down the country except that they did not even line up. He could scarcely credit it when I told him they just bypassed the queue as if it didn't exist. He was astonished but even more astonished when I revealed to him that there were some mourners who formed queues of their own when faced with joining a long queue which had been there already.

'They should be prosecuted,' he said angrily. 'A few months in jail wouldn't be long curing gurriers the like o' them.'

We both believe, after lengthy discussion, that most of these funeral queue-breakers belong on the stage. They show tremendous acting ability as they approach the funeral parlour. They give the impression that they do not know what a queue is. The expressions on their faces would have their victims believe that they have never seen a queue before. I have seen them myself as they paused with wry expressions on surprised faces. Their lips seem about to frame the question: 'what manner of contraption is this? Let us ignore it for God's sake and pass on. Let us not encourage these foibles in those inconsiderate eccentrics who would have us do as they do and misbehave by joining this long obstruction!

'Let us not suffer these fools gladly but rather let us go on our own way no matter how inconvenient it may be for those guilt-ridden louts who would expect us to behave like them!'

Let us now look at the inside scene, where the next-of-kin are gathered. The deceased naturally holds pride of place where it lies in the coffin at which everybody pauses for a moment or two before moving on. Some pause to have a good gander at the clothes and the coffin and to value the latter so that they may carry the news far and wide that the coffin was an inferior one or an expensive one.

Others pause to say a prayer or two and still more pause to see whether the corpse is handsome or emaciated. They like to be informed of such aspects of the obsequies.

About one in every three pauses out of reverence and respect for the dead and particularly for this individual cadaver. You see, the fact of the matter is that most people enjoy funerals and the sense of loss is secondary. I personally don't enjoy funerals because of the behaviour of certain mourners, the most obstructive of all being those who stop and start conversations with the next of kin while a huge pile-up of would-be mourners delays the proceedings no end so that funerals often run late, causing great distress to mothers of families and others who have vital commitments.

These obstructors are female for the most part and they show no consideration for those in their wake. They bend over the seated mourner with large posteriors extended as they pose questions about living members of the family of the deceased. So extended is the posterior that it is impossible to pass. The obstructor, male or female, heeds not the whispered pleas coming from behind. Instead the posterior is seen to flicker indignantly at the slightest touch.

Outside the funeral parlour the queue grows longer and longer and still the indoor obstructor does not budge an inch. Finally the next-of-kin to whom she is addressing herself closes her eyes and pretends to fall asleep. Reluctantly the obstructor moves on, seeking another source of information. These people make ordeals out of funerals and turn many genuine mourners away. The cure is to bypass them and to ignore the member of the next-of-kin who suffers them, for she must shoulder a fair share of the blame. It could, in fact, be said that she could also be prosecuted for aiding and abetting. After all, she encourages the obstructor to loiter in the first place by not reminding her of her obligation to move on and make way for other mourners.

Worst of all is when a pair of obstructors, upon recognising a familiar face among the ranks of the next-of-kin, greet her as thirsty Arabs greet an unexpected oasis. They enquire about all manner of things, from the quality of the year's potatoes to the condition of the silage. While it is sometimes possible to slip past one, it is physically impossible to slip past two, so that the queue lengthens. In many respects it resembles a traffic jam, except that there is no recourse to members of the Garda Síochána. Funeral parlours are places of peace and repose and forcibly removing obstructors, however provocative, would be a distinct let-down to the next-of-kin.

The ideal answer is, of course, an MC. There are MCs at weddings, and why shouldn't they be at funerals. I foresee a drastic drop in the number of funeral-goers unless things change in the very near future. Young people these days have neither the patience nor the energy to survive marathon funerals.

This is not my first time holding forth about time-wasting inside and outside funeral parlours. We must not lay the blame on the proprietors. You cannot walk up to a person at a funeral and tell them to move on. I have never met a funeral-parlour proprietor who was offensive.

They have to remember, I dare say, that everybody dies sooner or later and a body who has been pushed about, so to speak, at a funeral parlour will not be likely to nominate the proprietor of the parlour in question to take charge of the removal of his or her remains.

On the other hand, the proprietor who has a friendly smile for all, whether they are obstructors or not, will be rewarded by the ultimate favour at the end of the day.

Old Cars

Old cars are like old people!

They need to be rested occasionally. They need sympathy and understanding, for great age is often the breeding ground of great bitterness but if a car is looked after with care and love it will grow old gracefully and give as good as it gets.

Recently, I went to Limerick city with a friend of mine. It was a fresh frosty morning as we set out, and it was decided that we should travel by the coast road since my friend and I both like a bit of scenery.

The light wind on the Shannon was like a young girl whispering and my friend whistled happily while we sped over the tree-lined roadway at twenty-five miles an hour.

'She's in good order this morning,' he said, 'and what harm but she has had a hard week of it.'

The doors rattled merrily at this unexpected compliment and from various place in the back came a succession of clanging noises. As we neared Foynes she stopped, for no reason at all.

'That's all right,' my friend said, 'we'll give her a rest till she gets her wind back.'

Ten minutes passed and he started her again. All went well until we reached Askeaton, when our noses were assailed by three distinct burning odours.

'All she wants is a drop of oil,' my friend explained reassuringly. 'We'll have a drop ourselves, too,' he said, 'but a good cowboy always waters his horse first.'

At the petrol pump the attendant looked the car over without change of expression.

'Throw a pint of oil into her,' my friend said.

The attendant returned with a pint of oil, and when the bottle was empty he shook his head without the least sign of emotion. 'She'd take more than a pint!' he announced.

'She would not!'

'She would!' the attendant said, as if it was none of his business.

'She would if she got it!' my friend said, and we drove off, a defiant cloud of blue smoke rising behind us. Several uneventful miles passed and finally my friend announced that we were near Limerick.

'How do you make that out?' I asked.

'There's the smoke from the cement factory in front of us.'

'That's not the cement factory,' I said. 'That's the carburettor.'

We pulled up at a labourer's cottage and a small curious man hurried out to inspect us.

'Is she on fire?' he enquired.

'Is there any chance you'd oblige us with a gallon of water?' my friend asked, ignoring the question.

When the gallon was empty we thanked the kindly cottier who was still regarding our conveyance with a mixture of amusement and ridicule. 'She takes a share of water!' he laughed.

My friend sat behind the wheel again and looked his benefactor straight in the eye. 'If you were after running from Listowel you might like a sup of water, too,' he pointed out.

That night, as were leaving the city, I was a little apprehensive. My friend sensed my worry. 'You won't hear a word out of her now,' he said; 'she knows we're on the road home.' As we neared home she seemed to grow younger. Now and then she lurched a little to left and right. 'If I give her her head now,' my friend boasted, 'you wouldn't catch her with a jet but it wouldn't be fair to her and besides I want her tomorrow.'

'Did you ever think of trading her in?' I asked.

He looked at me with unconcealed astonishment. 'A new car is no good to anyone,' he said defensively. 'It's no good to the garages because it doesn't need repairs, it's no good to the owner because he's afraid he'll tarnish her and it's no good to a man looking for a lift because new cars are in such a hurry they haven't the time to stop and pick up a person. This ould car gave me the best years of her life. I courted in her and I proposed in her and I was accepted in her. I took her on our honeymoon and I drove my five children to be christened in her. She never let me down. I know her weaknesses and she knows mine. She knows my pubs and she'll pull up outside them without my having to touch a clutch or a brake. There's no fear she'll be stolen because she'd frighten the life out of a car thief. But I suppose I'll have to get a new car soon because my sons are growing up to me and there's no one could handle her but myself. But I'd better shut up,' he concluded, 'because all this praise isn't good for her and she'll probably sulk in the morning.'

THE TIME I WAS DEAD

I don't believe I ever told you about the time I was dead. Despite this I have never felt more alive than I do at this moment. In fact the captious old midwife who brought me into the world informed my father that I would live to be a great age if intoxicating drink didn't get the better of me prematurely. In this respect it has been touch and go for many a long day now. You might say that, drinkwise, I'm just ahead of the posse. The bother is that this particular posse catches up with everybody sooner or later, regardless of whether one drinks or drinks not.

One balmy evening recently, after returning home from a stroll by the river, I sat myself down on my favourite stool in my favourite bar, which is my own, and treated myself to a pint of beer. As I sat imbibing at my leisure a good-looking girl, from Mayo it transpired later, sat down beside me. She noticed a painting of me on the wall behind the counter.

'Is he long dead?' she asked the barmaid.

'He's dead a nice while now,' the barmaid answered, 'although you couldn't trust him. He could reappear at any moment.'

The visitor swallowed a little from her lager and addressed herself to me. 'What got him in the end?' she asked.

'I wish I knew,' I told her truthfully, adding to myself that it was just as well I could not forecast what I might eventually expire from although if it wasn't one thing it would most certainly be another.

A week passed and a busload of German tourists arrived. I was seated on my favourite stool, only this time I was drinking whiskey. The Germans too believed me to be dead. Even the courier, who was Irish, said a prayer for me when he was confronted with my painting.

'God he was an ugly-looking customer,' said the courier.

'Lak a vervulf,' said a German female.

'Nein. Nein,' said another, 'more lak a wampire.'

'What did he die of?' the courier asked the barmaid.

'Thirst,' she answered.

'Thirst!' everybody echoed incredulously.

'How could he die of thirst in the middle of a bar?' the courier asked.

'He was too drunk to come downstairs,' the barmaid explained.

This seemed to satisfy courier and Germans alike.

'There is wuss ways off goingk,' an elderly German gentleman announced and he called for a whiskey.

No week passes but somebody asks how long I've been dead or what did I die from. The barmaid always dispenses the same answer. Those present who know I'm alive keep their mouths shut. It all began after I underwent major surgery. Some reports said I was dead, others alive. I suppose the best description of me at the present time is to say that I am dead and alive.

The question arises as to whether I am worth more dead than alive. That, of course, will not be resolved in this place or at this time but I will be spoken of highly because it is the fashion never to say a bad word about the dead in this part of the world.

I must be the only man around who knows how Lazarus must have felt when he was raised from the dead because I have been consigned to the dead and I have risen. I rose yesterday morning at twenty past nine, was pronounced dead at half past twelve and rose again on a bar stool at quarter to ten that night.

DEAD PLUCKER

If I had not sprained an ankle recently I would never have heard of what is possibly the most outlandish part-time career of all. It is not the first time while compiling this book that these quirks of fate have come to my aid. There were times when I despaired of ever finishing it but then unexpectedly and quite by chance something would turn up and set me off on my merry way once more.

Having sprained the ankle, I was consigned to quarters for four days. While I was indisposed, Davy Gunn the bodhrán-maker called to see me. Neither grape nor orange did he bear but he came laden with fresh news from the countryside.

He had spent the previous day plucking chickens for a neighbour. I reminded him that I too had been a part-time chicken-plucker during my fowl-buying period back in the late forties. As I recall, I joined the fowl-buying fraternity around the same time that Ireland was declared a republic. This declaration constituted the severance of the last remaining tie with Britain. In one magical pronouncement every man, woman and child in the country was turned into a Republican and all were legally as republicanised as any diehard Republican of the time.

When Davy Gunn presented himself in my private quarters, I produced a bottle of Jameson (Davy's preference) and poured him a generous dollop. He swallowed the potion *in toto*. After a moment his eyes moistened and a deep sigh escaped him. The Jameson, obviously, had been dead on target. I replenished his glass.

'Speaking of plucking turkeys,' Davy reminisced, 'it's a few days now since I went on a dead pluck. Myself and a cousin of mine, Nonie Cahill from Tubbertarrive, was sent by my mother to oul' Cait Granville's a week after she was waked and grounded. We went for the dead pluck.'

Davy savoured his Jameson, removed his cap and elevated his left eyebrow, as is his wont while awaiting a question.

'What is a dead pluck?' I asked.

'A dead pluck,' said Davy, is the clothes and footwear that's left after a corpse.'

Apparently in Davy's youth it was common practice for the plain people of the countryside to present themselves at the worldly abode of the faithful departed, there to lay claim to a particular article of clothing belonging to the deceased, that is if anything can be said really to belong to those who are deceased. All Davy Gunn wanted was a black shawl for an old woman who lived next door to him.

'Faraor agus faraor,' said the new woman of the house, 'but isn't that same shawl spoken for.'

That left Davy nonplussed. Having been provided with no further instructions, he stood with his hands hanging to him while his relative Nonie Cahill, of the Tubbertarrive Cahills, waited to intimate her wants.

'And pray what ails you aweenach?' asked the new woman of the house.

'Could I have her black satin blouse, the Lord have mercy on her?' Nonie Cahill whispered in the most devotional of tones.

'And pray leanav,' asked the new woman of the house unctuously, 'what black blouse would that be?'

''Tis the one,' Nonie Cahill recalled the details clearly, 'with the bows and the flounces and the collar with the two motifs.'

'Spoken for, too,' said the new woman of the house without the batting of an eyelid.

'And is everything spoken for then?' Nonie Cahill asked with no deviation from the devotional.

'All that's left now, aweenach, is bloomers and shifts.'

'No thank you,' said Nonie Cahill with a smirk, 'you might be wanting them for yourself.'

According to Davy Gunn, there was no demand for shifts and bloomers, it being widely believed that these might be too contagious to the anatomy and might harbour some dreaded disease from their former proprietors. Demand was for skirts, shawls and coats, blouses, hats and brooches, and shoes if they were available, or waders and wellingtons if the deceased was male. A truly professional dead plucker need never enter a draper's shop. Adequate clothing over a lifetime was always available to those who knew how to ask.

Most male cadavers were buried in their Sunday best although in that part of the world where I was reared it was felt that there was no need for new shoes. This may have been because transportation of a divine nature was provided at the moment of death. I put this to Davy Gunn while refilling his glass. He tendered a valid reason for the absence of new shoes.

The first wake which Davy ever attended was in the townland of Coolcawboon. He went there with his father to inspect the mortal remains of one Thady McCarron, who was reputed to be a distant relation to the Gunns. They said a prayer or two in the wake room and afterwards repaired to the kitchen, where the drink was being given out.

It was a flahool household and the liquor flowed free. Out in the night Davy revisited the wake room to see how the corpse was faring. There was no change in that area except for one. Instead of the black, patent, span-new shoes with which the corpse was originally shod, there was now a pair of well-worn hobnailed boots encrusted with mud. There was no sign of the new shoes, although several weeks later shoes of a similar design and size were seen on the matrimonial trotters of a light-fingered neighbour as he wended his way from the altar of God where he had just been united in holy wedlock. It wasn't the first time a pair of shoes was stolen from the ice-cold feet of a corpse.

There was no great outcry over this. It was simply held that a man who never did a turn to anyone while he was alive was merely making up for his omissions in death. It also helped to reinforce the widespread belief that the dead did no harm, that all they did was good.

Therefore, if a man in need relieved a corpse of his shoes, he was not only doing himself a favour but also he was subscribing to the traditions and customs of the countryside. He was a dead plucker of the first water.

WAKES

Now we will deal with wakes, funerals, graveyards and things of such a nature. Do not hasten away I beg of you. There is a lighter side to everything.

One of my favourite pursuits is strolling through graveyards. It is a recently acquired pastime and it comes, I have no doubt, from a subconscious necessity to familiarise oneself with the sort of location where one will be forced to reside unt il Gabriel sounds his horn on the last of all days. There is, of c fact that there are few places more peaceful but I pre lieve that it comes from this submerged need to ide the last resting place.

I used also to like to attend wakes where the acce: relief rather than grief, that is to say wakes of a cheerl where the departe have been a migh a woman you were expected to embrace and kiss the female members.

Then one knelt to pray in the room where the corpse was laid out. Seated in this room would be several local women who always maintained serious and even cross faces lest some drunken intruder misbehave in the presence of the dead person. Some of these, the more intimidating, would be well positioned at the head of the bed, from where every visitor would be visible. Sometimes they would engage in whispered conversations but only when they wished to enquire about the identity of some strange mourner who might not have been seen in the district before. These doughty women were very necessary when the pubs closed and when every type of blackguard was let loose on the countryside in search of diversion. They were the vigilantes of the dead.

The wake-room was an ominous place where one first briefly examined the corpse and his manner of dress. Then one knelt down at the side of the bed, bent one's head and subscribed a decent number of prayers towards the heavenly welfare of the dead person. Then one rose slowly and exited to where the drink was. People with special claims would squeeze the dead man's hand or bend over the bed and kiss his brow. In the kitchen or the 'Room', which were the areas where the drink was in fullest circulation, one tendered still more sympathy to whosoever might be in charge of the drink. I remember once being present at the wake of an elderly man who had succumbed to an unexpected heart attack having returned home from his first holiday abroad. The gentleman in whose company I happened to be was a great man for protocol, and after we had said our prayers in the wake-room we proceeded leisurely to the drinking room. Here he shook hands with a woman who was handing out mugs of porter to all and sundry. He waited till she was about to dip an empty mug into the sudsy surface before he tendered his summation:

'God bless us and save us,' said he to the woman, 'but he's as handsome a corpse as ever I seen in my life.'

'He's all that,' said she, 'but of course the fortnight's holiday done him the world of good.'

Because of this astute comment we were handed glasses of whiskey so that our stomachs would have the requisite bases for the large draughts of porter which were sure to follow. We drank several mugs of the nourishing stuff and at the hour of midnight a Rosary was said. After that the older and more sensible of the mourners betook themselves to their own homes.

S₁

o₁

w

fc

g₁

w

the porter ran out that cnamhshawling was to be heard. There
are very few wakes these days, for the good reason that most
corpses are taken to funeral parlours and there are countless
other diversions, such as television and bingo.

WHERE HAVE
ALL THE OLD FOLK GONE?

There are no more old people and amen say I to that and oh
how women have changed especially women who used to be
called old!

Nowadays they drink gin and brandy and vodka and pints
of beer, and they have every right to do so but in my boyhood
they used to be their own worst enemies.

When I was a *garsún* they wore sombre shawls and long coats
and dumpy costumes. They never used make-up and why would
they when it was condemned from the altar. Painting one's toes
was the last of all and going off on a holiday was unheard of.

Didn't I hear them in my very own street when a woman
walked in or out of a pub and how they would raise their eyes
heavenwards whenever an unfortunate female passed by wearing
trousers! Didn't I listen when a woman walked down the street
in her figure which only meant that she was wearing a dress
with no corset underneath.

'Oh the hussy!' they would say.

Secretly they longed for her gumption and disregard for
convention. It would come in the course of time – a long time.

Women in their sixties, seventies and eighties now have
their hair done regularly, whereas in my boyhood they would
be considered daft should they dare to have it done more than
four times in the round of a year. These days they flirt and court
and paint their nails, toes and fingers and age has nothing to
do with it. They have discovered that being old is purely and
simply a state of mind.

How long since you heard anybody criticising a woman for drinking a pint of lager! for wearing a pair of trousers! for swearing or for staggering! For generations these practices were confined to men.

In my boyhood the women who wore bikinis on the beaches and in their own back gardens suffered the hardest onslaughts of all. I even knew a girl who lost her job for wearing a bikini during a sultry weekend in Ballybunion. Even in my twenties, if a woman walked into a public house on her own she would be the talk of the place. The only female who would dare walk with impunity on her own into a licensed premises would be a nun collecting the contributions from a donation box.

I haven't seen an old woman in a month of Sundays. Where, you may well ask, have they gone?

They have gone the way of haycars and ponycarts and long Sunday sermons, gone the way of black teeth and carbolic and castor oil and hairy bacon. They have gone the way of pannies and griddles and duck eggs, of suspenders, money balls and blackjack pipes, of hobnailed boots and haipneys and home-filled puddings, of flour dip and bloomers and potato cakes.

Will they ever return? Who is to say! All I know for sure is that these days you're as old as you feel and I can't say for sure whether this new trend is for the better or for the worse. I'm not ancient enough yet to know. I'm only seventy, on the threshold of a bright new future, barring a fall or a bit of bad luck, another one of life's passengers dependent on God's will.

These days it's as good to be old as it is to be young and isn't it high time the old came into their own. It's great to see them out and about and mixing with the young. They make great listeners and they fully understand the fears and worries of the young too, whereas the young have yet to be old.

girth and protuberance, stomachs that wobbled precariously like blancmange when they hastened and lent authority to statements which were laden with inaccuracy when they pontificated. They were men who could harrumph importantly like sea lions and frown like hippopotami. They were men of settled outlook, but they could be unpredictable, too, when it suited them.

They could wink imperceptibly at small boys who turned to look at the choir during Mass and they could, without animosity, paralyse a streetful of disrespectful delinquents with a single paralysing glare. They sported genuine brass chains and they possessed real turnip watches. They were, for the most part, men of few words. They were great artists also.

They had, when called upon for a song, the grace to stand, moist-eyed and stricken, while they lamented the sad fate of an exiled maiden who expired inevitably upon a foreign shore. The veins would stand out on their faces like purple picture-cords, and globules of moisture would glisten on their foreheads. If a man of substance, such as Tony Weller, were present, he would most certainly have nodded discreet approval, turned his head to hide his feelings and would most certainly have invited the author of the rendition to join him for a noggin of grog in the snug.

Please to remember that I am speaking about men who learned their art scientifically from tuppenny songbooks, men who scorned elocution but who could quote by heart, under duress, every line and lament of 'Auburn' and the lesser-known stanzas of masterpieces like Gray's 'Elegy'.

Let the great strut stages for audiences who pay to hear them, but every day of the week give me the man who has the power to make his fellows turn away from porter, the power to quell with a regal sniff disturbances which might intrude upon their pronouncements and the ability to impress their fellows by virtue of dignity alone.

each other next to the deathbed. Their comments were inaudible for the most part, and indeed, knowing some of the fair ladies in question I guessed that the whispered asides were far from complimentary.

In fact, the only person in the room to receive any form of praise was the one person to whom it was of no use, to wit, the corpse. For her there were gasps of admiration every time they looked her way. If a wayward draught chanced to disarray a rib or two of the corpse's hair they lovingly laid them back where they belonged, or if an ill-mannered housefly alighted on the hands around which rosary beads were entwined they were quick to send him off about his business.

'Isn't she handsome?' they said to each other with fervent piety. These were the only words that came across although it seemed to me at first glance that the corpse in question was run-of-the-mill. I took a second look to see if there were anything I had missed. There was nothing. In my book she was another corpse and nothing more than that.

'Isn't she handsome?' they said again in bold tones, high above the less pronounced and less endearing appraisals of the living.

Before rising from my prayerful posture I caught the eye of one of these obsequious matrons. In an instant she analysed me as no computer could. The eyes flickered and every exposed bit of me was subjected to the most rigid scrutiny. It was like being photographed from every side all at once.

Then the truth of the whole business dawned on me. This woman was a reporter. She took stock of my shoes, clothes, hair and general appearance swiftly but so comprehensively that I guessed she would be making a report of her findings when she returned home to her own hearth or when she met news-hungry neighbours in the days ahead. She was in her natural habitat and we may be sure that for years she aspired to such a position. Nothing would go unnoticed while she sat there. Her husband would probably be in the kitchen slugging a bottle of porter with his neighbours, happy in the knowledge that she was faithfully recording all happenings in the wake-room for his benefit.

To the uninitiated it must seem somewhat inexplicable that a woman sated by television and radio reports should be so anxious to determine the type of shoes, clothes and hair condition sported by common-or-garden mourners at a country wake. This can be simply explained by the fact that radio and television do not cater for local tastes and, most times, there is no known method of ferreting out information regarding the physical and mental conditions of enigmatic locals. As these kneel by the bed they are at their most vulnerable. From the point of view of physical exposure, a discerning deathbed reporter can look down on the crown of a head which otherwise would never be presented to her.

At a glance she can discover if the subject is greying or if she is losing hair and, while these may not be momentous observations in themselves, they form part of a complete picture which is always finished and framed before the visitor leaves the wake-room. Also allow for the fact that the head which had been investigated is partly covered by a scarf or hat and one fully realises the extraordinary perception of these deathbed attendants.

Female mourners, of course, are subjected to a far more intense study than mere males. Females are not above accentuating the natural colour of the hair, and this is their entitlement. In their exposed kneeling positions much can by the gleaned by the experienced deathbed investigator who is already more than familiar with the track record of the lady under scrutiny. She would know, for instance, what sizes she takes in hats and

has suffered the loss. Neither must the gentle reader get the impression that the author is opposed to the idea of deathbed reporters. On the contrary, he believes that they make a valuable contribution to community relations and can be regarded as part-time career women.

Erected to the memory of Thos. Pope Hodnett, died Dec. 26th, 1847. They say he was an honest man. Erected by his son Thos. Hodnett, Pastor, Immaculate Conception Church, Chicago.

In the same graveyard, which is ever open to passers-by, there is perhaps the best-penned epitaph in the country. When I last saw it, less than a month ago, the characters were as clear as could be on the stone:

Erected to the memory of Timothy Costello, died June 4th, 1873:

This is the grave of Timothy Costello
Who lived and died a right good fellow.
From his boyhood to life's end
He was the poor man's faithful friend.
He fawned before no purse-proud clod.
He feared none but the living God.
And never did he do to other
But what was right to do to brother.
He loved green Ireland's mountains bold,
Her verdant vales and abbeys old.
He loved her music, song and story
And wept for her long-blighted glory.
And often did I hear him pray
That God would end her spoilers' sway.
To men like him may peace be given
In this world and in Heaven.

WORDS, WORDS, WORDS

The Makings of a Book

Once upon a time my wife disclosed that she was going to write a book called *In the Round of a Day*.

In it would be detailed the fads and fancies, all the sayings and descriptions of the apparel worn by the customers who visited the bar from opening time to closing time. When the day came to an end she discovered that not a memorable human being had called.

It was just one of those days. I told her she should try another day but she never bothered. When I was left in charge of the bar for the better part of a day last week I decided to take up where she had left off. I did not start recording the sayings and antics of my visitors till half-past three in the afternoon but by the call of time many hours later I had the makings of a small book.

It was that kind of a day. The first arrival was a man made like a totem pole except that his face was more intimidating. He was as drunk as a brewery rat so I sent him on his way. He covered me with assorted curses before he left.

Then came a party of three people from Clare. They required ham sandwiches with their drinks so I invited the youngest of the party, a ten-year-old girl, into the kitchen and we made the sandwiches together in jig time. When the sandwiches were made I asked her if she could dance a step.

'I'll dance if you didle,' she said. So I didled while she danced. The oldest of the Clare men told of a time when every house in the Clare countryside never missed the Rosary.

'My mother,' he said, 'was very slow so what did my brother

some crumbs from the plate where the sandwiches had been.

'The man with the axe, apparently, followed the soldiers as far as the cross but don't ask me what cross it was.

'"Ye're nice militia,' he crowed after them. "Ye're the bucks what's supposed to fight the Germans and ye running from an oul' man with a hatchet!"'

So the day wore on, and by the end of it I had the makings of two books, not to mind one.

THE REAL MORAL

We had a chap in the extended family one time who endeavoured to make fun out of everything. The bother lay in the fact that what was fun to him was quite painful to others. I remember the day his aunt got the fit. The news was broken to him on the street by a relative.

'Your aunt is after taking a turn for the worse,' he was told.

'Was it a right- or a left-hand turn?' he quipped. When the relative upbraided him he apologised on the ground that he misunderstood.

'Well you know the kind of turn I mean,' the relative put in hotly. Now it transpired that the aunt in question was a great warrant to feed birds. When in the city she would purchase a pan loaf and disburse it among the ducks and coots of St Stephen's Green. At the seaside she would feed seabirds.

'Was it,' asked the quipper, 'a common tern she took or an Arctic tern?'

When no answer was forthcoming he announced that he knew it would happen sooner or later.

'A tern!' he mused, 'I always thought she'd take a duck. She was closer to ducks.'

When he arrived home the first thing he did was change his socks.

'Your aunt is failing,' his mother advised him.

'So what!' he responded. 'I failed in my time and look at me now. I have several pairs of high-quality socks. I failed my Inter and Leaving and I even failed the breathalyser but that's all behind me.'

PROVERBS

Recently I found an old exercise book which belonged to my late father. In the very last page was a collection of proverbs. The fact that he was a schoolmaster all of his life may have influenced his choices, and I don't know whether he made the selection on his own behalf or on behalf of his pupils. All told there were one hundred and eighty, and each was accorded so many ticks. The best were awarded three, the second best two and the ordinary only one. All made sense, however. The first to receive three ticks should make us ponder: 'Our last garment is made without pockets.'

The test of a worthwhile proverb lies in the number of meanings or interpretations which may be drawn from it. Many may be drawn from the following: 'One enemy is too many and a hundred friends too few.' It's from the German and it should teach us that it's folly to make enemies when we might easily make friends. The bother arises when we make friends with those who do harm instead of good. Still its better to convert a man to friendship if such a thing is possible. Would this have worked with Hitler or Stalin, however?

Now here's a biting one that begs comment: 'Old age, though despised, is coveted by all.'

Here's a sad one but how true alas: 'Old men go to death; death comes to young men.'

Here's another one all the way from the fourteenth century: 'Of little meddling comes great ease.' Ah how very true! I have always maintained that we should not concern ourselves with what others are doing but should be getting on with what we have to

AFTER THE PLAY

The playwright stood defiantly on the stage and listened with contempt to the howls of a disappointed audience. He held his head high and in his eyes was the long-suffering look of the truly great artist. Try as he might, he could not make himself heard above the boos of the crowd. Unexpectedly, a head of rotten cabbage came soaring over the heads of the audience from the end of the hall. It struck the author fairly and squarely on the nose and put him sitting on his behind. Loud laughter followed and derisive yells rose everywhere. Then there was a strange quiet. Rising, the author picked the head of cabbage from the boards and looked at it sadly. In a low voice he said: 'Somebody has lost his head. I'd better leave before you all do.' He exited with considerable dignity.

When an author faces the public after the presentation of one of his own plays he is placed in an extremely difficult position. Entering from the wings, he smiles weakly at the assembled cast as if they were complete strangers to him. They return the smile fearfully and turn towards the audience apologetically, thereby giving the impression that they are not prepared to be associated in any respect with the subsequent revelations of a man who, as everybody knows, is utterly irresponsible.

Some of the more thirsty members of the company breathe silent but fervent aspirations, hoping for a mercifully brief speech. Under the new licensing laws, every minute counts, and the longer the address lasts the more murderous the expressions on the faces of those who are not used to doing without a few pints at night. The terrible realisation dawns on them as the flow goes on that the author himself is well-primed for the occasion and doesn't give a tinker's curse for the misfortune of others.

The secret of the successful first night is to speak shyly, haltingly, apologetically and, above all, disparagingly about the play in question. Throw in the odd joke but never give the audience time to think. Ply them with regretful reminders of the play's failings and look downcast and sheepish, as if you were thoroughly ashamed of yourself. It is not a good idea to appear on stage with a baby in one's arms but crutches may be used legitimately or, if this seems like overdoing it, a success-ful ruse is not to shave for a week beforehand and to climb on to the stage assisted by friends. Nobody will jeer at a sick man. However, the safest bet is the apologetic tone, the air of perfect humility, the dejected appearance. People will leave the hall, saying: 'Well, now, wasn't he a very unassuming fellow, so natural. Sure, you'd think he never wrote a play at all.' The fact is that he never did but he has cunningly gained a brief respite until the morning papers catch him out. It is no harm to point out that, if this procedure is exaggerated, there can be disastrous results.

There is the classic example of the too-modest playwright who received his just deserts for laying it on a bit too thickly. On the first night he appeared on the stage with a devout expression on his face. He had the appearance of a man who has been interrupted in the middle of his prayers. He looked soulfully and piously at his audience and started his address. 'Ladies and gentlemen,' he began, 'if there is any credit due for the writing of this play, it is due to God, not to me. So thank God instead of me.' Religiously, he stood his ground while the audience applauded hysterically. Suddenly an old woman jumped to her feet and shouted: 'Ah! the blackhearted blackguard! He won't even take the blame himself!'

Long Sentences

Listening to the radio I was struck by the fact that politicians are masters of the long sentence. By the constant use of 'but's, 'if's and 'and's, to mention but a few overdone conjunctions, they seem to go on *ad infinitum* even when frequently interrupted by other politicians and by the person conducting the debate.

When asked for an answer such as 'yes' or 'no', they accept the question as a licence to go on and on with the end result as inconclusive as ever. Good as our southern politicians are, however, in respect of marathon formulations they wouldn't hold a candle to their northern counterparts but I will concede that they are catching on fast.

The idea is, of course, that the longer the sentence the fewer the interruptions since it is considered bad manners to break in at the middle of a sentence. Just as one believes that the northern politician is about to cease he unexpectedly comes out with: 'and if I may say so', or 'on a point of order', or 'but on the other side of the coin'. These short phrases are merely the links that assure longevity. I have listened while those waiting in the queue, so to speak, made bold bids to get in their tuppences worth but it's all to no avail once the speaker is in his stride. Fear of interruption is the motive and the content of the sentence does not seem to matter as much, in the final analysis, as the length.

You can have sentence after sentence after sentence with nothing being said but there is with the solitary, long sentence always the possibility of a candidate for *The Guinness Book of Records*. I don't know what the longest sentence is at this precise time,

FALSE ACCOUNT

There are tale-carriers whose slightest utterances cannot be believed. There is no community without one, and indeed there have been standard names for them down the years such as Dick the Liar and Tom the Liar and so forth and so on.

Then there is the tale-carrier whose tales have become so distorted in transit that nothing remains in the end but a parody of the original.

Then there are what I call natural tale-carriers. Everything you hear from the natural tale-carrier should be divided by at least two or even three. The net result will provide you with a semblance of the truth.

Only last Sunday week I was at a football game in Ballybunion. There was a good crowd and the game which was contested provided high-class entertainment.

That night in these here licensed premises a man held forth about the same game until I was forced to draw the conclusion that we were at two different games. According to him the fare was substandard and there was hardly anyone present. I contradicted him and informed him that where I sat in the sideline there seemed to be quite a good crowd.

'Well,' said he, 'I was in the stand and there wasn't enough of us there to put a ring on a sow.'

Instead of dividing by two or three, in this instance one should multiply by a hundred. The problem with this tale-carrier was that he didn't care for Ballybunion, and why should he, for wasn't he the victim of several bad decisions there during the Pavilion dances for which the resort was once famous.

On one particular night he devoted all his attention to one girl. She was only half interested but that's a lot as far as females are concerned. He collared her for every dance and when he was excused during the excuse-mes he excused back without delay. Normally you'd give the round of the hall to the man who excused you but this man didn't allow him as far as the first corner.

The girl decided to make enquiries about the fellow in the cloakroom.

'What kind is your man?' she asked an acquaintance who chanced to be from the same townland. What she did not know was that this acquaintance was an extraordinary tale-carrier, totally incapable of transporting one iota of the truth even if her very life depended on it. She was, in short, a pathological liar and while her tales were never less than entertaining, they were rarely based in fact and, when they were, the truth itself was drowned in the flood of red lies which she manufactured on a non-stop basis.

'Your man, is it?' she asked.

'Yes,' said the girl who had asked, 'your man.'

'If there was ten more of him there,' said the acquaintance, 'he wouldn't amount to one man.'

Disappointed, the unfortunate girl sought out confirmation. She asked a relative of the man who had been so attentive all night.

'I know nothing about him,' said the relative, 'except that his father was cashiered out of the Black and Tans.'

No wonder our friend had little time for Ballybunion. After hearing two such belittling descriptions the girl ignored him for the remainder of the dance.

But you wouldn't have to exaggerate to do damage to an innocent man or woman. What's that Alexander Pope said of his friend Addison:

I remember once a cousin of mine enquired about a neighbour of hers who happened to be married next door to the patient in the next bed. What my cousin heard was better than any tonic. Instead of being married into a place with fifty cows she had only married into nineteen. The farm was up to its hocks in debt and not rotting with money as my cousin had been led to believe. The patient in the next bed of course was exaggerating for she sensed that my cousin was interested only in a bad account of her former neighbour's circumstances. The patient was prepared to falsify the accounts on the grounds that my cousin needed cheering up and how better to cheer a person up than provide them with bad news about those who would rise above their station without any right to do so.

My cousin left the hospital a new woman. Even the doctor was mystified for his prognostications were all wrong. He had forecast a long stay and was happy to admit that he had diagnosed wrongly.

He hadn't. The cure lay in the news she heard: the distorted, unfair, untrue account of another's misfortune. No great harm came about as a result. The end, you might say, justified the means.

he told me that I was always writing about him and that was enough.

'Anyway,' said he, 'the whole truth cannot be told about any man and must never be told.'

'But,' I said, 'the whole truth is so well known to all that it doesn't matter. It's so inherent in us that it goes without saying: the bodily functions, the notions, the lunacies. These are so much a part of us that you would only bore your readers or maybe disgust them by adhering to such mundane, everyday balderdash.'

'It's all in my face and in my hands,' Sonny Canavan told me when I said he should record his life from start to finish.

'Wouldn't you like to know what people think about you after they hear your story?' I asked.

'What I'd like,' said Canavan, 'is to know what my goats think about me. Now that's something. What do the dogs think about me and the birds?'

Those of you who have come this far with me might be induced by what you have read up to this to consider writing a book. If you have a few scores or more of years put behind you there has to be the makings of a book. I knew a man in Listowel who wrote to his daughter before he died. In the letter he told her he loved her and that he was leaving her all he had. Then in a postscript he wrote 'I was.'

He was wrong. He still is in her memory and indeed in mine because I liked the man and sincerely miss him. He was a despondent fellow in life but this, I feel, was because he did not think enough of himself. I knew nothing about his personal life or of his experiences. All I knew about him was that he stood his round and went to Mass regularly, that he had a hot temper which cooled instantly and that he had two songs which he sometimes sang, 'Shenandoah' and 'The Black Hills of Dakota'.

I didn't know enough about him and that's not fair. I should have been privy to more if only to satisfy my curiosity. I feel deprived because I liked and enjoyed him and his ways. Now, if he had written a book, I would know a lot more about him and indeed I honestly feel that this is my entitlement. When I spoke to his daughter she agreed that he had a book in him for when she was young and when he'd be drunk he would spin for her romantic tales about himself during his journey through the world. At least he left her fragments of what might have been a book. He left the rest of us nothing.

So, dear reader, take your friends and those who love you or even hate you into account and start somewhere on your own or with the help of others.

Don't delay. Put it down bit by bit and in no time at all you will have a worthwhile testament to leave behind you.

folded. One of their group had written a short new play. He further compounded the crime, according to one local critic, by acting in it and producing it.

As we discussed the play afterwards in a local public house we invited the opinion of an amateur actor from the area who generally never had a good word to say about anybody or anything.

'This drivel,' said he, 'is an insult to our intelligence. The author should be hung, drawn and quartered. He should be hung for acting in it. He should be drawn for producing it and he should be quartered for writing it. In another country,' he concluded, 'he would be taken out and shot.'

Then there was the night I met a holidaying priest in Ballybunion. This took place a long time ago. It happened in the Central Hotel of the time, a great haunt for visiting clerics. He was seated despondently on a stool with his back turned to everybody except the barmaid.

'Finish that,' I advised, 'and have another.' He declined graciously for all his despondency. It transpired that he had not long before attended a performance of Othello. 'I will never be in the better of it,' he said, 'and imagine I was fool enough to fork out a florin in order to sit for nearly two and three-quarter hours in suffocating conditions listening to an arrant scoundrel massacring Iago – Iago, that gem of parts which has never been truly mutilated until tonight.'

I sympathised with him, for I have seen bad Iagos in my time and bad everything.

'Never mind,' he said as he attracted the barmaid's attention and instructed her to proceed with the filling of two small Paddies. 'I had,' he went on, 'intended visiting a retreat house for the remainder of my holidays, a prospect which I cherish not. Fortunately I have tonight amply repaid for my occasional transgressions during my agony watching and listening to Iago.

Pernounciations

Some men are born to be great, others to be failures. There is, however, the consolation that the failure has the same chance of being happy as the great man. Greatness is no guarantee of happiness. Of course, neither is failure. It must be said at once that some words, like people, are born to be great. Others, alas, are born to be failures.

Let me explain. You have words like beautiful and you have words like brilliant. They are much in use and, most important of all, they are pronounceable. Other words, for instance, like investigation and recognition, to mention but a few, while easily pronounceable to some are unpronounceable to others.

A man arrived into the pub one day bearing a plastic bag which carried the remains of an ancient timber plough.

'I wants this westergasted,' he said, 'and someone said you'd be the man to do it.'

At the time I did not know what westergation meant. I stole into the kitchen and consulted my wife.

'That's easy,' she said. 'To westergate is to investigate. Some people call it westergate,' she continued, 'and cannot see what's the use in putting an 'in' before it.'

So that was it. He simply wanted me to investigate his wooden plough.

Recognition is another unfortunate word which has suffered from many different and incorrect pernounciations – sorry, pronunciations. The late Jack Faulkner, the great travelling man, used to say that he had a cousin in Clare who was a brilliant man, 'but,' said Jack, 'he can't even pernounce his own name.'

I sympathised, and Jack proceeded to inform me that he knew hundreds who went to school and who could not pernounce the simplest of words.

'When I was in the army,' said Jack, 'you had to pernounce your words properly or you could be killed. There was a drunken corporal coming home one night and refused to halt when I ordered him. I was on sentry duty and I had a loaded gun.

'"Advance to be reckernised," I called.'

'"What do you think he called back?" Jack asked.'

'"I give up," I answered.'

'"Is that Faulkner?" he shouted.'

'"'Tis me," said Jack.'

'"I'm so drunk," said the corporal, "that I don't even reckernise myself."'

'"'Tis a good job,' said Jack, "that one of us knows who he is or you'd be a dead duck by now."'

There was another occasion in the bar when two teachers were discussing a trigonometry paper which their pupils had found extremely difficult. There was a third man in the bar at the time who had considerable difficulties with pronouncing long words. The man was drunk and aggressive. He persisted in interfering with the teachers.

'Do you know something about trigonometry?' asked one of the teachers.

'Triggernomerty is it!' he said disdainfully. 'Nomerty is a cowboy, I'd say, and don't every fool know what a trigger is.'

The teachers enjoyed the input but the man who inputted did not. He was one of those individuals who believes that when people laugh in his presence they are laughing at him. A row followed, and one of the teachers who had a short fuse floored Triggernomerty, as we'll call him, far better than any sheriff ever could.

well before we deliver verbal broadsides which could provoke the same reaction as shrapnel.

I remember well to have been loitering in the vicinity of an ice-cream stand at Ballybunion many years ago. A small man, accompanied by a wife and five children, placed an order for seven cartoons of ice cream.

'Cartoons!' the youngster behind the counter scoffed. 'Go up town to the cinema and you'll get all the cartoons you want.'

The small man shot out a left fist. The youngster fell. The small man moved with his party to the next stand and was accommodated without comment. If the small man had said carton instead of cartoon there would have been no trouble. If the youngster had used his imagination he wouldn't have been floored.

Questions and Answers

Frequently after a lecture the master of ceremonies asks the audience if they would like to put relevant questions to the lecturer. This is a sound idea but, alas, lurking in all audiences are persons male and female who are themselves well prepared to answer the questions they pose.

For years now I have been bored into semi-insensibility by these opportunistic predators. There I am, having contributed my quota of applause after the lecture has been concluded, in the act of pulling up my socks before departing, when the MC falls into the age-old trap.

He may suggest that the questions should be pertinent and the answers brief so that the whole business might be concluded in a fifteen-minute period. Alas there is no containing the man who would answer his own questions. He might not seem to be answering his own questions because he starts off by saying things like 'would not the lecturer agree' and follows up with a long dissertation which reveals all his personal philosophies. He will explain that under no circumstances would he be presumptuous enough to give a lecture himself but the simple truth is that he has a captive audience albeit gathered in the first instance to listen to another. He is going to hold forth *ad nauseam*, no matter how many times the MC may look at his watch.

I suggest that there should be a blacklist of these insufferable bores who have no regard for the feelings of others and whose only concern is that they unload their tedious vacuities on an audience too polite or too cautious to object. These brash buttonholers – and buttonholers they are – are forever on the lookout for inexperienced masters of ceremonies who foolishly presume that the rules they impose will be observed by all. Not even a tidal wave will halt a man who knows that it might well be years before he is provided with another opportunity.

On a number of occasions I have been obliged to play the role of chairman. Luckily I had a rogues' gallery of post-lectural criminals firmly framed in my mind's eye and I was able to ignore them by the simple expedient of pretending they didn't exist or by looking through them and afterwards apologising profusely when confronted with the accusation that I had deliberately ignored them.

'Never!' I would say in horror. I had no misgivings about such fabrications. I had a duty to the audience and I would protect them at all costs from being bored to tears. As a former victim myself it was my bounden duty to do so.

In appearance, these lecture-hall miscreants are harmless and self-effacing. Apologetic is another word which occurs to me but given the slightest opening they can be ebullient and abrasive over long periods. It is the absolutely innocuous and gentle manner in which they lift an index finger to claim the MC's attention which is the most misleading and deceptive aspect of these seemingly harmless procrastinators. To the uninitiated MC, here is a mild-mannered, easily controlled dilettante who can be swatted like a fly if he persists beyond the allotted minutes. Believe me, gentle reader, once the scoundrel gets under way it would be easier for a group of old ladies to subdue an All Black scrum.

A friend once suggested to me after we had been subjected to a question twenty minutes long that it might be a good idea to lock the speaker into a soundproof room for a whole day and to replay for him at least forty times his own humourless outpourings.

LONG SERMONS

We will now turn aside from worldly matters and address ourselves to things ecclesiastical. Not by bread alone doth man live,
although you'll find few bakers to agree with such a sweeping
statement. Indeed, as shall be seen, we are more indebted to wine.

Believe it or not I have no objections to long sermons in
church. I always wake up from them feeling greatly refreshed.
On the other hand, short, instructive sermons keep me awake
and present no opportunities for dozing. The days of the long
sermon, however, seem to have vanished forever. Consequently
I was amazed last Sunday to hear a succession of faint, happy
snores coming from the pew in front of me. The sermon was
short and to the point so the snores could not possibly have
been induced by boredom. Then came the unmistakable whiff of
recently consumed whiskey and all was made clear. The alcoholic
fumes had blunted the sharpness of the poor fellow's wits, and
he had succumbed to slumber.

We once had a parish priest in Listowel, many moons ago,
who specialised in long sermons. Oddly enough, nobody objected.
He had a soft voice which did not carry very far and since
microphones had yet to be introduced to pulpits the majority of
his listeners accustomed themselves to the sonorous drone of his
preaching, folded their arms contentedly and drifted quietly into
the land of half-sleep. These long sermons did them the world
of good. At the conclusion they blinked happily into wakefulness
and approached the rest of the Mass with revived interest. To
them the long sermon was what half-time in a football game
was to the tiring midfielder: a well-deserved lull, a chance to